MW01127273

Dark Visions

A collection of 34 horror stories from 27 authors

Edited and compiled by Dan Alatorre

Dark Visions
A horror anthology with stories from over 30 authors

© This book is licensed for your personal use only. This book may not be re-sold or given away to other people. Thank you for respecting the hard work of this author. © No part of this book may be reproduced, stored in a retrieval system or transmitted by any means without the written permission of the author. The individual authors herein maintain the Copyright © to their respective story or stories. This anthology collection book is Copyright © 2018 by Dan Alatorre. All rights reserved.

This is a work of fiction. Names, characters, places, and incidents either are the product of the authors' imaginations or are used fictitiously, and any resemblance to actual persons, living or dead, businesses, companies, events or locales, is entirely coincidental.

This anthology contains some previously published materials. Prologue and epilogue by Dan Alatorre.

Compiled and edited by Dan Alatorre

Cover by DAVID DUANES DESIGN

Warning!

American _and_ British spelling ahead. It's not typos. Probably.

A few Aussie stories might have snuck in here, too, and one from the Great White Canadian North. It happens. They're sneaky.

To enhance your reading experience and prevent confusion, I have noted the country of origin for each writer. I agree, it's sad I had to do that.

Each story appearing in this anthology is meant to be a complete, stand-alone short story. If you enjoy the piece and want more information on that author or their other works, a link has been provided near the title of the story. For many of the contributing authors, this is their first and only published work, and I am proud to introduce them to you here.

If you enjoy this anthology, please post a review on Amazon

READ ORDER

195	69	14	213 (5)	3
221	107	21	75	58
210 (3)	160	41	98	113 (12)
84	204 (6)	132	182 (9)	28
124		153	48	227 (14)
128		168	88	
139		175	143 (10)	
191		197 (7)		
223 (4)				

Contents

PROLOGUE: Now Comes Death
part one

A somber conversation had
Two brothers from the hospice bed.
Traveled far to see young Blane,
A chance that would not come again.

Just thirty years was this grown child
But older, much, from cancer's trials
And in this brother's eyes did see
The arc of life soon to complete.

We talked of pleasant stories past
And as my brother breathed his last
A favor, holding hands, I asked;
And one which he agreed would pass.

"Always protected me," he said
As tears fell on the hospice bed.
"No one protects me now from this."
The journey, all alone, was his.

The favor asked, agreed, and done,
My brother, with the setting sun,
Did go ahead to that which waits
To tell me what's past Heaven's gate.

No more for me to do but leave
And in my solitude, to grieve.
And so I left that cold, hard place
A dark hotel room now to face.

As sleep upon me later came
The night now dark, began the rain
A rustling to my ear did make

Dark Visions

To pull me from my restless state.

Outside my room and through the glass
A hooded shadow figure passed
Awaiting me in dark and gloom.
I rose to cross my hotel room.

And solemn was the face inside,
A glimpse the black cloak did not hide,
Three globes did he hold out to me
- To gaze upon my destiny?

A face of peacefulness and pain,
No message could I ascertain,
Just holding out a crystal ball
For me to gaze upon it all.

Past, present, future? Who could tell?
Or hope and fear? The depths of hell?
And so I gazed upon the ball
And saw a glimmer in its walls.

The stories that the globes did say
Were mysteries to come my way
And if mistakes the tales contain
I did my best to ascertain.

And once this information gained
The figure disappeared again.
The shadow and the crystal balls
As if they'd never been at all.

A promise kept? Or lies for show?
The crystal told me in its glow.
"Beyond is but for Death to know."

The Corner Shop
Dan Alatorre
Tampa, Florida, USA
Copyright © 2018 by Dan Alatorre. All rights reserved.
DanAlatorre.com

I'd never held a human skull in my hands before.

It was lighter than I expected, with a texture like polished wood. Not plastic or heavy resin—like I was expecting—and the longer I examined it, the more uncomfortable I felt. Disrespectful.

Parker leaned against the wall, hands in pockets, sighing loudly. It'd been almost fifteen minutes since his last beer. No concerns of disrespect there.

The bell jingled as another person came into the dimly lit shop. An old African-American woman, wearing a long, straight dress of a colorful but thin material. The kind that didn't get too hot in New Orleans. She made her way through the rows of glass jars and stacks of boxes, past the hanging tied herbs to the painted counter. A slow curl of incense rose up from a ceramic holder as she spoke to the woman I assumed was the owner.

"C'mon man, let's get going." Parker slid a tiny glass bottle onto a wooden shelf, relatively close to the spot he'd plucked it from. "You're not seriously thinking of buying that thing, are you?"

As he walked over to me, I gazed at the skull, turning it around. "I don't know." No price tag. No made in China sticker. "Depends on what it costs."

"Dude, look." Parker grabbed the skull and glared at it. "You can see the glue on the edges where it's holding the jaw in place." He tapped the teeth. "These are all wiggly. They'll fall out

3

on the plane ride home." Dropping the skull back onto the small wooden shelf, he turned and headed for the door. "I'll be in the bar across the street with the Carlie and Sissy."

"Hold on." I picked the skull up and took it to the counter. Parker stopped, sighing loudly for my benefit as he waited. The whole place was bathed in a twilight glow from the blue paint on the windows, so even though it was only about 2 P. M. outside, the inside had a constant feel of oncoming night. The rows of close tables with all their oddly named bottles, the stacks of shelves holding little brown boxes and plastic bags of dried plants, the stink of the incense, and the owner who didn't speak—that added up to a definite voodoo feel that I bet the owner enjoyed. Drunk tourists would buy a little something-something in a plastic baggie with a handwritten tag, and be convinced they'd have the magic bedtime energy of an eighteen-year-old, or the brain skills of an MIT mathematics professor, or whatever. Restored looks and—

The dolls behind the counter caught my eye, but having a seven-year-old daughter, dolls often did. Colored yarn tied with twine and stuffed with beanbags, they stared at me from their miniature gallows, all dressed in their little painted burlap clothes and little twig arms.

The shop lady busied herself with something out of sight behind the antique cash register, a drawn, somber expression etched onto her aged face.

I held up the skull. "How much is this?"

She lifted her hand and inspected her long nails, lifting an emery board and running it across the side of her index finger.

The putrid smoke of the little ceramic incense holder seemed to know just how to find me. I stifled a cough and resisted the urge to pull my t-shirt collar over my nose. "Ma'am, I'm curious about the price of this."

As I lifted the skull, it became bathed in light. I glanced toward the shop door. The customer exited the shop, allowing the bright light from the street to illuminate the room as she stepped outside.

A small girl appeared from a room through a partition of beads. She was dressed similar to the shop owner, but with long, tight dreadlocks and a youthful, round forehead. "May I see?" She

4

had an island accent. Jamaican, more or less. She held out her hand.

I gave her the skull. She turned it over in her hands, but her big brown eyes looked only at me. "Two hundred."

I blinked. "Two hundred? Dollars?"

The tiny head bobbed up and down. "Two hundred, cash." She glanced at the shop keeper. "American."

"Well, yeah, I'm not from . . . wow, two hundred, huh?"

With bony arms that stuck out from her dress like the twig arms on the dolls, she held the skull out to me. Her big eyes were neither happy nor sad. They were businesslike.

She seemed about my daughter's age. About the same height, but older looking than Tira somehow.

"Brett, check it out." Parker had lit up a cigarette and was using the flame from his lighter to read a beige flier. "They have haunted tours at midnight."

"Not haunted," the girl said, lifting the skull from my hands.

He blew smoke toward the door, casting a white, fog-like haze in the dim room. "It says they go through the graveyard. What else would they be?"

The girl moved past the rows of tables and placed the skull back on its shelf. "They not be haunted."

"Hmm." Parker took a puff on his smoke, the red tip glowing against the faint light of the store. "Well, whatever they are, do they allow drinking?"

The girl nodded. "You can drink."

He grinned at me. "Wanna do it?"

I sighed as the girl returned empty handed, the skull back in its proper place. "How much is the haunted—I mean, not haunted—the tour?"

"How many of you go?"

"Two." Parker chuckled, coming toward the counter. "The Carlie and Sissy will never go anywhere except a bar that late, and they definitely ain't going anywhere near a graveyard after dark." He snorted, sucking another big draw on his cigarette. "Besides, you have Tira."

My girlfriend's sixteen-year-old sister was babysitting our daughter on the trip, and it had turned into a disaster after only two days. "Yeah, lucky me. Kylee had no interest in actually being a babysitter, and Tira had no interest in being babysat."

I'm seven, Dad. I don't need a babysitter.

So far, they'd limited the feud to the four walls of the hotel, but since she was just like her sister, the sixteen-year-old wanted to go out at night in New Orleans. By herself.

Can't say I blame her. The city had it all. Great food, great bars—the hurricanes at Pat O'Brien's were a red, fruit punch frozen rum drink, the kind of happy beverage that helped fight the blistering heat and soggy humidity of the Crescent City. So sweet, it didn't even taste like drinking, and as soon as you ordered a third one, you realized you hadn't even needed the second one. You needed a cab ride home.

'Nawlins also had the dance clubs that have the drugs and other mischief a young girl could get into at night on her own— also like her older sister. But Carlie would be happy with a little weed and a few hurricanes, and then some drag queen burlesque, while she and Sissy helped squander our work bonus.

"Maybe . . ." I walked to the shelf with the skull. "Maybe a smaller one? Would that be less?"

Parker shook his head. "Are you thinking they're real? They tell you a crazy high price just so you'll think they're authentic. They're fake. Ten bucks at the local Wal-Mart. Maybe five."

"More."

The little girl's voice cut through the din of Parker's smoke and clatter. Her big eyes locked on mine. "The small ones, they cost more."

Tira could take business lessons from this kid.

"Yeah, of course." Parker grumbled, heading toward the door. "I bet the little ones do cost more—now that he asked about them."

I sighed, staring at the skull. I can't say why I liked it. I always wanted one as a kid, and as an adult we were allowed to give in to some kid fantasies. A real skull, not like in the magic set I got when I was ten.

6

Parker was right, though. It was probably a fake. It was too light and papery feeling. That, or some poor Chinese guy in a slave labor camp got starved to death and they sold his freaking bones off to voodoo shops. Kinda gruesome, really. And it's not like I needed it.

But I wanted it, and the bonus money wouldn't last forever. It wasn't the kind of bonus you could stick in a bank account, after all. I slid my hand into my pocket. The folds of cash pressed hard into my fingers, like the edges of a book. Sharp, but not cutting.

"What about this?" Parker held up the flyer. "How about we take two tickets on the haunted tour and you sell us the skull for a legit price. Like ten dollars."

The old lady behind the counter stared at her hands, inspecting microscopic flaws in her long fingernails. Then she set the file about its work again.

"Four." The little girl held up the fingers on one hand.

I knew what Parker was going to say before he did.

"Four dollars? Now you're talking."

"Four tickets. You pay now, come tonight. I give you the skull then."

"Four tickets, huh?" Quite the little negotiator, this kid. "Park, how much we talkin' for four tickets?"

He sneered. "Doesn't matter, the girls won't come. You—aren't gonna take the kids . . ."

"No, they can all stay in the hotel. But what's the cost?"

"Fifty bucks a pop." He shook his head. "You've negotiated yourself back up to two hundred. Shrewd."

But it wasn't. It was the price I was willing to pay to own something gruesome enough to not ever be owned, by me or anyone else. The nuns from grade school would've had my hide for even thinking about buying such a thing. *It's a sin.*

"It's a free graveyard tour for us, after I pay their price for the skull." I eyed Parker. "Even you can't argue with that deal."

"It's your money."

I fingered the roll of bills in my pocket. Yep. It's my money.

As I peeled off fifty-dollar bills and handed them to the girl, the old lady reached behind the counter and pulled out a plastic baggie. The kid held out four tickets to the graveyard tour—printed on paper that matched the flyer.

I reached for the tickets. "Any sales tax on this?"

The old lady glared at me.

"Dude, when you pay cash," Parker snatched the tickets from the kid's hand, "there's no tax."

I slid my wad of cash back into my pocket. "Just wanna pay what I owe."

The old lady looked at me and nodded. "You will."

Her voice was old and cracked, like the dingy walls around us, stained with smoke and incense and darkness just like her shop.

Parker headed for the door when the kid held out a baggie with a sample from the old lady's stash. "For your friend."

Parker didn't stop, but I took it for him. A little *lagniappe*; something extra, like how a donuts shop gives you thirteen in a baker's dozen.

The bright afternoon light didn't help *Rue Bourbon's* seedy back quarters. The worn brick pavers still held the stench of the prior night's stale beer—spilled or urinated or vomited—onto the tiny alleyways between drinking establishments, and the business owners who hosed down the sidewalks every morning didn't seem to do much except push the putrid sludge into the street where it festered all day in the sweltering sun.

Drunk tourists didn't seem to mind, though, and I personally thought it added to the ambiance of the city. The place wasn't afraid to be who it was: clean and pretty in the right light, down and dirty at other times.

Our dinner consisted of shrimp *po' boys* and hurricanes. The girls were happy; they'd been drinking and shopping most of the day—normally a bad combination—but since we were temporarily flush with money to spend, we all spent it.

So it wasn't a big deal that the stupid skull cost two hundred dollars. My bonus couldn't go into a savings account. It went into a safe deposit box at Miami Federal and it was all cash, just like the drug dealers do until it won't fit in a vault drawer anymore.

It needed to be spent on vacations and nice clothes and fancy hotels. Toys for the kids and trips for the parents. Good food, good drinks, good parties—and much too much of all of it.

That's why the girls said no to the graveyard tour, and yes to dessert at the Court Of Two Sisters. That's why Parker said yes to the baggie. He was ready to get a little back after getting the shaft in our skull scoring deal, and he felt he'd earned it. It was good stuff, too, according to him. Not as good as the stuff he got from our friends in Miami, but for free he wasn't complaining. Much.

By 2 A. M., we'd be home, the girls would be back from the clubs, Tira would be asleep, and Kylee would be . . . well, Kylee would be pissed. But Kylee was always pissed.

So we headed out to the dark street on the back of *Rue Bourbon*, ready to tour the graveyards and take home my prize.

The old man who met us on the corner at midnight—our tour guide, according to the flyer—seemed to try his best to act the part of someone who truly believed the garbage he was spewing. He wore a tuxedo jacket and tails, with a dark shirt and tie. His mannerisms were stiff and formal, and his accent a kind of watered down British. The kind snooty guys on TV spoke, but not quite the queen's English.

"Nobody else showed up?" Parker sneered.

The man handed us flashlights. His boots shined even in the dark of night. "I'm afraid you gentlemen are it tonight."

Parker mumbled to me as he clicked his flashlight on. "Man, you are such a sucker."

It was a walking tour, and the night was just as hot as the day had been. We traveled along a few famous streets, as Tremont, our guide, explained in his aged, faded English voice what historic indiscretions had happened there. Within a few blocks Parker and I were sweating, but not Tremont. The old guy had grown accustomed to his job and the heat in which he performed it.

Parker and I were accustomed to air conditioning.

By about 1 A. M., we'd seen the creepy above-ground cemeteries and listened to all of Tremont's lame ghost stories. It seems a lot of bad magic happens after midnight around New Orleans, and even if it didn't, everybody still believed it did.

9

The tour would have been fun for regular tourists looking for a scare, but it was only delaying me from getting my prize and delaying Parker from getting to bed. Too many hurricanes or too much partying, courtesy of the *lagniappe* from the old shop keeper, but my man was tired.

He was half awake when our guide announced the end of the regular tour. At the edge of the city, a horse drawn carriage awaited.

"If you are so inclined, you may take the advanced tour, gentlemen."

"What's that gonna cost us?" Parker was close to slurring. "Another fifty bucks?"

"The advanced tour is at no additional charge, sir. It seems your hostess at the shop wishes you to receive the maximum benefit from your tour."

I glanced at Parker, shrugging. "Well, if it's no additional charge . . ."

He placed his hands on the sides of the carriage and slogged an unstable foot inside, hoisting himself aboard. "Do we get to ride in this back to our hotel, Truman? Like Cinderella?"

"*Tremont*, sir. And you will have full use of the carriage for the duration of your trip tonight." Tremont was atop the front seat, buggy whip in hand, in the smooth, graceful move of a much younger man. "The lady of the shop insisted."

"I'll be darned." Parker settled into his seat, his eyes half open. "The old bag was taking care of us after all. Throwing in a horse ride and a skull and Truman here and everything."

The crack of the whip shot through the night like a gunshot.

Parker snapped upright, his eyes wide open. My stomach jumped as our guide turned to face us from his perch on the carriage driver seat.

"*Tremont*, sir." Another crack of the whip sent the horse lurching into a trot, jerking the carriage forward. "If you please."

My racing pulse settled a bit as we rode. I took a deep breath and tried to calm myself while the big black mare pulled us down a dirt path. Lanterns on either side of the carriage swayed and bobbed, sending eerie white shadows to dance on the passing trees and hanging moss. Fog gathered at the base of the ancient oaks, the gloom allowing for thoughts not often considered in daylight.

Ghostly thoughts, in the shadow-filled void of night. Whispers of voices disguised as a slight wind in the trees.

I felt it, the power of this place. No wonder the old woman had me come here to receive the skull. It was to be appreciated in ritualistic fashion, given in the darkness, to convey its dark origins. I understood that now.

It made me want the skull all the more.

Beside me, Parker had gone to sleep—at best. Passed out, most likely, but then he had enjoyed most of our hostess' *lagniappe*. I didn't care. I knew what awaited me in the darkness ahead.

The nuns were right. It was a sin.

It was evil, to be sure, to acquire the skull of another human person, man or woman, slave laborer or thief. It was wrong.

And the price was right.

Two hundred dollars to own and understand, to have and to hold, that which no man should possess. The bones, the dignity of the dead.

Their spirit. Their magic. The secrets they alone could reveal.

I licked my lips, wanting it like nothing I'd ever wanted before.

Ahead, the lanterns illuminated shapes—one tall, one short—against a clearing in the trees. Our hostesses from the shop, no doubt, and the finale of a tour worth every penny.

The swampy sound of crickets and bullfrogs filled the air as the carriage pulled to a stop. The strong horse shuddered, her long black mane whipping against her neck. A steadying hoofbeat or two and she found her spot, ready for her passengers to disembark.

I was first out the door, breathing hard in anticipation now, my heart racing as I stepped toward the old shopkeeper.

"Your friend will be staying in the carriage, sir." It was as much a statement as a question. Tremont glowered at Parker, eyes shut and body slumped against the black silk backrest. His mouth slightly agape, he was done for the night.

"Yes, I believe he will, Tremont. Thank you." I walked to where the shopkeeper woman stood, the air thick with anticipation. Her young assistant held a lantern. At their feet, an incense stick burned in a ceramic holder, and a burlap bag like the ones from which the dolls' clothes had been cut and painted, lay on the dirt. It's top sagged over, flopping down over the box it held inside.

My heart thumped hard, rising and beating against my collar bones, so ready was I to receive my gift. Around me, the fog crawled out of the swamp, a thick white smoke that hugged the ground, reeking of incense and the same vile stench of the washed-down backstreet sidewalks.

I glanced at the bag, then to the old woman, raising my eyebrows. "Is that for me?"

She stared into the black spaces between the trees, the picture of stony silence. It was the child who answered.

"This box be for you."

I didn't know the custom, whether to take it or wait for them to offer it to me. The loud groaning of the bullfrogs gave no indication, their raucous rasping ebbed and crested like police sirens in a summer traffic jam. Deafening.

But I had paid. It was mine.

"Shall I carry on, then?" Tremont's aged voice managed to reach me through the swamp noise. Without waiting for my reply, he cracked the whip and set the horse in motion pulling the carriage away. In a moment, the clouds of fog swallowed them up, Tremont and Parker and the big black mare, all disappearing into the dark.

I rubbed my hands on my khaki shorts, eyeing the bag and the burlap silhouette contained within it. "What happens now?"

The child stepped toward me. "Now we wait for the skull."

"Wait? But I paid."

"And you will pay." The old woman cackled. "But not tonight."

She heaved her hand into the air. A massive knife glistened in the light of the lantern, raised high over her head. Its sharp edge gleamed as the old woman held it. Her eyes were wide with demonic rage, red as the setting sun and burning with fire.

My stomach lurched as I stepped backwards. "Do you mean to kill me?"

"No."

I let out a breath.

"Not tonight."

She was on me with the speed and intensity of a woman half her age, her strength overpowering me as she knocked me to the ground. I kicked and flailed, gritting my teeth and twisting my face away from the knife, pushing and shoving against her—but she was ten times as strong as me. With the knife pressed hard against my cheek, its tip massive in my sight, the only thing visible out of my left eye, she leaned into me. She rammed her hands into my shoulders and pinned me to the ground. She held me while the child rushed to bind my hands and feet, finally tying a rag over my mouth.

Each breath was a fight. Fear and adrenaline surged through me.

"Tonight, we wait." The old woman wheezed and gasped. "When your friend get home, your woman ask questions. And they will come to Tremont."

I shook my head, choking on the gag, straining against the ropes that now held me. Sweat gathered along my forehead and ran down my cheek.

The shopkeeper smiled as she slipped one hand around my throat and raised the knife to my eye, daring me to move. I froze, my heart pounding. The gaps in her black, rotting teeth allowed the stench of the swamp to wash though her, like they were one and the same. "They will come, the *womans*. The children."

"They will come for you." The girl whispered, a fierce rasp like a storm through a tree top. "Your friend bring them to Tremont, and he will demand to come to here."

The old woman leaned closer. "And we will be waiting."

"We will take the skulls, all of them." The little girl's words were a hiss in the night, an echo in the dark woods, as she dimmed the lantern. "The smaller ones always bring more."

The Stranger
Allison Maruska
Colorado, USA
Copyright © 2018 by Allison Maruska. All rights reserved.
allisonmaruska.com

"I found another box back here!" Coughing, I shove the dust-coated cardboard across the cement floor of the crawlspace and out to my brother. "This has to have something."

He pulls it into the family room as I brush my grimy hands on my jeans, trying not to cringe at my beat-up manicure.

"Why?" Aaron pulls the crackling tape, a simple task given the adhesive's age. "Fourteenth time's the charm?" He shoots me a satisfied smirk.

"Ha ha. Let's just get to it. We're down to . . ." I check my watch. "Half an hour before Dad has to have whatever pics we can find."

"Thirty minutes to go through sixty years of memories? No problem." Aaron lifts a shoebox from the larger cardboard one. "Here."

I grab and open it while Aaron shuffles through whatever loose things are in the big box.

Surrounding us, Grandma's things lay strewn across the floor, and like layers of ancient rock, they show more age as we dig farther into the crawlspace. On the far end of the room rest the newest finds, including programs from our graduations, birthday cards from the past few years, even Christmas gift tags. The next layer included framed pictures of us as young children, starting around the time Mom took off, and after that came the bracelets

14

from our birth and the program from Dad's college drama production.

So many items showed a life I had no clue about, despite the fact that she had a large part in raising us. The weight that insisted on sitting on my chest the past four days returned, so I do what I've done almost non-stop since then: keep busy.

"This is full of canisters of undeveloped film." I take one out and shake it. "Think anyone still develops this stuff?"

"Doubt it." He removes a stack of papers and pictures and flips through them. "Hey, these might work." He holds them out to me.

I take the faded, yellowing photographs, images of a young family—our father and his parents—on a beach. A twenty-something version of Grandma wearing a bikini and huge sunglasses is sitting on a towel, her legs stretched before her as our preschool-aged father buries her feet with sand. Behind her are other families, all looking like they're in a show about summer in the sixties.

I set the picture aside and flip through the others. "Grandma isn't in many of these, huh?"

"I noticed." Aaron flips through his own stack of square photographs. "I guess moms are usually the ones taking pictures. Oh, here we go."

He hands me another shot, this one featuring young Grandma standing beside a Thanksgiving table. Behind her, pressed against the wall, is a man I don't recognize. He isn't smiling.

Squinting, I hold the picture close to my eyes, looking for anything familiar. Failing that, I set the photograph with the beach one.

By the time the alarm on my phone goes off, Aaron and I have a stack of five photographs featuring Grandma as a young mom. I grab them and jump to my feet. "Come on. We'll drop these off with Dad and clean up after."

As Aaron drives us to the funeral home, I analyze the pictures, wishing I could reach into them and pull Grandma back to us. I remember tracing an old scar on the side of her hand, the one she got cutting vegetables years before, with my finger when I was a kid. These prints are rare treasures, capturing something I haven't seen in the more-recent digital shots. "Did you notice Grandma is never alone in these?"

"What do you mean?" Aaron pulls into the funeral home's lot and parks in the space closest to the street.

"Exactly what I said. Look." I hold the pictures up, slowly flipping through them. "There's a guy in all of them." In the Halloween picture, where Grandma sits with our pirate-costumed dad in what looks like a church basement, I point to a brown-haired man dressed in tan slacks and a shiny, green button-down shirt. I flip to the Thanksgiving pic and point out the same man. In all of the pictures, he wears the same clothes and stares straight ahead, unsmiling.

"Huh." Aaron takes the stack from me and flips through them. "Maybe Dad knows who he is. He must have been a close friend if he was around on Thanksgiving. Come on. We need to get in there."

* * * * *

The next day's service comes too soon, though I suspect any time would feel too soon to me. I check my lipstick one last time in the bathroom mirror before heading into the crowded hallway. While I'd love to say goodbye to Grandma in comfortable solitude, I can't wait out these people forever.

The first eyes to connect with mine belong to someone I haven't seen in decades—of course, those eyes are much older than I remember. "Uncle Frank?"

My great-uncle offers a half-toothless smile. "Mariah. My goodness." He approaches me with an uneven gait, though I'm not sure if it's caused by his aging joints or by the huge, archaic camera around his neck. He takes my hands in his, smiling and nodding. Moisture sits at the bottom of his eyes, as if he'd been mourning his sister just before I joined him. "You're all grown up."

"Yeah." I smile gently, patting the back of his hand. "Did you see the display Dad set up?" As I haven't seen the display myself, I hope doing so with company will be easier.

He shakes his head.

16

"Let's go, then. It's in here." I pull him toward the sanctuary.

"One second, dear." Releasing my hand, he steps back and raises the camera. "I'd like to get your picture, if that's all right."

"Sure." I stand straight and smile half-heartedly, assuming this is a photograph no one will see.

The old camera clicks, and Uncle Frank cranks a dial.

"How old is that camera?" I ask as I reach for his hand again.

"Oh, older than you, I think." He chuckles. "I never got into those newer, fancy things. This one works just fine."

I hold the door open for him, and together we make our way to the front of the mostly empty sanctuary. Lilies, Grandma's favorite, surround the urn centered on the front table, covering it and the floor around it. On the table farthest to the right are photographs, including the ones Aaron and I found yesterday, now framed and arranged chronologically alongside the newer pictures. I bend over, analyzing them again, looking for the stranger in each like I'm looking for Waldo. He only appears in the older photos.

"Uncle Frank, do you know who this man is?"

"What's that?" He shuffles over to me, lifting his glasses and putting his face inches from the pictures. "Oh sure, I think I remember him. A neighbor of theirs, I think. I met him at barbeques once or twice."

Putting his glasses back on, he stands straight again and moves to the front pew, expressing a long sigh as he settles into the seat.

"Did you know his name?" I sit next to him.

"Oh, no. You know how it is with people. They come and go."

"But he was around on Thanksgiving and Christmas."

He shrugs and takes a hankie from his jacket pocket, wiping his nose.

In the minutes that follow, family and old friends join us, pausing to appreciate the display. An older lady wearing a long, floral dress stops at the pictures, leaning close. "Well, I'll be damned!" she says more loudly than I think she realizes. The man behind me stifles a laugh.

She puts one hand on her chest and fans herself with the other, looking like she might fall over.

I hurry to her side. "Excuse me—are you doing okay? Can I help you find a seat?"

"Oh, no, dear." She takes my hand and smiles at me. "I was just surprised is all. We were so young in these pictures." She points at the beach picture, to a young woman behind my grandma—and next to the stranger. "That was me. Sylvia and I were the best of friends."

Butterflies rush to my stomach. "Who was the man next to you?"

"He was my husband. Only . . ." Narrowing her eyes, she leans toward the photograph again. "No, that can't be right."

"What can't?"

"Your father, there. He was about four. But my Jimmy was gone by then." She shakes her head. "Silly. I must be losing my old marbles." With another smile, she leaves my side, heading for the pews.

I follow and sit next to her. "Can I ask what you mean, that he was gone?"

"He disappeared when your dad was a baby. I remember it very clearly because your grandmother had to console her crying baby at the same time she consoled me." She laughs a little as moisture pools in her eyes. "The police found him about a year later."

I swallow past the lump in my throat. "Found him?"

She nods slowly. "He'd been murdered, I'm afraid. Stabbed and tossed into the lake. They never found who was responsible."

My face falls, regretting making her relive such old pain. "I'm so sorry. Would you like me to sit with you?"

"That would be nice, dear. Thank you."

As the service begins, my eyes go to the photographs again. The beach picture was the oldest. If her husband was already gone by then—or near then, if her memory wasn't quite accurate—how was he in all the later ones?

* * * * *

18

A few weeks after the service, a knock at my door pulls me away from my book. Not expecting anyone, I peer through the peep hole, then open the door. "Dad! What are you doing here?"

"I have some things from the service I thought you might want. Uncle Frank sent it over." After a hug, he steps into my living room. "How have you been doing?"

Without waiting for an answer, he hands me a large, yellow envelope.

I open the clasp. "What is this stuff?"

"I don't know. I didn't look. I've been busy clearing out Grandma's house. Finished what you and Aaron started."

"Find anything interesting?"

He shrugs. "Why don't you come out to the car and have a look? Maybe you'll want to keep something."

I set the envelope on an end table and follow him out. Three boxes sit neatly in the back of his SUV.

"This is all you've got?" I ask.

"It's all that I thought you guys might want."

The first two boxes hold a few vases, wine glasses, and framed pictures. The second has a tarnished silver punch bowl set. The last box has more random items: yellowed doilies, ceramic dolls, and something that didn't fit with any of the other things—a hunting knife.

I pick it up, studying the heavy case. "Why did Grandma have this?"

"Beats me. Maybe your grandpa hunted before I could remember. I found it in the back of the bedroom closet—I almost missed it. Do you want to keep it?"

I pull the knife from the case, eyeing the shiny blade. At the base, near the handle, is something I'm sure shouldn't be there: a small drop of blood.

He'd been murdered, I'm afraid. Stabbed and tossed into the lake.

I gasp at the sudden memory. This knife could be from anything. Grandma couldn't have been involved with her friend's murder.

Could she?

With shaking hands, I slide the blade back into the case and drop it to the box. "No, my apartment has enough clutter."

"Are you okay?"

I nod, maybe a little too rapidly.

"Okay." He stares at me as he makes his way to the driver's door. "Call me if you need anything."

After he drives off, I go back inside and pick up the envelope. It holds a program from the funeral, some thank-you cards, the guest book, and a photograph.

"Oh my god!" I fall back against the wall, my eyes glued to the image and my heart pounding. The photograph is of me, the one Uncle Frank took in the hallway. And though I'm sure I was alone that day, according to this picture, I was not.

Behind me is a man I only know from pictures, a man with brown hair wearing tan slacks and a shiny green shirt. Only this time, he is smiling.

The Right Time To Move On
Jenifer Ruff
Charlotte, NC, USA
Copyright © 2018 by Jenifer Ruff. All rights reserved.
jenruff.com

The odor of disinfectant chemicals and urine fills my nostrils. I don't usually notice it unless I'm wheeled from the room and brought outside for a bit of fresh air, but it's been days, maybe weeks since that's happened.

Torrential rain drums a steady beat on the roof and lashes against the glass window I can't see. I knew it was coming long before the first drops descended. A chill creeping inside my brittle bones. A flare of arthritis in my aching joints.

A bitter exhale of breath that no one else hears escapes my throat. That's me laughing. If I could shake my head, I'd do that too. I'm especially melancholy. The incessant rain reminds me of lost opportunities.

My life wasn't supposed to end this way. When the right time arrived, I was to move on.

Long ago, when my mother, wise beyond her years, first explained what would happen—*what could have, should have happened*—I drew back in horror, unable to swallow my disbelief. I couldn't imagine ever going through with it.

I remember sunlight flashing off her remarkable diamond as she placed a gentle, reassuring hand on my shoulder. "I know, I know. It does sound horrible, but mark my words, a time will come when you'll know it's the right thing to do. I promise you. The time will come."

I put aside a substantial amount of my inheritance. I called it my "rainy day fund." Quite the understatement. The stash was more than enough to sustain a new life. Tucked inside a large combination safe beneath the hayloft on my farm, it's highly unlikely the money will ever be found.

I trusted my mother. I trusted her right up until the moment I realized she was wrong.

My stroke gave no warning. It didn't politely call to make a reservation or mail a "save the date" notecard a few months in advance. It didn't knock on the door and quietly wait for a signature. It rudely appeared, with no regard for my current or future plans, and kicked the door in. One day I was out walking and weeding, pushing a wheelbarrow across one of the fields, and the next I was an invalid who couldn't speak or move.

And now, I've had enough. I'm ready to go.

A young nurse's aide with sleek cornrows enters my room. I'm pretty sure her name is Sarah. They're supposed to wear name tags, but they hardly ever do. And with cataracts clouding my vision, I can barely read them anyway.

"Afternoon, Mrs. Laprade."

I don't hear a good in the greeting, but at least she has acknowledged my existence and I'm grateful for that because sometimes I wonder if I'm really laying in this bed or if it's all some horrible hallucination.

The fat one, Louisa, stands in the doorway, blocking the light from the hallway. Her wheezy breath gives her away. She's terribly out of shape. Maybe I'm like the pot calling the kettle black, except that I have no control over my condition.

"I always get a strange feeling in this room," Sarah says to Louisa.

Her words warm my near empty heart. She can sense there's something special inside me even if she has no idea what it is. It used to happen all the time, but as I've aged, people don't seem to sense it so much anymore.

Sarah yanks the sheet down from under my chin. Exposed to the air, my pale, papery skin prickles with goosebumps.

Sarah sighs, long and loud. "Louisa, you gonna just stand there?" Sarah is already tired of this place and I believe she's only been here a few weeks. They never last. It's hard work. Hard on the legs, hard on the back, and hard on one's capacity for compassion. It's work best left to others, but someone has to do it.

"Louisa? I need help moving Mrs. Laprade." Sarah presses her hands against her hips. I can tell she's exasperated with Louisa and I can't blame her. Louisa's lack of responsibility is shocking.

"Just leave her there." Louisa wipes her forehead with the back of her hand then scratches her belly. "She don't know what's what. Ain't no one gonna care if she don't get moved around today."

Sarah frowns. "That's what you said yesterday."

"Right. And see, ain't nobody complained yet and ain't nobody going to. Where she got to be? Important appointment? Got a big date?" Louisa laughs and slaps her huge thigh. This represents my only glimpse of humor, and it's hardly funny. She plops down in the corner chair, her bulk spreading and settling. "Lordy, I'm beat. Just gonna sit here for a few."

Louisa's lazy attitude astounds me. On my farm I performed healthy, hard physical labor every day from the crack of dawn until the sun went down. No complaining, no shirking your duties. Louisa grew tired of her work here long ago, but didn't have the decency to quit and leave. Instead she quit and stayed. The worst combination for all of us at the Havencroft Nursing Home who exist here at her mercy.

Sarah scowls at Louisa and turns back to me. Her eyes scan my body. Most of her bottom lip is hidden under her top teeth. She's thinking there's no way can get me out of this bed alone, and she's not supposed to. Louisa is a lot stronger than she is.

"Okay." Sarah exhales loudly. "I'll just change her, turn her over at least." And then she looks at me, really looks at me, something hardly anyone does anymore. "Mrs. Laprade? I'm going to clean you up now, okay?"

Perhaps she hopes I will say, "Don't bother," to save her the trouble. But I can't respond and I would very much like to be changed indeed. I'm certain I smell terrible and the persistent, sharp sting on my backside, another bedsore, is almost unbearable.

Mentally, I brace myself for the indignities to come as I'm rolled from one bony hip to the other like an old sack of rotting potatoes. Enduring the tugs and shoves, I remind myself that when people are completely dependent on others, they must be grateful for whatever care comes their way.

After a few minutes, the ordeal is over. I feel more comfortable. Or, to be more accurate, less miserable. The momentary embarrassment has come and gone.

Now that the work is done, Louisa pushes herself up from the chair with a grunt.

Leaving me uncovered, Sarah is halfway out the door. "I'm going to get new pads."

I'm alone with Louisa.

She plods toward me and hovers. Lifting my small, vein-covered hand from the bed, she holds it in her big, puffy one. The stale smell of cigarettes and coffee floats on her breath. Sometimes I wish my sense of smell had faded.

"Hoo-boy! Will you look at that rock."

She's talking about the ring my mother gave me on her death bed. An ancient family heirloom, the large diamond surrounded by blood red garnets.

Louisa glances at the doorway and the empty corridor beyond before staring right at me, her big eyes gleaming. "Whatch you be needing this for?"

Without having the faintest idea of the power it wields, she clutches my ring with her meaty fingers and tugs.

She isn't the first or the second to try. I've lost count of the failed attempts, but I do know she won't succeed. I'm not sure if that knowledge is a relief or a disappointment. The ring won't come off. After so many years on my swollen finger, the platinum band has become a part of me. It's not leaving unless my finger goes with it. My gnarled joints crack and scream out with her efforts, but the ring doesn't budge.

She lets go. My aching hand drops back to the bed, infused with fresh new pain. I think she's given up, but I'm wrong. She returns to my bedside with the hand soap from the sink's edge. I hear the squish, squish of the pump. The cold slimy liquid surrounds my finger and oozes down my wrist.

With her fat features scrunched in concentration, she seems determined. Perhaps she has children at home who need new shoes, an electric bill she can't pay. And her question is a valid

24

one. What *do* I need the expensive ring for? It doesn't help me move or talk, it isn't a key to my memories. The time for its purpose has long passed. At the very least, the ring is worth tens of thousands of dollars. If she manages to get it off, I should be happy that even in my condition I'm still able to make someone's life a little better. Although I would prefer the ring went to anyone but her.

She keeps pulling, perspiration coating her forehead, droplets rolling down her temple and over her cheek.

"Excuse me?" The soft, rarely-used voice of my neighbor, Mrs. Murphy, calls out from behind the curtain that separates us. "Excuse me?" She is a sweet elderly woman. Like me, she lays in bed day after day and never has visitors. Often she is kind enough to talk to me, even though I can't respond. I have much to share, but my end of our conversation remains locked inside my head. She coughs and clears her throat. "Can you please bring me some water, when you have a chance? I'm very thirsty."

"Later." Louisa's voice sounds harsh, irritated. "I'm doing something else right now." But that's not all Louisa says. As she grips my finger and yanks with all her might, she mutters, "You ain't thirsty from just laying there, you old bag. Maybe I'll let you find out what real thirsty feels like."

A powerful crack of thunder shakes the walls and something inside me changes. I cannot stop myself. There's something rancid and festering inside Louisa's core. I steel my mind and recite the spell I learned on the same day my mother bestowed me with the ring. The spell I only recently believed I would never ever use.

Poor, stupid Louisa. Not in her wildest nightmares could she imagine what will happen if she succeeds now.

The wind wails outside, as if it means to come in, and a flash of lightning illuminates the room. Louisa wrenches my finger at an angle, with no regard to the fragile wrist and arm attached to it.

I hear soft cracks, like dead sticks crunching underfoot. My brittle bones are crumbling. The ring departs my finger, tearing away layers of my dry skin as it goes. An agonizing and overwhelming vertigo spirals inside me. Raw pain sears my nerves. My weak heart beats so fast, I can't tell where one thump stops and the next begins. I'm choking on a torrent of acidic bile rising inside my throat. Gray clouds close in around my vision and turn black. A final sputtering moan escapes my cracked lips.

It is done.

The pain disappears.

I blink. Open my eyes. Blink again.

My eyesight is sharp and clear.

I'm staring at my extraordinary ring on a fat pinky, the only finger it fit. I splay my fingers wide, then flex them. Lifting my arms overhead, I stretch toward the ceiling, shift my weight from side to side, shake out my legs. A smile begins to form at the corners of my mouth.

I should have never doubted my mother.

Cringing, I look down at the gaunt, almost skeletal figure in the bed and can't repress a shudder. Did I really look that pitiful? My instinct is to turn away, but I don't. I look deep into her eyes, circled with dark shadows like a corpse. Sections of her spotted scalp are visible between thin wisps of dull gray hair.

Leaning closer, I whisper. "Louisa? Can you hear me?"

She cannot answer. Eyes wide with terror, beads of sweat dotting her brow, fear emanates from the frail old woman's every pore. Except she's not an old woman. Not really. Only her body is old.

I can't imagine what she is thinking, and I do feel for her, I know exactly what it's like to be trapped inside a useless body. And once it's done, it can't be undone. Not for her.

I stroke the ring in appreciation, such a small, simple action, but something I haven't been able to do for years. I can keep moving forward and I will. I have every intention of finding a body more suitable for hard work, the type of work I enjoy.

I smooth my hair back, square my shoulders, and straighten up.

Thunder rumbles, echoing outside the little room as I bring Mrs. Murphy some fresh water.

Sarah returns with fresh pads and I reach out to take them from her. She raises one eyebrow and looks at me strangely.

I smile. "I'll finish taking care of Mrs. Laprade today. I want to put something on this bedsore of hers, prop her up so she's not laying on it. We have to do a better job turning her."

Sarah's mouth drops open. "You hit your head or something while I was gone?"

I laugh again as I unfold the pads, delighted by the clear sounds I'm able to produce with ease. "I might have to leave a little early today. So let's not waste any time."

I'm going back to my farm. Everything I need is waiting for me there.

It is after all, a rainy day.

Devil's Hollow, Holy Water
Adele Marie Park
Originally from Rousay, an island in the Orkneys, U. K.
Copyright © 2018 by Adele Marie Park. All rights reserved.
Firefly465

A community that hides a secret, sticks together. It binds them like glue and smells just as evil.

Holy Water is one of those towns built upon the bones of those we took it from.

Oh, they'll tell you that the settlers wandered for months without water when they came upon the river. The founding father fell on his knees and declared it a miracle. Hallelujah, Holy Water was born.

I'm smiling at you, Doc 'cause your last name was his, too.

Don't patronise me with your hollow chuckle; you ain't amused.

It's nice and peaceful by this window. I can see the gardens and the trees. Don't mind having no shoes on my feet.

When I returned home that terrible day, my feet were so swollen they cut my boots.

Lord, I was screaming like a wild animal. They paid no attention. If they had, Benji might've been saved. I doubt it, but in the early days that one thought kept me from dying.

Here come the tears again. Like Mama's, on the morning it happened.

She'd had no money from Mr. Aitken's for a month. Oh, he kept saying things would get better, but he was lying and she knew it.

Benji tried to sit on her knee but she was shaking so bad he fell.

He hit his head on the table and hollered like a baby goat.

So, Mama told me to get on out and take Benji with me.

I got us bundled up in our new winter coats. The last of Mama's money went on them, but she said we needed em'. I'd have done without but that's a Mama's love for you.

The day was full of the promise of snow. You know, the kind of sharp, crisp morning when jack frost is just waking. Peaceful if it weren't for Benji and his screams.

They echoed around, shaking stubborn leaves off the trees and scaring the crows.

He stopped crying when I gave him the last of my candy from Halloween.

Anyways, we was heading towards the park. Even if it only had one swing, it was better than getting under Mama's feet.

Benji was chattering like a baby bird, but I wasn't hearing him on account of Doug coming towards us.

Doug Johansen. The boy that made my hormones come alive, despite his braces.

My sixteenth birthday had come and gone with nothing changing but the weather. I'd been this way about Doug for two years.

Sometimes when I laid quiet in bed on nights when sleep was missing, I imagined what it might be like to kiss him.

Would his braces cut my lips?

Would it be like kissing a dead fish or would it steal breath from me and set my heart pumping blood so fast I got dizzy?

I would press my face against the pillow and giggle like I was Benji's age.

I remember Doug saying hi, and us looking at one another, not saying a word.

Benji found something up his nose and I swatted his hand away. It made Doug and me smile at one another, flipping my stomach like a pancake.

Doug's older brother, Bart came along on his bike. Laughed and said we was idiots.

The brothers got into an argument.

29

Bart called Doug a coward, and I asked why. Wish I'd kept my mouth shut but I guess I never could.

So we got the story from Bart. Last weekend, Halloween night, Bart and his stupid friends dared Doug to go into Devil's Hollow and search for the mine. Doug refused to go, and I don't blame him.

Devil's Hollow is in the middle of the woods that edge Holy Water. It's a mean looking place. Dangerous, too. An old mine lies buried, the entrance lost to time.

There're stories about that mine. You know 'em.

How a hundred years ago or more there was a pack of miners and their families living in Devil's Hollow. More of 'em came building homes like it was a small town. Fragile homes, Mama said, made from sticks and planks of wood which was no good come the winter. They came because some fool said the mine was full of gold. They found nothing but death.

My granddaddy used to say they dug something evil outta that mine.

Anyway, the miners caused a huge landslide that buried the mine and the houses. The ground just opened and swallowed them.

Old folks say its cursed land, while others say they triggered an earth quake.

On this day I told Bart we'd go with them to look for the mine. I guess the day was just started, and I didn't want to go home yet. Or maybe it was because of Doug.

I carried Benji in my arms, while Doug walked beside me. Bart peddled on his bike, scouting ahead, he said.

God damn. It started out so innocent. We were bored kids trying to find treasure or something. Isn't that how they say it in the books?

We talked about things that might bore most folks, but for me, it was a golden moment. I keep the memory locked inside my head. No one can take it away from me, no matter what they do.

The nearer we got to Devil's Hollow my breakfast turned to rocks in my stomach.

Healthy trees gave way to ugly, mean stunted things, all twisted and overgrown so that the sun only pierced the tops of 'em.

I looked up once. Without their leaves, they was just like skeletons and I could imagine them reaching out with bony fingers, snatching me up and shaking me til I died.

It got colder, too. Not winter cold, but bone chill. That's my granddaddy's saying, and it's a true one too. I was glad mama made us put on our new coats even though the wool itched any skin it touched.

I didn't put Benji down even when he wanted to 'cause the ground was all mulch and smelled like a blocked toilet.

You ever smelled that? Nope, suppose you ain't.

By this time, we went quiet.

Bart was pushing his bike but took a temper on it and left it beside a tree. He took a flashlight with him though. Should've realised how serious he was.

I got my coat caught by brambles, but Doug got me free.

My new coat ripped, and I remember wanting to cry as the button tore.

The fear of mama's tears and pain made my heart tremble.

The spikes kept a hold of the pink button, guess they still have it.

Bart kept shouting for us to hurry or he would find the mine and keep everything for himself.

The deeper in we got, the worse the ground got.

Green muck oozed over the tops of my boots, making my feet squelch. The stink changed to rotten wood and dead animals. We had a racoon die on us in the woodshed, so I knew what dead animal smelled like.

Bart kept ahead of us. Despite the stink, I was enjoying talking to Doug until, Bart screamed.

We ran towards his voice, me bumping Benji on my hip to keep a hold of him.

Bart was stuck in the ground right up to his middle.

At first, I thought he'd fallen in a bog, but then I saw the broken bits of wood he was trying to grip. He said his feet had gone through something and his legs were dangling in space.

We hauled him out and pulled the bits of wood away from where he'd fallen.

I remember staring into that black hole and I thought someone said my name. I should've turned back, but hell, I'm as nosey as the next person.

Bart and Doug were arguing again. Bart asked me what we should do. Go down or go home.

He had a way of sneering. It always got my temper rising, so I told him to go down.

Benji cried; there was no way he wanted to go down, but I shushed him and dried his tears.

Bart shouted for us to come.

His feet hit something solid, and the stink got worse. Like rotting mushrooms or meat gone rancid.

Doug looked at me real funny. He whispered it wasn't too late to back out, but I wanted to see. I needed to like an itch that wanted scratching.

He jumped down and the beam of his flashlight wavered. I prayed that the batteries weren't going out. His feet hit something solid, and the stink got worse. Like rotting mushrooms or meat gone rancid.

I handed Benji down to him. Oh, God, why did I do that? It hurts so much inside; my baby brother.

No, I've got to finish this. I'm old now and it'll be the last time I recall it. You can do what you want with it when I'm done.

I jumped in after them, and if the stink was bad up in the fresh air; it was disgusting here. The reflex to vomit was strong, but I swallowed hard enough to banish it, holding my breath until my ears popped.

We stood on damp, rotting wood that looked like floorboards. We thought it must've been part of the shacks.

That scared the hell outta me. We were walking on graves. People died here.

Doug shined his torch around the walls, yep, walls, made of the same type of rotten planks.

Them walls disappeared into blackness. A tunnel that might never end.

Bart was far ahead of us and his voice echoed back saying he'd found something.

Careful of the flooring, I picked up Benji, and we walked on real slow to where Bart waited for us.

Bart came into view when the flashlight shone on his face. The light made his skin white but with a kinda green tinge to it.

Then we saw them.

Skeletons.

I hid Benji's eyes, but he seen 'em and started to whine.

Bart was touching 'em, excited, he pointed out the rings on their fingers.

Doug and me shouted to leave them alone.

He agreed too quick; it showed how scared he was.

Someone piled up the skeletons at a corner. Who had done that?

Why the hell was there a corner?

The more we questioned what we'd found, the more my nerves shot through me. I remember saying I would be sick and we should go back.

Benji was hiccupping tears every so often. His senses told him he shouldn't be here with them long dead bones.

God damn, everything in those moments are so clear, they replay in my head all the time.

Doug took hold of his brother's shoulders and shook him like a bag of popcorn. He cursed at him saying he would tell his mama everything.

Bart yelled at him to shut up.

The silence after made me hold my breath. I heard nothing but my heart echoing in my ears. I hurt inside, wishing I'd never eaten breakfast as my stomach surged like a roller coaster.

It's so weird all these things happening in seconds. Normal reactions to a situation which was anything but normal.

Then the sound came.

It reminded me of chipmunks, but what the hell would they be doing down here?

We stared at one another.

You know when you read "their eyes were wide"? Well, that's true. It looked like Doug's eyes would pop outta his head.

Nothing could be alive down here, could it?

He shone his torch further down and the light never reached the end of blackness.

"We've found the mine. We'll be rich."

I remember Bart saying those words, and taking off like a jackrabbit.

We'd no choice but to follow.

Doug's flickering torch picked out more floorboards, and the walls packed up with dirt and more wood.

Bart's feet shuffled onward and I'm thinking how far is he going to go?

The footsteps kept going, and the air hurt my lungs. It was like breathing in damp fog that burned.

The tunnel narrowed, and Bart's footsteps stopped. He didn't call out like before, so we wondered what the hell he'd found this time.

When we caught up with him, the tunnel opened out into a large cave with lots of tunnels leading off.

We stood gawking at what was in the middle of the cave.

An old table dominated the space. What gave me terror bumps was someone had dressed the damn thing.

Plates and cutlery. A teapot sat in the middle like a short, stout, commander of the cups.

On the rickety chairs, sat like royalty, were two skeletons, dressed in rags that held likeness to clothing.

Benji had gone quiet with fright, but I held his hand and walked back the way we'd come—but stopped. It was black as tar without a flashlight.

There was a sudden loud noise that made me jump and Benji wet himself.

"You stupid idiot," Doug shouted at his brother.

Lord, when they gave out brains Bart must've been absent that day.

He'd touched one skeleton and the damn head rolled onto the floor making an almighty racket.

It echoed around us and slid down those other tunnels carrying, Lord knows how far.

I held my breath until I couldn't any longer for fear of passing out. Even so taking in breaths so fast made me dizzy.

Terror froze us. I know it's a saying but until you feel it creep into your bones, you don't know how real that saying is.

Benji laid his head on my shoulder, his breathing making a song, a wheeze, as if the damp and mould were lying in his lungs.

I remember thinking that mama was gonna beat me for getting him so dirty and ill.

Bart opened his mouth but shut it again, waving at the rest of us to keep quiet, too.

He pointed to one of the tunnels and cupped his ear.

I figured out from his bizarre behaviour that he was hearing something, so I listened.

At first, all I heard was blood rushing around my body and the fast beat of my heart. It thumped like a resurrection preachers drum.

Slow at first, the sound trickled into my ears.

It sounded as if someone snapped their fingers, but not in time. A disjointed rhythm, it grated on my nerves and my mouth filled with saliva.

I backed up holding onto Benji so tight he grunted.

Doug glanced around before he joined us. I turned my back at the entrance and I swear there were spiders crawling down my neck. Doug took a hold of my elbow and we moved faster until we entered the dark tunnels again. Bart's footsteps kept pace with ours. The clicks got fainter the more we kept moving. Something wet dripped down my face and I held up a hand to touch it. They were my tears that was falling. "Can we go home now?" I whispered hoping he caught my words above the shuffling of our feet.

"Yeah," Doug said and turned his head towards Bart. "We've seen enough. Hurry up."

We walked back through those damn tunnels except now they seemed to go on forever. We jumped at every noise and the shadows the torch threw up.

Benji's wheezing got worse and my teeth chattered. I longed for fresh air on my face.

I remember a song kept going 'round in my head. "This train is bound for glory." More like we was running outta the mouth of hell.

Our eyes got used to the darkness 'cause we could see daylight ahead of us.

Heaviness pushed on my chest as if someone tied a stone around my neck and it crushed my bones.

We stopped just out of reach of the hole, I guess we thought we was safe.

I turned around and noticed tiny trickles of earth flowing through the rotten planks like rainwater. Fixated by this, my brain trying to process why, when a plank fell from the wall and landed at my feet with a dull thump.

I glanced upward and my eyes widened as something pink tried to push through the earth.

Worms? They were like fat worms, wiggling in a way that made me feel sick.

Benji screamed and made me jump.

Bart poked the wall where another plank had fallen out.

I looked at Doug, my heart beat now up to the speed of a freight train.

"Run!" he said.

I tried to move but the ground underneath me heaved in waves.

Bart screamed.

My gaze fixed on him as the worm things protruded from the earth walls capturing Bart. Dozens of them wrapped around him like pink ribbon.

Doug tried to help him but there was nothing for him to grip. God damn, they pulled Bart into the earth. His screaming went on for what seemed ages, but it must've been seconds.

There was a gurgling sound before it stopped. I swear to God, they was eating him.

We could hear the crunching, oh God, the snapping of teeth. They were grinding up Bart's bones like a wood chipper. Sniffing and gulping like a pack of animals eating their dinner, snarling over who got the juiciest piece.

Doug just stood there, staring at where his brother had been as if nothing was real and we'd all wake up and laugh about what'd we'd dreamed.

Something grabbed my hair, and I screamed like a fox caught in a trap.

Doug pulled me towards him, and through fear I dropped Benji.

I turned around, safe in Doug's arms, and saw my hair, like cobwebs, dangling from pink fingers. They twitched, rubbing my hair with the finger tips as if they used them to see.

Benji sat on the ground, howling.

"Give me a minute, Jesus, just wait a moment, will you?"

I was just reaching for him-and I would've got him-but a head pushed out of the earth.

It's burned into my mind.

A bulbous head with no hair reminding me of a rotten fruit someone had left out in the rain. Soft and squashy. It might have been human once.

The eyes, Jesus, pure white, blind, and it opened its mouth letting out a gurgling, wet sound. Pointed, sharp teeth, like those of a shark, filled its mouth.

I couldn't move, my fingers were so close to grabbing Benji, but I couldn't take my eyes off that head.

Quick as spring showers that thing moved.

It pushed out of the earth and grabbed Benji.

It took my baby brother.

His screams didn't last long. He was so tiny, so afraid.

Benji.

Everything that happened next is blurry.

I screamed, and Doug shouted at me because more of those things pushed through the walls.

The ground heaved, they came from every direction.

The earth flew around in great globs that hit us, as they dug through like moles.

Doug pushed me real hard, and I fell face first onto a plank of wood.

As I looked back I wanted to scream at him in temper. Ask him why he pushed me, but they'd caught him. Grasped him in their fat, pink fingers, pulling him further into the earth.

His eyes, the expression in them... I'll never forget. He opened his mouth and screamed at me to run.

I wasn't quick enough because I saw one tear out his tongue, hold it up as if it were a piece of candy dripping with strawberry sauce.

It fixed blind eyes on me as it bit off the tip of Doug's tongue.

That did it.

Fear and flight took over me and I scrambled over broken planks and soft squashed stuff. I didn't want to know.

Just as I reached the place where we first jumped down, something snagged my foot.

One of those monsters crawled after me.

It mewed like a kitten, its fingers scrabbling, trying to get a hold on me. Its body was as bulbous as its head.

I saw veins pulsing through the creature, carrying blood to a huge black heart, and I wanted to have the courage to rip it out of the thing's chest.

Anger flared up inside me, giving me strength.

I screeched, kicked out and got free. My boot caught the thing in the face and a sound like a dying cat left its mouth.

Revulsion caused me to gag as green goo dribbled from the corner of the gash that was its mouth.

By now the need to escape flooded through me, giving me speed. I shimmied up the wall.

I got to the surface and threw myself on the wet grass. My lungs were bursting as I drew in deep breaths.

Below me, I heard them. They were swarming like ants. Oh, God, I ran like the hounds of hell were chasing me, not caring if branches scratched me or holes in the ground tripped me up.

The sound of my feet pounding on the road, matched my heartbeat, thump, thump, thump.

I burst through the front door, Mama screamed and dropped whatever she had in her hands.

Mama couldn't understand me.

I was shaking so bad that no words that came out of my mouth made sense. Then Mama realised Benji was missing...

The cops came. Well, Deputy Francis, being the only cop in town, arrived.

Neighbours pushed into our house. Someone trying to calm mama.

They forgot me for a moment; bad for me 'cause I replayed everything over.

Screaming ripped my throat, but I couldn't stop. I howled like a wolf.

Someone must've called the paramedics. I didn't feel the prick of the needle, but my body went to sleep.

Inside my head, I was still screaming, disconnected from my body and existing in a floating nightmare.

You say disassociation. I say drugs.

Give me a light. Thanks. I didn't use to smoke, but it helps now. Nothing else on this earth can scare me now, apart from the creatures.

Everyone looked for Benji, Bart and Doug.

Never found 'em. Didn't even find the hole we'd exposed.

They called in the FBI. I could've told 'em not to waste their time. People scoured Devil's Hollow with big machines, and men in white paper suits took away samples of the earth. To check if there was poison coming from some government base.

Nothing was found. Not even a scrap of clothing.

Mama put me in an insane asylum; said it would be safer for me. I believe she knew the truth but got scared. The illusion that I was crazy was easier for her.

I soon learned to stop talking about what had happened. It stopped the constant round of doctors, drugs and other stuff.

Do you know what it's like to be held under a cold shower? Oh, no, you don't do that now, these days you invent different tricks.

When the drugs didn't work. I'd lay awake at night, and I swear, I heard them underneath me. I'm never gonna forget the sounds they make.

I imagine what it would be like to stomp on their heads. Hearing the squelch as their skulls burst and the satisfaction I'd get.

Don't worry Doc, those clowns in white won't let me out.

It's my minds way of trying to make sense of what happened that day. I got real good at saying that to them until it satisfied them I wasn't a risk to myself or others.

They closed the damn asylum, and I got shifted around for a while until I landed here.

So, you got me, Doc, and like I said this is the last time I'm gonna talk about this.

What do I think they were?

I think a few miners and their families never died, they ate the ones who did and became something non-human. Or they were a forgotten race only remembered in legends.

Even the forgotten crazy relative hidden away hears news from the outside world.

I've heard kids and adults went missing in Devil's Hollow. Where do you think they've gone?

Them ghost hunter people investigated.

I wasn't allowed to watch the tv show; the old doc said it would bring back too many memories. He was right.

We opened something which should've stayed deep in the earth.

It is torture to be the only survivor of a horror so not of this world it haunts you.

It happened. They are real. They took my baby brother.

I heard they're talking about bulldozing Devil's Hollow and building houses on it. They can't do that. Decent folks, they won't suspect a damn thing.

You gotta tell my story Doc. You have to believe me. One night when it's black dark they'll crawl outta the ground.

It's safe in here. No wooden floors.

Where The Black Tree Grows
MD Walker
Breckenridge, Tx, USA
Copyright © 2018 by MD Walker. All rights reserved.
https://plotmonster.wordpress.com/

My dress clung limply to my body, drenched in sweat, as I rushed through the pitch-black alleys and side roads. Trash littered the walkways and mysterious shadows lurked around every corner. Still I hurried on. Mama always said that New Orleans after dark was no place for proper young ladies, but proper young ladies don't set out to do what I had planned.

I whipped around the final corner and scanned the alley for the entrance. Dark intentions rarely walk through the front door, and this was no exception. A candle flickered in a window to my left, and I knew this must be the house. Carefully, I crept to the back step. There was no turning back once I stepped over that threshold. I took a deep breath of balmy night air and knocked on the door.

The woman that answered the door was an ancient, wrinkled creature with twisted limbs and gnarled hands. Her stringy gray hair hung in tangled clumps about her neck and her bent broken figure filled the doorway.

"What do you want?"

"I'm here to see Marie."

"She ain't here."

Before she could retreat, I shoved my foot between the door and the frame. "It's important."

She shook her head and gestured for me to enter, opening the door wider and grumbling, "Always is."

41

I followed her into a kitchen overflowing with pots and pans, of course, but also herbs and spices. Strange relics hung from the ceiling and miniature statues lined the shelves. Dominating the middle of the room was a monstrous table covered with a brilliant blue cloth and a cavernous stone bowl situated in the center. Despite the heat outside, there was a large pot with some type of bubbling liquid boiling on the stove. It filled the room with an enticing smell and my stomach rumbled in response.

She gestured for me to sit down. "I ain't lyin'. Missus ain't here."

Disappointment must have been written all over my face because she smiled, almost warmly, and asked if I would like a bowl of stew. I nodded as I breathed a sigh of relief. I had been nervously wondering what was in that pot and more than a bit relieved to know it was only supper.

She pointed toward the table and I sat on the sturdy bench tucked beneath it. The spicy aroma of onion and garlic filled my nose while she ladled the steaming soup into a bowl and placed it on the table before me.

A loud commotion outside the tiny kitchen caught my attention. Moments later a beautiful, mulatto woman entered the room. Her hair was plaited down the side and she was wearing a dress in vibrant hues of orange and yellow. Two small children hugged her skirt hem. She took one look at me and quickly scooted the children into the next room. The crone followed them, hobbling with her withered walking stick.

I swallowed hard, barely able to force words from my mouth. "Marie?"

She nodded. Her eyes were a striking blend of brown and gold and she stared at me like she was peering straight through to my soul. A chilly sense of foreboding flooded my senses, my pulse quickened and every nerve in my body crackled to life. The hair on the back of my neck stood on end, sending a shiver through me. "I need your help."

She raised her chin with an arrogant smirk, "And why would I help you?" Her voice was silky smooth but there was no denying the danger that lay beneath her words.

I pulled a worn velvet pouch from my pocket and sat it on the table. Eyeing it greedily, she moved closer and retrieved the pouch. She quickly looked inside before pulling the drawstring closed and slipping it into her pocket. "Humph. You don't look like you need a love potion. So, then? Why did you sneak to my house in the dead of night to beg favors?"

"Do you know of Madame LaLaurie?"

Her body went rigid at the mention of LaLaurie and she moved to the table, bracing her hands on it before lowering herself onto the bench. "I have heard the name," she replied.

I pushed the bowl away from me, suddenly losing my appetite. I focused on the purpose that had brought me here. "She is our neighbor. I work as a freed person for the Abellard family across the street from the LaLaurie mansion."

Marie said nothing but stared at me, her unblinking eyes holding my gaze. She leaned a bit closer as I continued, "My uncle Ezekiel is a slave in her household. I have been trying to save my money to buy him but have not earned enough yet."

She nodded. "What does that have to do with me? I can't spin straw into gold."

My voice quivered, "It's getting worse. Her slaves are scared, and I just don't have any more time to wait. I… I came to you for a curse."

"Why do you think that I can help you?"

I lowered my eyes unable to meet her steely gaze, "I just know that I need to save my uncle. I'm desperate."

She stood up and moved to a row of shelves in the back of the room. There she pulled a small black bag from behind one of the statues. "You are not the first to come here about LaLaurie. What makes you think you have a better chance to get what you want?"

She didn't wait for my reply as she walked back to the table and emptied the contents of the bag. Shreds of green and brown herbs drifted to the bottom of the bowl. She struck a match and tossed it in. A flame flared up, popping and hissing as the herbs smoldered. She snatched a knife from the table and held it to the fire before swiping it across her hand.

Then she gestured for me to do the same. I gasped in surprise but slowly moved my arm in her direction. She made a quick slice across my palm and then smashed our hands together, dripping our mixed blood into the bowl.

Marie bowed her head and began to chant in a language unknown to myself. When she once again lifted her eyes, they glowed with a sort of fire that did not seem wholly human.

My body trembled at the unnatural sight and yet I swallowed my fear. It was too late to be deterred. I watched as she scooped ashes from the dying flames and placed them into the little black bag.

"Here." She handed me the bag and explained what I must do for the curse to work. "What's done is done."

I would have to hurry if I wanted to see my uncle before Madame LaLaurie returned. I needed to talk to him about the plans I had made. He would no doubt try to discourage me, but the wheels were already in motion. I could only hope he would go along with it. Madame Delphine LaLaurie had to die and Marie Laveau had helped me decide how.

A skinny slave-girl about ten years old answered the door. She looked half-starved, wearing a dress at least two sizes too big. Her bones stuck out at strange angles and the dress did little to hide the grotesque thinness of her body.

"Yes, ma'am?" Her voice was barely more than a whisper and she refused to look me in the eye.

I smiled warmly at the child trying to put her at ease, although it didn't seem to work. "Can I see Ezekiel for just a moment?"

The girl's eyes widened in fright and she shook her head vigorously. "Oh, no, ma'am! What if missis comes home?" Her little body trembled so violently that she almost lost her balance.

I knelt and took her hand. "He is my uncle and I really need to talk to him. My mistress will not allow any harm to come to either of us."

The little girl didn't look convinced, but she pushed open the door to allow me access. She led me through the house, winding a path through room after room until we came to the kitchen. It was a massive area with an impressive cast-iron stove

44

taking up most of the space. The cook was busy rolling out biscuits and paid little attention as we cut through her domain. As I passed by her, I noticed the chain cuffed around her right ankle. She was chained to the stove! I shook my head in disbelief but kept moving as the little girl led the way out back.

Ezekiel was repairing a damaged wheel for the LaLaurie's prized carriage. He was bent over his work and never even looked up until I was practically standing over him.

"Eva! What you doing here? You know what the missus will do if she finds you here?"

I looked at Ezekiel. He should be a handsome man in the prime of his life. Yet, here he stood, starving, neglected and abused.

"I just wanted to see you and let you know that all of this will be over soon."

"What will be over soon?"

"I have a plan to get you out of here." He started to object but I continued talking. "Don't worry. It's all taken care of. I went to see Marie Laveau and she gave me this." I pushed the black bag into his hands and detailed her instructions.

"And what if it doesn't work?"

"What's done is done. This'll be over soon one way or the other."

Ezekiel's eyes grew as round as saucers and his mouth dropped open. He pointed over my shoulder as I heard a voice behind me.

"Yes, it will."

I turned to see Madame LaLaurie wielding a hammer. She flung the hammer at my head. I tried to dodge her aim, but it was too late. My vision swirled in blurry circles. I felt another blow hit my head. Then another. Then nothing but darkness all around me.

As I laid there, my body limp and twisted, I couldn't help but question the choices that led to this. Marie had warned me that these spells could be unpredictable. I hadn't cared.

I tried to move but it was no use. I tried to scream but no sound came out. I heard her coming, trudging along the garden path with heavy steps.

Plop. Plop. Plop.

The sound stopped and she was standing above me. She grabbed my arms and dragged me towards the garden. My arms felt like they were being ripped from my body but still I couldn't move. When I once again opened my mouth to scream, a garbled choking sound was all that came out.

I watched her pick up a shovel and start digging, dumping shovelfuls of dirt in a pile.

Plop. Plop. Plop.

She kicked me, and I rolled into a shallow hole. Shock and horror filled my mind as I realized what she was doing. I tried to stand up, to kick, to scream. Anything. But, I still couldn't move. The dirt landed on top of my broken body. It entered my mouth and my nostrils. I couldn't breathe.

Plop. Plop. Plop.

Then all at once, the pain stopped. I couldn't feel the weight of the dirt crushing against my chest any longer. My throat was no longer burning as it filled with soil.

Suddenly, I was outside of myself watching as LaLaurie buried me. She shoveled dirt on top of my corpse. She stamped down the earth. Then it was all so clear as I understood my fate.

The flames rose higher and higher in the night sky as the LaLaurie mansion burned. The frightened screams of slaves desperately trying to escape filled the air. There was nothing left that I could do for them, so I watched as that monstrosity of a home went up in flames.

Shouts of "Fire, Fire!" could be heard up and down the street as the neighborhood turned out to help douse the flames. Madame LaLaurie scurried in and out of the house carrying as many of her possessions as she could but none of her slaves were anywhere to be seen. The people began to grumble and ask questions. *Where are the servants?*

LaLaurie's cook had carried out her part of the plan perfectly. Chained to the kitchen stove, she doused the kitchen in oil and struck a match. Then she tugged at her chains, trying to break free but the effort was futile, and the stove was too heavy to move. The flames grazed her skin and the heat of the fire took her breath away. Coughing and sputtering, she choked on the smoke filling the room. Her screams pierced the air but there was no one to hear, no one to help her and all I could do was watch as she writhed in pain.

Dr. LaLaurie was refusing any help. He was ordering everyone to stay out of his house. However, a large group of people paid him no mind as they rushed in to find the missing slaves. Some ran up the stairs to the sound of terrified screams and painful moaning, while others ran toward the now silent kitchen. As they discovered what the occupants of 1140 Royal Street wanted to hide, the LaLauries got into their newly repaired carriage. Amidst all the chaos, I was the only one that saw them drive away. The only one that noticed Ezekiel was driving. Everything was going as planned.

Ezekiel would take them to the swamp and leave their bodies hidden in the cypress stumps where the black trees grow. Maybe the gators would get them. Maybe not. But either way, the LaLauries would never leave Louisiana.

Marie sat at her table eating breakfast and reading the morning headlines: "House of Horrors Goes up in Flames." She took a sip of coffee and smiled.

The Storm
J. A. Allen
Prince Edward Island, Canada
Copyright © 2018 by J. A. Allen. All rights reserved.
JAAllenAuthor.com

"It's too hot to sleep."

I swept Cruise's hair away from his face. He lay on top of the blankets, naked except for his slightly worn Spiderman underwear. Staring up at me in the candlelight, his seven-year-old features gleamed under a sheen of sweat.

"You won't notice the heat once you fall asleep." I leaned in with a kiss for the top of his head before returning his book to the shelf. "They'll probably have the power on by morning." I took the candle from the top of his dresser, which was littered with the sidewalk chalk he used to draw all over the room's blackboard painted walls. It seemed he was a natural born artist, just like his father. "Would you like some toast with cinnamon and brown sugar for breakfast?"

"You're trying to bribe me," he said, pulling a stuffed dragon with oversized eyes close to his chest. "It won't work."

"It's time to sleep, kiddo. I love you."

"Good night, Momma."

Ben tossed his cell phone on the coffee table as I entered the living room. Placing Cruise's candle next to it, I sank onto the opposite side of the couch.

The discarded phone reflected the candlelight. "Who were you talking to?" I asked, forcing an air of lightness into the question.

"Just playing Sudoku. The battery's out now. I'll have to wait for the power to come back." He offered a strained smile. Something had been bothering him all week. He'd been playing it off, but after seventeen years together, the signs were easy to spot. The strained conversation. The way he rolled toward the opposite side of the room when we went to bed.

I lifted my feet onto the ottoman. "I wish we had a generator, at least to run the air conditioner. I can feel your body heat from here." Fanning myself with a magazine from the basket on the floor, I asked, "What do you think happened to the power, anyway?"

Living so deep in the country had its advantages. Cruise, Lily, and Grace were free to roam the meandering trails on their four-wheelers in summer and snowmobiles in winter, paid for with the money left over after trading the cramped, million-dollar condo in Vancouver for a sprawling acreage in Saskatchewan. Nestled so deep in the woods, we had no neighbors. Ben had converted the old barn across the yard into a studio with large windows that allowed the natural light he so coveted to brighten his herculean canvases, and I had turned the spare bedroom into an office to complete my second novel, having quit my job as a content writer. The kids all had their own rooms. The move had granted us everything we wanted out here, and while I never once regretted leaving British Columbia the year before, I did miss how easily accessible information had been in the city. The power had been out for three hours, and we still had no idea why.

"The heat probably blew out a transformer," Ben answered. "Are Lily and Grace asleep?"

The basement stairs appeared dark. "I think so. But, it's nearly midnight, they'll be tired at school tomorrow."

Ben's gaze wandered back to his phone on the coffee table. He masked a frown with his hand.

"You sure everything's okay?" I prodded, knowing it was her. It was always her.

He stood. "We should go to bed. Not much to do without the power."

I let out an annoyed groan, rising to my feet. "Why's it so hot, anyway? It's mid-October, for Christ sake." There had been no mention of the day's spiking temperature in the forecast. Our summer clothes had already been packed away.

"Who knows," Ben said, his shoulders taught. He made his way to the living room window in a paint-spattered pair of shorts that had somehow eluded my last trip to the donation box. I enjoyed the sight of him staring into the night: the way his naked back tapered so neatly to his waist. "Seems to be shifting though. There's a breeze now, at least."

I joined him at the window. He was right. A cool stream of air filtered through the screen. Closing my eyes, I enjoyed the feel of it against my face.

"Tell me the truth," I said, turning to face him. "Has she been messaging you again?"

The candles flickered behind us, caught in the breeze. Ben sighed. "I'm not encouraging her, Terra."

"What's she saying?"

"She's . . . in a dark place."

I crossed my arms, suddenly thankful his phone had died. We had explained the move to Saskatchewan easily enough as a means to escape the traffic, hectic lifestyle, and endless cycle of day after day of gray skies back home; but, the real motivation behind it had been keeping our family intact by getting Ben away from Helena.

"She's depressed?" I asked.

He lowered his head. "Before the phone died, she said . . ."

I waited, saying nothing, refusing to prod him on. It was a mess he had gotten himself into. A mess he promised to leave behind us.

Ben cleared his throat. "She picked up some sleeping pills."

"Do you think she would . . . " I couldn't bring myself to say the words. I'd been trying to forgive Helena for stealing Ben away. Not because I felt she deserved forgiveness, but because my hate had consumed me the past two years. Changed me. Ben was doing everything he could to save our family. It was only fair that I tried, too.

Ben shrugged. "I don't know."

The world would be better off without her. I bit my lip, holding the comment in. "Would you like to call her?"

"Is there any charge in your phone?"

"No," I answered, suddenly relieved that Cruise had drained the battery playing Minecraft. It seemed seventeen hundred miles wasn't enough to keep Helena from my husband. Maybe if she killed herself it would be over and done with. Let her beautiful face and her flawless body rot six feet under the ground if that was what it took to keep her from my husband. My family. Mine.

Ben absentmindedly rubbed the back of his neck, flexing lean muscles along the left side of his body. Even in paint-spattered shorts he was a sight to behold, his blond hair ruffled and jawline speckled with stubble. He was, objectively, one of the most handsome men I'd ever seen, and a brilliant artist. I doubted I could have forgiven another man for the pain his affair had caused me. Of course Helena was depressed. I had been depressed too, when I found out about her. Would I have killed myself? No. But then, I had the kids. Helena had nothing.

"You're right," I said finally. "We should go to bed."

By the time we completed our nightly rituals of face-washing and teeth-brushing, the breeze had picked up substantially.

Ben closed the bedroom windows halfway while I peed in the en-suite. He peered across the yard. "It's getting wild out there."

The shrubs surrounding the outer wall of the bathroom scraped the siding in the wind. I rose, allowing my nightdress to fall to my knees while I flushed the toilet. Out the small window, I caught sight of the trampoline in the yard. "We should take the safety net down. If the wind picks up any more that thing will end up on our roof."

Ben's shoulder slumped. "Oh, hell. I'll do it."

"I'll come with you."

"I'll be right back." He grabbed a flashlight from the closet and pulled a shirt on before making his way down the hall. In a minute, the back door slammed shut behind him. I sat on the bed. The sound of crisp autumn leaves rustled noisily outside. I strained to see Ben climbing onto the trampoline to wrestle the ties of the safety net in the darkness. The slivered crescent of the moon was white and bright above Ben's studio, and then it was covered by a thick patch of quickly moving cloud. The earthy smell of fast approaching rain filled the air.

Footsteps shuffled on the floor behind me. I turned to find Cruise. The hair rose along the back of my arms. His face had paled since I'd tucked him in. His eyes were empty. Hollow.

"Cruise?" I asked, coming toward him. "Are you all right?"

He didn't respond. His little belly protruded slightly over his underwear. Despite a recent growth spurt he still had a fair amount of baby fat. The innocent expression that usually brightened his baby-blue eyes was gone, hidden behind heavy lids.

"Are you sleeping, baby?" I asked. How long had it been since I'd left his room? A half-hour at most. Apparently, that was all it took. This was the second time I'd caught him sleepwalking that week.

He mumbled indiscernibly in garbled, halting vowels and sharp consonants that made my pulse race. Ben handled Cruise's sleepwalking better than I did. It seemed to me that he inhabited a different world when he was like this; a world meant to be unknown to the waking, living beings on earth.

"Do you need to use the bathroom?" I asked.

He seemed to look right through me. "It's going to storm."

My hand flew up to cover my chest. His lucidity shocked me. Cruise had talked in his sleep a hundred times before. But, his words were always mangled. I'd never been able to understand him.

He reached out blindly to softly grip my arm. "Careful, Momma."

"Let's get you back in bed, baby." I swallowed.

"Momma." Cruise beckoned me closer with a wave of his little hand. When I knelt before him, he leaned in with a worried whisper. "She's coming."

A chill rose up my spine. I hesitated, staring at my only son. My sweet boy. "Who?"

The back door slammed. I jumped to my feet. Ben lumbered up the stairs. He came into the room breathing hard. "It's going to pour out there," he said before catching sight of Cruise. "What's he doing up?"

"He isn't up." My attention returned to Cruise. "He's still asleep." The older Cruise grew, the more he looked like his father: the same broad shoulders, square jaw, and puckered lips. He was my baby. A perfectly unspoiled replica of the man I'd fallen in love with so long before.

"I'll take him to his bed." Ben laid his hand on Cruise's back to usher him slowly down the hall. "Let's go, buddy."

I waited, listening to the wind wail against the outer walls of the house. Something was banging in the distance. A door, maybe. An open gate. I retrieved the discarded flashlight and slipped past Ben, who was speaking softly to Cruise while tucking him safe beneath his blankets, and descended the stairs to the entryway. Pushing firmly against the closed door, I turned the deadbolt sideways at the top. Ben had installed one on all the outer doors when we first moved to the acreage. The last thing we wanted was Cruise sleepwalking out of the house and getting lost in the woods. I glanced into the front yard through the window. The trees swayed violently in the wind. Rain droplets spotted the glass.

Moving systematically from one room to the next, I closed the windows and locked the doors to the garage and the patio. Grace and Lily lay still in their rooms in the basement, breathing heavily, blissfully unaware of the coming storm.

Back in our own room, Ben stripped to his underwear and laid down on the bed. "This rain is exactly what we need. It'll take some of the humidity out of the air. Cruise will be fine tomorrow."

He was right, of course. Cruise's sleepwalking somehow always grew worse with humidity. Laying next to Ben I let out a long breath. "I hate when he talks in his sleep. It's like he's communicating with another dimension."

Ben tried to hide a smile. He lay his hand over mine. "He's fine, Terra. Don't worry. It's natural. Weird, but natural."

We blew out our candles, but Ben remained restless beside me. I was certain he was thinking of Helena. I could practically feel her in the bed between us. There was nothing he could do for her from here. I turned to face the window. Rain broke in waves against the pane. We listened to the storm until almost two hours had passed, and Ben's breathing became heavy. Sleep came slower for me. Now and then my body became weightless, my thoughts setting adrift as the edges of my consciousness began to soften.

I'd only seen Helena once, across a busy street. She'd been with Ben, coming out of a hotel paid for with our credit card. She was prettier than me. A couple of years older. He told me she was an artist, like him. An artist like Ben, who felt deeper than other people. Loved harder. Could she have loved Ben more than I did?

Did it matter?

He was mine, after all. Bound to me by the silver ring that encircled his finger.

And maybe Helena was lying to him about the pills; using whatever means necessary to pull him back into her web. Perhaps she wouldn't take them.

Maybe she would.

Oh God, I hoped she would.

I imagined her sitting in her condo, her shining black hair pulled into a perfect bun on the very top of her head, rolling the bottle of pills back and forth across the coffee table with the beautifully manicured tips of her perfectly slim fingers. I willed her to remove the cap. To wash the bottle of pills down with a bottle of Malbec.

It'll be easier if you do it, Helena.

A slow roll of thunder moved through the trees outside our room like an animal approaching in the night. Rain pounded against the roof. Wind whipped at the siding. My awareness drifted: euphoria closing in as sleep worked to erase Ben's lover from my mind and I became weightless, weightless, weightless.

My eyes fluttered open. I had lifted from the bed. My arms and legs and head hung loose, as though I was dangling from a rope knotted around my stomach. Ben lay below me, breathing steadily. I tried to scream. No sound came out. My chest and lungs constricted involuntarily as if to expel my soul, to force my consciousness outward. Into what? Where would my soul go if not locked inside my body? Uncontained, it would spill free, separate, disappear. I would be gone. And then? My body would be as empty as an old house, waiting for a renter.

Waiting for her.

Another slow roll of thunder tumbled across the field, carrying with it a resonance like a woman's voice, a scream, a battle cry in the night. I tried to yell for Ben again. Air poured freely from my lungs, frustratingly unencumbered by sound.

Ben let out a stammered snore beneath me. Adrenaline pumped from my heart. I swayed slightly, a pendulum swinging to the left and the right.

"Ben," I managed finally. It was a little more than a kitten call. It was enough. There was a sound of blankets stirring. Was he patting my side of the mattress? Did he see my nightdress swinging overhead? He launched from the bed to flatten himself against the wall. "Terra, what the fuck?"

"Help me!" I reached toward him before being swung back violently. "Get me down!"

Electricity flashed through the lights, and I caught a snapshot of Ben, face white beneath blonde stubble before it died, leaving the room even blacker than before.

Cruise's warning rang in my ears. She's coming.

No. No, no. I was dreaming, wasn't I? This wasn't real. This was my body. My house. My husband. Mine. Helena didn't kill herself. Even if she had, she wasn't here, forcing herself inside my body. She would have died three provinces away.

"Terra!" Ben's voice came closer. "Grab my hand."

It was too dark to see. I swung in and brushed the tips of my fingers against his before being ripped back. He grabbed me at the elbow when I came in again. My movement grew manic. I was swung back and forth and back again on an invisible line to the roof.

"Tell me what to do, Terra!"

What could he do? Maybe there was nothing. It didn't mean she'd win. Not when the prize was my body. My life.

I imagined myself as a sponge with every cell opening, blossoming outward to reabsorb my soul. Focusing all my energy, I breathed in and out and in again: using my lungs to pull the spilled me back.

It worked.

I was released. Flung onto the floor. There was a crunch. Something hard protruded from the ground beneath my back. Was it the flashlight?

Ben rushed to me. "What the fuck just happened?"

"I don't know," I lied, unwilling to say it.

A door slammed downstairs. Grace screamed, the sound muffled by distance. I scrambled to my feet. Pain screamed from my ribs. A warm stream drained down the back of my nightgown.

Ben moved to the dresser. A match flared across the room. The candlelit on his third attempt. We ran down the stairs, Ben guarding the wildly flickering flame with his hand. A roll of thunder shook the house, loud, and long, and close.

Helena was in it. She was all around us now.

Ben's opened Grace's door. I held his arm.

"Honey?" I asked.

Wind billowed through the open window, tangling the curtains. Our eldest daughter shuffled back in her bed, long hair wildly disheveled. Both girls took after me more than their father; with the same mousy hair and extra flesh around the waist and hips.

"Sorry," she panted. "I got scared. The wind blew my door shut."

At fourteen, Grace rarely looked like a child anymore. Now, her youth was all I saw. I raced past Ben to embrace her, eager for an excuse to hold another person, heart hammering heavily beneath my breast. Ben closed the window with a thud.

"Why'd you open the window?" I asked Grace, holding her soft frame tight.

"It was open when I went to bed."

"I know." I glanced at Ben. "I closed it."

Lily padded in rubbing her eyes. "What's going on?" She was two years younger than Grace, but unlike her older sister, she appeared unfazed by the storm. Thunder roared around us. The basement windows flashed brightly.

Slam, slam, slam: the bedroom doors blew shut upstairs. Wind ripped through the house. Had every window opened?

Ben blinked. "Cruise!"

Something changed. The wind shifted. Grace shimmied out from the blankets. Ben raced up the stairs to check Cruise's room. We followed. I slowed as I moved past the front door, noticing the safety lock had been turned vertical. The door remained intact. The bolt had to have been opened from the inside. But, by who? Cruise wasn't tall enough. He was only seven.

Only seven. Pure, and good, and mine.

"Ben," I yelled, rounding the corner to Cruise's room. "Is he here?"

"Yes," Ben answered. He was hunched over the bed, shaking Cruise's shoulder.

Lily took my hand. "What's going on?"

"Daddy's just checking Cruise," I answered as calmly as I could. "Ben!"

"He won't wake up."

"What do you mean, he won't wake up?" I came over. Cruise's face was inanimate, his eyes closed. The only part of him that moved was the slow rise and fall of his chest while he breathed.

Thunder sounded in the distance, retreating like a bitch with her prize. Seconds passed before the resulting lightning illuminated the room. Then we saw it, written on the wall in Cruise's discarded sidewalk chalk.

Mine.

The Bloody Dogwood Tree
Dabney Farmer
Charlotte, North Carolina, USA
Copyright © 2018 by Dabney Farmer. All rights reserved.
LifeWithLee

Sometimes the ones we love are the ones who hurt us the most, both in life and in death.
- Dabney Farmer

They say I'm crazy. Actually, they say a lot of things about me behind my back when they think I'm not listening. Shows what they know. I'm always listening.

They say I'm depressed, anxious, a homebody, a loner, or just a cranky jerk. They didn't say that about me before, but now they do.

It all started when I went to a small plant shop and bought a simple, skinny, seven-foot-tall, dogwood tree.

It was a normal-looking tree by all accounts, with white flowers that weren't pretty, but weren't ugly, either; and a few blood-red berries about the size of peas growing on only one branch. Not a lot, as it was small at the time.

I planted the tree in my backyard as a tribute to my late wife, who had died earlier that year. She had always wanted a dogwood tree when she was alive, but one fateful day her long-standing illness took her—sooner than we both expected.

It took forever to dig the hole. I never knew how many rocks were in my yard until I started digging. You'd think I'd have remembered that, since I'd needed to dig holes in my yard before

58

for making a fence, but of course, wouldn't you know the spot I picked for the tree had the most rocks in it.

Once dirt was packed around it, I took a step back. It was a rather plain thing for all the work it took. But for my wife's memory, it was worth it. When she'd been alive, planting the tree for her was the furthest thing from my mind. But now that she was gone, it felt like the least I could do after all we'd been through together.

My late wife and I fought over a lot of things that seem stupid now. She always wanted a dog. I didn't, as I hate things that crap in yards. She always wanted to go to the movies. I didn't, as there is always something for free on TV, like Sports Center. She always wanted me to wipe my feet when I came in, as she was such a clean freak. I just didn't; it was my house, after all. So what if its dirty? Deal with it! She wanted me to get rid of all my old junk. I didn't. What's the worst that could happen if I kept my old stuff?

She always wanted a garden in the backyard, and I... Well, you get the idea.

Whenever my late wife got mad at me, which had been more frequent during last year of her life, she would scrunch up her face, showing off all her wrinkles. It reminded me of one of those Chinese Shar-Pei dogs.

I'd have to bite my lip hard not to laugh when she did that, or from blurting out she didn't need a dog, she already looked like one.

It would always end with her stamping her foot and waving her fists in the air, like a spoiled brat. I used to hate it when she would throw tantrums, but now looking back on it, I see she was pretty funny when she was mad.

The last fight we had, right before she died, had been the worst. I realize to late that I'd overreacted. I don't remember exactly what I said to make her so mad, but it must have been something bad to make her so angry she couldn't concentrate in the car accident that took her life. I always thought her illness would do her in the end—the one she spent her whole life fighting—but it ended up being a car crash instead.

The really sad thing is, I don't remember what that last fight was about. The second to last thing I do remember fighting with her about was getting a dogwood tree, but that was weeks or maybe even a month ago. I think… My mind isn't what it used to be. So, I thought, why not? It's just a little tree, what harm could it do? But it turned out to be the biggest mistake of my life.

The first thing it did to piss me off was grow like a weed. In no time, its stupid, pointy roots stuck out of the dirt, all over my yard like an octopus stretching its tentacles over its prey. Its roots grew and looked alive, as if they had a mind of their own. Just like something out of a damn nature documentary, the kind that they force you to watch at school.

Those damn roots would cause bumps in the lawn. They would even get stuck in the lawn mower. That was a chore I hated to do anyway—mowing—but those stupid roots made it even worse. When I wasn't cleaning splinters out of the lawnmower, I was buying new blades for it.

Those damn freaking roots forced me to wear shoes in my own backyard, which was something I'd never needed to do before I got that damn tree. If I wore sandals, those damn roots would poke right through them like a dagger through butter.

Whenever I'd step on those bastard roots I would let loose with my sailor talk. Which is what I always do when I get hurt by accident. It's a guy thing.

Wouldn't you know my luck, my neighbor's kids would always be right there when it happened. Those damn kids would overhear me and run to their moms and say, "Mommy, guess what that man just said?"

Then I would get dirty looks from parents, who were never that far behind from their little brats. Glaring at me with those judging eyes. As if it was my bloody fault I stepped on a freaking root in my own backyard. Even if it was, it was my god damn backyard anyway.

So I should be able to say whatever the Sam Hill I want. If I drop a meat cleaver on my big toe, it's my God-given right to swear to high Heaven and Hell. That's what being an American is all about. Give me truth, justice, liberty, and the right to swear freely. But did I ever get any sympathy? I was the one with bruised, banged up feet. Sometimes they were more than bruised; they might even be bleeding. But even then, did I get sympathy? NOOOOO… of course not. God, I hated my neighbors.

As if my damn neighbors weren't enough to put up with, I also had those damn leaves all over my lawn.

So I had to rake my yard every single freaking day. I tried shaking the damn tree so those bloody leaves would all fall down for good and I'd only have to rake once. But no matter how hard I shook that tree, none of the leaves came down. It was like they were superglued on or something.

I even tried throwing rocks at the tree branches just to get the leaves down, but I have terrible aim and I kept hitting my car windows. You know, the only thing worse than stepping on animal crap is stepping on broken glass in your driveway when you go to pick up the paper.

Part of me felt like my late wife was somehow part of this, as if somehow beyond the grave she'd gotten the leaves to stay on the trees as long as possible, just to piss me off. I know that sounds crazy. But she knew how much I hated raking. That was the whole reason I didn't want a damn dogwood tree in my backyard in the first place.

But, of all the things I hated about that damn tree, those awful blood red berries were the worst. They grow right next to such white flowers, that only makes them look brighter and redder.

They just looked creepy, like little drops of blood from a nosebleed, or a head wound. People say blood isn't really bright red, it's more of a dark brown. It's true, bloods only looks bright red when it's next to something pale, like those damn white as ghost flowers, or skin wearing a white dress. My wife loved that damn white dress, wore it all the time. She had it on the day she died. Not sure If I told anyone that before.

They were the kind of berries that are poisonous for humans to eat. However, that didn't stop every damn bird and squirrel in my neighborhood to come and feast on them. As apparently, they're are not poisonous to vermin.

Do you know what happens when you've got loads and loads of squirrels and birds in your back yard? You get cats. Stray,

61

mangy cats. Do you know what happens when you get stray, mangy cats in your backyard?

You get stray, mangy dogs, too. If that wasn't bad enough, when you get stray, mangy dogs in your yard, you get a bunch of crap all over your lawn.

As if I wasn't having enough fun stepping on roots and occasionally broken glass, then I got to step in something warm and smelly. That's a great way to start the morning. But of course, when you have stray cats and dogs hanging around your yard, the other neighbors' dogs and cats come to make friends, so I got even more crap from them. Whenever I complained to my neighbors, they would just laugh it off and say, "You should be thankful of the free fertilizer they are giving you."

That was easy for them to say; it wasn't on their lawn. They all would have thought differently if I'd gone in their yard, pulled my pants down, and let them have a big surprise on their front porch. I was two beers away from having the guts to do it, but I didn't feel like going to the store to pick up another six-pack.

Not one stinking animal was the least bit scared of me. Every time I yelled "Get the hell off my lawn, you spawns of Satan!" They all just looked at me for a second, then would go back to their business of crapping on my yard.

People say deer and dogs are incapable of laughing, but I knew they were all thinking about it. You can just see it in their mangy eyes. I hate animals, but I'll be the first to admit they're a lot smarter than we give them credit for. My late wife was a lot smarter than I gave her credit for, too. It wouldn't surprise me if she was somehow a part of this.

Now, this will sound crazy, but I felt all this crap (both literally and figuratively) that was happening—from the roots hurting my feet, the berries, the animals, and especially the crap—was all somehow my late wife's fault.

As if somehow she was controlling these events through the tree she'd wanted so much. I know when you're dead, you can't control things. I know that. I really do. But, then again, I also know my late wife could be so madly controlling it would drive you insane, just like this tree was driving me insane. She'd always find a way to get her way, so it made sense this tree was finding a way to do everything it wanted, whether I liked it or not.

It was almost as if she was getting revenge on me for her death. Which was ridiculous; she had an incurable illness. She was going to die anyway. How is it my fault?

Most of the time I was yelling more than stomping around. Which actually pissed off my goddamn neighbors. They'd yell back at me. "Don't yell at those poor innocent animals, they are not doing anything wrong!"

Wouldn't this kind of thing affect them too? It'd bring down the property value of the neighborhood. "Oh yeah? Come look at my yard and tell me they're not doing anything wrong!"

But you know what I hated even more? When the neighbors would look over into my yard and say, "Aww look at that cute little squirrel. You are so blessed." They talked about it like the Queen of England was coming to my yard or something.

But the worst part of that evil, nasty, putrid tree, even more than the berries, even more than those roots, even more than all the other literal crap in my yard, were those damn white flowers. I remember when I first plopped that damn tree in that hole in my backyard, I got a good whiff of the flowers and instantly couldn't stand the smell of them.

They smelled just like this god-awful perfume "Desert Storm," my late wife's favorite perfume of all time. She practically bathed in it.

All perfumes smell like toilet bowl cleaners to me. However, for me, "Desert Storm" smelled like the worst gas station bathroom you'd ever been in.

When I met my wife, I thought I could learn to love her perfume. Instead, her perfume only grew to smell worse for me, to the point where having her in the room irritated my nose so much, I felt nauseous. Come to think of it, that might've been what our last fight was about. As I might have thrown that damn perfume out the window and she got in her car to buy more.

I don't know how, but somehow those damn white flowers smelled just like my late wife's perfume. A perfume I thought I'd never smell again with my late wife gone forever. Only she wasn't gone, as far as my nose was concerned. It was like she was here, in my backyard. Waiting to come in and get me in my sleep.

Most people will try to tell you those white flowers on a dogwood tree don't smell like anything. But I'm not like most people. I know better.

They have a sickeningly sweet smell, just like my late wife's perfume did. It matched her personality, that's for sure.

I got so sick of smelling those damn flowers, I cut every last one of them off the tree—which, I learned later, is a felony to do. Apparently, since it's the state tree, there's some law out there that you're not supposed to hurt it, at least in Virginia. But what the hell do I care, my family was originally from Canada anyway. It was my tree, so I could do whatever the hell I wanted with it, thank you very much.

But even with all those goddamn flowers gone, I could still smell that god-awful sickly-sweet smell everywhere in my house. The smell started to seep into the house like a bad septic tank odor. I tried to keep all the windows shut, but I could still smell it. I tried having my windows nailed shut, but I could still smell it.

So I got a couple of air fresheners. I'd never used air fresheners before, because my late wife hated them—big surprise. She thought they smelled like gas station toilet cleaners, whereas as I thought her perfume smelled like toilet bowl cleaner.

I finally had enough, and I hacked that damned dogwood tree to bits with an axe. It was kind of like that Mickey Mouse "Fantasia" short, only replace the enchanted broom being cut up with a demon tree that deserved to die.

When I was too tired to hack anymore, I donated what was left of that evil tree to a mulch charity, where they turn lawn clippings into mulch for needy families. My wife always wasted her money on that charity, even though I told her they used most of it in prisons yards instead of habitat for humanity. Not that she ever listened to me.

They all looked so surprised when I came in with the hacked-up tree. You would have thought I brought them a mutilated body, the way they stared at me.

I never forgot what they said when I brought them the tree's corpse. "Gee, sir, you didn't need to cut it up that much, we have a thrasher in the back that does that."

I burst out laughing, as if I'd let them have all the fun. I did ask if I could see them throw the tree in the thrasher, but they seemed uneasy around me for some reason. I guess they couldn't take a joke.

Finally, the damned evil nasty dogwood was gone. She was finally gone. Well, almost gone. All that was left of that damned tree was to rip up the damned stump. I tried doing it myself, but despite the fact all the roots seemed to be poking out of the ground, they were deeply stuck in my yard.

The stump's roots didn't seem to be dying after the tree was gone. If anything, they were getting stronger and sharper. I had to hire a stump removing service to get it. It took six goddamn weeks for them to even show up. They kept making every damn excuse in the book. "We had another delivery, so it's too late to come now."

I tried not to lose my cool. I really did. I kept reminded myself that they were taking it away and it would all be over and done with. I was almost giddy when I thought about the stump being gone, as well as my neighbors leaving me alone.

When the stump people finally came, they couldn't get it out either. Even when they attached cables from their truck to the stump, it didn't work. The truck almost overheated when they tried flooring it.

Those bastards still wanted to charge me anyway. I had to fight back the urge to not come after them with an axe. Then I got an idea that would be both efficient and satisfying. I went out and got some dynamite and stuck it between the evil roots of what was left of the evil tree. Even that was a pain in the ass to do, as I had the hardest time shoving the dynamite into what was left of the stump.

Turns out old those old "Loony Toons" cartoon lied to me as a kid. Dynamite is not easy to buy, not even online. I found a guy who sold it to me out of his van. It didn't look that great. I didn't think it would even work, so I bought more than I should have.

It was as if she knew I was going to destroy her, and she was fighting back. But I was stronger, baby. I couldn't be stopped.

I dug holes around it. I even got more dynamite, as I wanted to make sure this tree was gone for good. I set the fuse and ran to my house, to watch it go off like the 4th of July. But I think in my excitement, I used too much dynamite. The explosion was deafening.

Everyone and their grandmother could hear it for ten blocks, shattering my windows along with a few of my neighbors'. When the dust cleared, there was a huge smoking crater exposing my wife's body. That's when I remembered the whole reason I put that stupid tree in that exact spot in my yard in the first place, as well as the whole reason I'd really bought the tree.

The neighbors had seen me digging the hole. I couldn't say I was making another fence; it was too close to the house. I had to lie, saying it was for a dogwood tree. That was the most believable lie I could come up with, after all. My wife was always loudly asking about getting a tree, anyway. Kind of ironic when you think about it.

You know, what's even more ironic is I might've been able to cover her back up before anyone even saw her body, or what was left of it. There were huge mounds of dirt everywhere, blocking everyone's view. With my bare hands, I could've probably covered her up before anyone noticed.

If only one of her bones hadn't landed in my neighbor's yard. Wouldn't you know it, of all my neighbors, it had to be the old woman who was always outside gardening.

I didn't see her face, but when a big white thing that kind of looked like a skull flew over the fence and landed in her yard, I knew I was screwed. It figures; my wife was always talking to her when she was alive, always telling me to be nice to her.

She would spend more hours talking to that old woman than she ever talked to me in a day. It was as if in her death she decided she would have one more conversation with her. I'm not even entirely sure it was really my wife's skull that landed in her yard. But I'm sure it wasn't a rock.

They say bones aren't really white unless you bleach them white; they're more brown—but not my wife's.

66

Figures. Even in death, she had to be as freakishly clean as she was when she was alive.

I had to laugh in spite of my situation. Even in death, she couldn't stand to get dirty. In spite of my situation, it felt good to laugh. Unfortunately, that didn't exactly make me look innocent, or sane.

I tried to explain she was going to die anyway with her longstanding illness, but the courts didn't see being a total bitch as a real illness the way I did. Even though she'd been suffering from it her whole life.

I pointed out I didn't kill her; the car crash did. But the lawyers said I'd been the one to crash my car into her.

Lawyers can be so touchy. So, in their mind, I had killed her.

I also pointed out it wasn't like I had lied to the insurance company. I had always said she must have not been paying attention to the road, and that a car accident took her life.

But I never said she was in the car when she had the accident. What difference does it make if a car kills you by driving it off the road or running you down in your garage? Either way, you die by car. It was her own fault for getting so angry she couldn't see I was in the car about to drive into her.

I guess it also didn't help that I had run her over more than once, which I wasn't aware would show up on bone tests. Guess I should have watched more CSI reruns.

Turns out, more than a few cops had been suspicious of me from the start, when they found my car in the river. The one I said she had borrowed, but not found her body inside it.

In retrospect, I probably should have had her body in the car when I pushed it in the lake, or not kept her so close to the house. I guess I've always been a bit of a hoarder, as my wife used to say. I couldn't even get rid of her.

But I didn't care, even when they took me to jail and the court decided to give me life in prison due to insanity. I was finally free of that damn smelly, evil, putrid, tree.

I was free from my neighbors, those blood-red berries, and those crapping, berry-munching animals. I was finally free of all of it. I was free at last.

Hallelujah, I was safe! Safe from her in my cozy cell which smelled like one big urinal, but who cares? Anything is better than that damn stupid tree.

People still think I'm crazy, even now, but if they had to live with her, they would have seen the crime would be not killing her. I've never been a people person anyway, so I liked being left alone in my cell. Even the other prisoners stayed away from me.

But, you know what? I like it that way.

I feel like a monk, being left alone in my own monastery. I was so happy here.

That is…Until the prison had to get the grounds re-mulched.

Mulch that was from the same company that took away the dogwood tree.

Mulch they spread all over the garden right by my cell window.

Mulch that smelled like that damn "Desert Storm" perfume, which I can now smell every day.

What are the odds of that happening?

Ghosts of Tupelo

Sharon E. Cathcart

San Jose, Calif.

Copyright © 2018 by Sharon E. Cathcart. All rights reserved.

http://sharonecathcart.weebly.com

The Elvis Presley Birthplace Center didn't look too impressive, to be honest. Still, my dad knows how much I love old music and thought it would be fun if we took a trip to see some historical places related to it. Dad parked the car in the lot just behind a tiny, white clapboard house. Rain was pouring down in buckets as we shifted in our seats and undid our safety belts.

"You go ahead into the main building," he said. "Your mother and I will be along directly."

I dashed across to the awning over the sidewalk, rain matting my hair in the process. Dad helped Mom down from the front seat, pulling the hood of her raincoat up over her dark brown hair as he kissed her cheek. He handed over her cane and gave her his arm so that she was supported both sides while they made their slower way around to the ramp. His black hair was plastered to his head, but he was more concerned about Mom's comfort.

I get tired of explaining to people that my mom is sick. I wish things were different, but I'm old enough to know that's never going to happen. I used to get really mad about her illness, but I don't anymore. I'm almost fifteen years old, practically grown up, and I know better now than I did when I was a kid. Besides, she hates it more than anyone, you know? I love my mom and dad, and I know they're doing the best they can with what they've been given.

Anyway, while I waited for them I watched a family loading things into the old green car parked under a gazebo-type thing near the museum. The man was tall and handsome, with wavy brown hair. The wife was pretty but careworn, her black hair pulled back in a bun that just touched the collar of her faded, calico dress. The third member of the party was a boy in denim overalls, the legs cuffed up. He had heavy brown shoes on his feet and his brown-blonde head was covered by a cloth cap. He was handsome, which might have been easy to miss in that old-fashioned attire. The affection among the group was apparent, and I couldn't help wondering whether the actors were a real-life family.

I turned to ask my dad what he thought of the little reenactment I was watching, but he was focused on helping Mom get under the tiny awning. After making sure she was settled, he pulled a handkerchief out of his pocket and swiped at his face and hair, focused solely on drying off a little before we went inside.

"Mom, did you notice the reenactors over by the car? I think that's kind of neat."

"I'm sorry, Evie. I was concentrating on not slipping in the rain. Where did you see them again?"

When I turned to show her, the people and their things were gone. The car was alone on display … and completely empty.

"I guess they went inside to get out of the rain," I said.

"We should do the same," Mom replied.

We went into the dark brown building and my dad paid for our tickets. We would see a little museum, a church presentation (of all things; I didn't think this was going to be a religious visit), and the tiny, two-room house in which Elvis Presley was born.

"Before we go into any of these places," my dad said, "I want to talk about why I think this trip is important. I know you love this music, Evie, but we need to remember that the legendary people whose records you listen to came from nothing. We're really fortunate with all we have, and sometimes it's worth a pause to remember. With that, let's look at this museum and then go over for the church program."

The Elvis mementos and memorabilia, all part of a private collection, were fascinating. No photos were allowed, but it was neat to see the clothes, books, and other things that had belonged to the man who really was the first rock star. I was still distracted by what I'd seen outside by the antique car that had belonged to Vernon and Gladys Presley. The reenactors surely did look like the Presleys; their photos were in the museum and I studied them for a long time.

After a few minutes of wandering around the gift shop and picking out souvenirs, Dad gathered us together to walk over for the church program. The little one-room building had been the Presley's family church, the docent explained, as people in both modern-day and period clothing filed in. I sat down on one of the rear-most pews while the guide explained the multi-media presentation that would simulate a Pentecostal service for the visitors.

Just as both the screens and the lights were lowered, the blonde boy I saw earlier slipped in and sat beside me, his cap in his hand.

"Sure is somethin', ain't it?" he whispered. "Course, that fella up on the screen ain't quite as inspiring as Brother Frank Smith was when he got to going, but he does tolerably well."

"We shouldn't be talking," I whispered back.

Dad turned around and gave me a puzzled look.

"Nah, it's not really church. 'Sides, we used to really make a joyful noise during services." He gave a little lopsided smile that lit up his hooded blue eyes.

"You're really into this role; I admire you for it. I'm a performer myself," I whispered.

The boy gave me that same smile. "I'm not a performer. Leastwise, not yet. I got dreams, though, and I aim to make 'em come true."

"Okay," I replied, and turned my attention back to the presentation. As the screens and lights came back up, I realized my companion was gone. I figured he'd moved on to his next reenactment.

Mom asked that everyone visit the meditation chapel next door to wait out the rain for a while, so we made our short way there. Along the sidewalk, we passed an outhouse that had been shared not only by the churchgoers, but by the families along what was formerly known as Old Saltillo Road. I couldn't imagine walking half a block to use the restroom. It must have been awful, especially if you had to go in the middle of the night.

"I thought it was neat that they had so many people in costume at the church," I ventured as I closed the chapel door behind us.

"That presentation was impressive, all right," Mom settled into one of the pews. Unlike the dark wood of the old church, those were golden and bright. "Having screens on the sides to help you feel like it was really happening was a clever way to bring the experience home."

"I wasn't talking about the screens, Mom. I was talking about the people. The couple I saw earlier putting things in that green car outside were there, and the fellow playing their son."

Mom and Dad both looked at me like I'd grown another head.

"Amos," Mom said, "why don't you play something on the piano?"

"I don't know, Diana. It doesn't seem right."

"Well, I don't see any signs saying we can't, and I'd like to hear one of Elvis' hymns if you don't mind."

Dad compromised and sang two verses and a chorus from "Peace in the Valley" a cappella. He used to be a professional singer back in the day, and Mom says she fell in love with him while he was singing an old Cajun song.

I closed my eyes and focused on Dad's voice. In my ear, though, I heard a second voice: the whisper of the boy who'd sat next to me in church.

"Tell your daddy thank you."

I'd always thought that the whole "hair raising on the back of your neck" thing was an old wives' tale, or something that only happened in scary books. But it happened to me right then.

When I opened my eyes, there was no one sitting next to me. However, the sun had come out and was peeping through the stained-glass windows to make colorful swirls on the carpet.

"Let's go over to the house." Mom gamely picked up her cane.

"You guys go ahead," I said. "I want to spend a few more minutes here. I promise I won't be too long."

"All right," Dad said, and helped Mom up and out the door. After they left, I closed my eyes and spoke aloud.

"I don't know exactly what's going on here, but I'm hoping you'll help me understand."

I opened my eyes, and that same boy was sitting next to me in the pew.

"I reckon your folks can't see me," he said. "They seem real nice, though. And I like that your daddy sang for a bit."

"Who are you?" I asked.

"You don't know yet? Well, you walk out that door down the pathway to the house and you'll see. Go on now."

I was puzzled, but I went out and followed the pathway.

About halfway between the chapel and the little white house was a circle of park benches and trees. In the middle of the circle was a statue of an overall-clad boy clutching a guitar around the neck. At the base was a plaque reading "Elvis at 13."

My jaw dropped open.

"It's an okay likeness, ain't it?"

The blonde boy materialized next to me, and I got the picture at last.

"But you were grown up when ..."

"When I passed? I surely was. But I left here when I was thirteen. That's why I look this way near the house. Man, I remember what a treat it used to be to sit on the porch and play some new song Brother Smith taught me, or maybe share a Coke and a funny book with one of the fellas. Not that I had so many friends, mind. I was kind of a timid kid. I surely loved Captain Marvel, Junior. He had black hair and wore a jumpsuit with a cape; I thought that was how a hero should look, boy."

Elvis went on to tell me about how no one had much, because all of their fathers were sharecroppers. So, if somebody got a funny book, they all passed it around "real careful-like", and how they would even share a bottle of soda pop.

"Oh, hey," he continued, "when you go into that house where I was born, it won't look like much. Hell, it ain't but two rooms, with no 'lectric or running water. They've got it lookin' like it did when we lived there for the most part. At least it's got real wallpaper now, 'stead of newspapers put up with flour and water paste. My mama and daddy worked real hard, and I loved them. We sure didn't have much to speak of, though, like I said. That's why I was so proud to buy my folks a house in Memphis when I got some money.

"Reckon it's time for you to catch up with your folks now, Miss Evie. Thank you for talking with me; sometimes I get lonely for a pretty girl's smile."

"How'd you know my name?"

"Heard your daddy say it, of course. And you knew my name before you got here." He gave me that same lopsided grin. "One more thing. I know what it is to lose my mama, and I know you're worried. Your mama's going to be okay, hear? It's just gonna take some time."

"Thank you, Elvis," I whispered, the tears I'd tried to contain rolling down my cheek. He leaned forward and kissed me where the tears fell. It felt like a gentle breeze against my skin.

I turned toward the tiny shotgun house and walked away from the little park where, if someone were to look closely, they might have thought there were two statues in the circle before deciding it was a trick of the light.

* * * * *

The author wishes to thank the staff of the Elvis Presley Birthplace Center, particularly hostess/docent Nina Kaye, and the staff of Tupelo Hardware, both in Tupelo, Miss.

Cabin 5
Heather Kindt
Woodland Park, Colorado, USA
Copyright © 2018 by Heather Kindt. All rights reserved.
www.heatherkindt.com

Brittney hefted her duffel bag from the trunk and swung it onto her shoulder. It must've been a half-hour on a one-lane dirt road to get out to this hellhole. She glanced down the hillside—cabins, canoes, and a lake. Everything that screamed *camp* to her. And it was exactly where she didn't want to be.

Her stepdad didn't even bother getting out of the car, just took a long drag on his cigarette before flicking the ashes out the window. "Don't do anything I wouldn't do." Cal smirked before spinning out his tires on the gravel driveway and taking off.

She loathed her stepdad, and her mom for that matter—sending her away to a stupid camp to work for the summer.

"Howdy-ho." A guy stood by the side of the road—tall, lanky with thick-rimmed glasses. He had a whistle around his neck and his pale white legs extended out from his khaki shorts. A clipboard was in his hands. "You must be Brittney Cahill."

"How'd you know that? Stalk often?" She swept her blonde hair off her neck and up into a messy bun using the tie around her wrist.

He raised an eyebrow before pointing to the paper on his clipboard. "No. You're just the only female counselor missing." He turned his back to her as another car pulled up. "Head down to the mess hall and get your cabin assignment." The dork called over his shoulder.

Anything to get away from you, nerd. This place had to get better.

Brittney longed for her gas station job from last summer. Even though living at home with her mom and Cal drove her crazy, she had discount cigs, free Slurpees, and of course Bobby— the number one reason she was sent away this summer.

The mess hall was down the hill from the parking lot and closer to the lake. No one was around when she pushed on the creaking door that she let slam shut behind her. A disheveled old man, walking with a slight limp, entered through a side door and lifted his glasses to his nose. He appeared frail and Brittney worried he might keel over at any moment.

The man sat down at a circular table and sifted through a stack of forms. "Name please."

"Brittney Cahill." She remained standing even though there was a metal folding chair across the table from him. Brittney shifted her weight from foot to foot.

He inspected her, making her wish she hadn't worn her daisy dukes and tight tank.

"I'm Ben, the caretaker of the camp. You'll be in cabin 5 in the village. No smoking, no drinking, no cellphones and no mixing with the male counselors. Staff meeting's at four, before dinner." He slid a box toward her. Numerous cellphones were inside.

Well, what kind of fun was this place going to be? She placed her phone into the box. "Can you define mixing?"

Ben straightened his papers. "I think, Miss Cahill, you know what I mean."

The creaky door slammed behind Brittney and she jumped, her heart racing. A tall, dark-haired guy entered—sunglasses still on. He was tan and his muscles were evident even through his loose t-shirt.

"Hello, Marcus." Ben started sifting through the forms.

Marcus sauntered over to the table giving Brittney a tiny grin. "I'm guessing I'm in Lakeside eight again." He emphasized his cabin number and lifted his sunglasses, before winking at Brittney.

"Yes, and same rules apply." Ben pushed himself up from the table, letting his chair scrape across the floor. "Don't want a repeat of last summer."

"No, we wouldn't want that." Marcus smiled at them as Ben hobbled back into the other room. He turned to Brittney. "I'm Marcus, and you must be . . . "

"Brittney." She set down her bag. Her hand instinctively ran through her hair and released her locks from the hair tie.

His eyes took her in from head to toe. "Nice to meet you, Brittney. Maybe we can catch-up later."

"Um . . . " She twisted a strand of her hair around her finger. "Do you know how to get to the village?" Anything to spend more time with him. She knew she could use the poor, new girl tactic at least for a few days.

"Past the road, hang a left, and then go across the field. You can't miss it." He grabbed his bag, gave her one more look-over, and was out the door.

The new girl. It had been a while since she'd played the role. Now, she was forced into it by her mom and her frickin' stepdad. Neither of them wanted her anymore. Her mom said it was so they could have a healthy environment. Her mom and all her new age, yoga mumbo-jumbo was driving her crazy. They couldn't have Brittney's smoking habit around. The second reason she was sent away—they wanted to replace her with a new baby.

Brittney crossed the dirt road alone and frustrated. She kept her head down, not wanting to make contact with anyone at this stupid camp. A large field spread out next to the parking lot. At the far end of the field was a wide, muddy path that led into the woods. A communal bathroom was on the left after the first cabin. She turned her nose up at the cobwebs clinging to the screened door and cringed at the foul odor that hung in the air.

Brittney climbed the stairs to cabin 5, the furthest cabin out. A spider darted across the wood causing her to let out a muffled squeal. She flung open the creaking door and jumped inside to avoid any further encounters with the insect world. She clutched her duffel bag to her chest, her heart beating wildly as she drew in a deep breath. Three bunk beds lined the walls of the musty room. The windows were mostly screened, so a few flies buzzed near a dim light. A single twin bed was to the left, next to a beat-up, brown dresser. She set her bag down on the bed with a sigh—her home for the next two months. Despite the forested, wild world of spiders and other nasty, creepy-crawlies outside, the cabin was fairly clean, and with a few Brittney touches would be passable.

A loud bell clanged in the distance a few hours later as Brittney checked out her work—heather gray bedspread with dark gray and pink furry pillows, pictures in matching black frames on the dresser, and a small area rug on the floor. The bell rang again.

She was at the edge of the woods, when another girl called out to her.

"Hey, wait up." The girl fell into step next to Brittney. "You must be the new girl. I'm Rachel."

She wore a Camp George t-shirt and ripped jeans. About an inch taller than Brittney, Rachel had dark French braids knotted in different color hair-ties. Her mocha-colored skin was flawless and her eyes shone bright set in her dark lashes.

Brittney swept a strand of hair out of her eyes. "Brittney . . . Maybe you could call me that instead of new girl?"

"Sure." Rachel made an indentation in her bottom lip with her teeth. "Where you from?"

"Cromwell." Brittney thought she should add a little bit more to the conversation, so she didn't seem like a complete jerk. "It's in Connecticut."

"I know." Rachel waved at another girl exiting a larger building behind a grove of pine trees. "I'm from Hartford."

"Oh." Brittney twisted the string bracelet on her wrist with her finger. "What's this meeting about anyways?"

"For the group leaders. It's so everyone can meet each other and go over the rules and everything." She waved and gave a wide smile to a guy hanging a towel outside one of the lakeside cabins. "Plus, it's a way to check out the new guy counselors."

"Sounds like a plan to me." Marcus was pretty hot, but she wasn't tied down to him yet.

The small staff lounge was in the same building as the mess hall, but they entered through a different creaky door. Most of the seats on the couches were already taken, so Brittney squeezed in where she could find a spot.

She introduced herself to the two people next to her and then took a few moments to scan the room. There were a couple of guys that caught her eye, one being Marcus. He smiled at her, so she ran the tip of her tongue over her cherry coated lips. His eyes grew wide.

Brittney turned her focus away from him and onto another guy with light-brown hair. She knew how to flirt and planned on driving Marcus crazy. She lifted her arms above her head to feign a stretch, revealing her more than ample assets.

She heard him cough across the room. Perfect.

"Hello, everyone. Welcome to Camp George." A woman with long, dark hair pulled into a ponytail stood at the front of the room in front of an old TV. "I'm Amy and I'll be the women's group leader this summer. This is Kevin and he'll be in charge of the men." A hefty man gave a half-wave from his chair next to the beat-up television.

"We know we've hired the best staff and we're ready to have a successful camp and forget all about last summer."

The room erupted into a bunch of side conversations.

Brittney turned to the girl next to her. "What happened last summer?"

She kept her eyes on Amy as the group leader started up again. "It's all in the past and no one has anything to worry about. Ben has been here all winter and he's assured us that the authorities have gone through this place with a fine-toothed comb."

Brittney stared around the room, trying to get a clue from someone about what Amy was talking about. Every set of eyes was either set on their feet, their hands, or on Amy.

"Whomever, or whatever was causing the . . . disturbances last year has left and I'm sure if we all follow the rules, there won't be any problems."

Disturbances? What disturbances? Vandalism—a sexual predator—a serial killer? Brittney wanted to raise her hand, but she didn't want to be such a new girl.

"So without further ado, Kevin is going to go over the rules for this camp season." Amy sat down in her chair near the front of the room.

"Welcome, counselors. It's so good to see so many of you returning this year. Especially after . . . well, you know." Kevin's face reddened before he continued. "We've added two new rules this year. As usual, no drinking. This goes for on or off camp grounds. And yes, even if you're twenty-one."

Groans sounded from a few counselors on the couches.

"No smoking anywhere. It might just be your summer to quit."

Brittney could already feel the twitch deep down for one of her cigarettes buried in her duffel bag beneath her bed.

"No men in the women's cabins and no women in the men's cabins, even on the weekends when the campers are gone."

Marcus raised an eyebrow at Brittney. She uncrossed her legs and then crossed them again, staring at him the entire time.

"And here are the new rules. No walking around camp by yourself at night and no swimming by yourself." After a couple of protests, Kevin added, "You need to use the buddy system this summer. It may be long gone, but we want to be safe." He chuckled. "Yeah . . . I know we've slacked off on the buddy swimming rule in the past, but this year it will be strictly enforced. No exceptions."

What may be long gone? What the hell happened last summer?

Brittney twisted a loose string on her shorts. She couldn't be the only new counselor who didn't know what Kevin and Amy were talking about. At the moment, Brittney longed to be back at the gas station sucking on Slurpees.

Amy stood back up. "We have two new staff members this summer. Colton Hewes from Worchester, Massachusetts."

The guy with the light brown hair gave a half-wave to the other counselors. When he glanced in Brittney's direction, she smiled at him.

"And Brittney Cahill from Cromwell, Connecticut."

Brittney smiled at the other counselors. "Hey."

The clipboard counselor from the parking lot rolled his eyes. Definitely not her new BFF.

"So, you all got your cabin assignments. Tomorrow, we'll be assigning your stations for camper rotations and planning out the first week of camp with your coworkers." Kevin rubbed his hands together. "But for now, let's go get some grub."

The group rushed through the door to the mess hall. After going through the line, Brittney brought her food to an empty table and sat down.

"Is anyone sitting here?" It was Colton, the other new counselor.

Brittney held her hand out to the spot. "No, it's all yours."

He punched open his milk carton and poured it into the plastic cup. As Colton forked his pasta into his mouth, Brittney saw some type of football championship ring on his finger.

When he stopped mid-scoop with his mouth hanging open, she smiled. "Either you don't eat much, or this is the best spaghetti you've ever eaten."

"Missed lunch today." He set his fork down. "So, you're the other newbie." Colton glanced over his shoulder before he leaned toward her. "What do you think happened last year?"

"I don't know." Brittney lifted her napkin to her mouth as Marcus walked in their direction. "But I intend to find out."

"Can I sit here?" Marcus set his plate down.

"Sure." Colton went back to inhaling his food.

"So what happened last year?" Brittney pushed her noodles around with her fork, but then looked at Marcus. "Because all this talk is really starting to creep us out."

Colton nodded.

Marcus leaned in this time. "Can't tell you. Classified information."

"What do you mean?" Brittney crumpled up her napkin and tossed it at him.

"But . . . I can come to your cabin tonight and let you in on a few camp secrets." Marcus grinned and then tossed the napkin back at her.

Colton shook his head, picked up his plate, and walked away.

Brittney ran her finger along her lips. She knew what he wanted, but maybe he'd let her in on what she really wanted to know.

"I'll see you after lights-out?" She smiled.

"Wouldn't miss it." He reached out and drew circles on her wrist with his finger. "What cabin are you in?"

"Village 5."

"Oh." He pulled back his hand and jumped out of his seat. "I forgot. I've got bathroom duty tonight. Got to make sure those toilets sparkle."

Brittney drew her eyebrows in, her mouth hanging open. What the hell just happened?

*****

The bell rang for lights-out around what Brittney assumed was ten o'clock. She carried her toiletry bag up the hill to her cabin and set it in one of the drawers of her dresser. Even though it was hot and muggy outside, she felt a chill run through her. She was sleeping alone in a cabin at night with only screens between her and the creatures of the forest.

Brittney slipped under the sheet and reached over to turn off the small lamp on her nightstand. She drifted off to a restless sleep.

The noise that woke her sounded like it came from outside the cabin. The leaves crunched just beyond the screen. Brittney's heart rate increased, but she didn't move an inch. *Maybe if it was a bear, it would go away. Was the door locked?*

The crunching noise grew louder and closer. She gripped the sheet tighter around her body. The sweat from the humidity encompassed her and suddenly turned cold.

She had to take a risk before her heart gave out on her. "Marcus?" Her whispered word sounded like it was shouted from a megaphone in the silent world.

The crunching retreated away from the cabin. *What happened here last summer? Was she going to be the next victim of the mysterious assailant?*

Brittney reached over and pulled on the door handle to make sure it was locked before pulling her sheets over her head hoping to deter any knife-wielding intruders.

First thing the next morning, she dug through her dresser for a t-shirt and shorts before reaching for the top drawer to take out new underwear.

She slid open the drawer, the thoughts of the midnight noises still fresh in her mind.

A bloody, severed finger lay on top of her pink thong, rolling back and forth.

Brittney screamed, adrenaline pumping, and slammed the drawer shut. She collapsed down in front of the dresser, her face in her hands and tears streaming from her eyes. She had to look again to make sure.

Edging the drawer open, she closed one eye and peeked again at the finger. The football ring was there. She hurried down the steps of her cabin and through the field, not stopping until she reached the mess hall. Marcus leaned against the building next to the door as she stood there, still trembling.

"Village 5?" He raised his eyebrows at her. "Catherine was there last summer. Broke rule 3. No hanging in guys' cabins. Didn't last two weeks. How long do you think you'll last, newbie?"

She flung the door to the mess hall open and every eye turned in her direction. It was silent. Brittney's eyes were wide as she searched the room for Colton.

Amy stepped forward with a stack of pancakes on her plate. "Looking for somebody?"

"Where's Colton?"

He had to have been put through the same type of initiation.

"Where's Colton?" Louder this time, more frantic.

"Oh, you only broke the first of the new rules." Amy placed a hand on Brittney's arm. "You know it's very dangerous to go walking around camp alone at night, even to your cabin. Make sure you don't do it again. Colton broke both of the new rules." She let out a soft laugh. "Thought it would be safe to go for a midnight swim."

It was only then that Brittney noticed Amy's hair was wet and her jean shorts appeared damp. Brittney looked from face to face to face around the room, her mouth hanging open.

Amy wagged a finger at her. "Just make sure you don't break any more rules. At the end of the summer, we want to send you home in one piece."

Bella And Button
Allison Maruska
Colorado, USA
Copyright © 2018 by Allison Maruska. All rights reserved.
allisonmaruska.com

"Gah!" Bella stood on the sidewalk, watching the yellow bus shrink as it headed down the street. If she'd left school a minute earlier, she wouldn't have missed her ride. "Guess I'm walking again," she said to no one in particular.

She tromped her aggravated self across the street and into the neighborhood. All of her friends had cars and were probably home already. The only reason Bella didn't have a license, much less a car, was her mom's irrational fear of . . . well, of everything. *It's not my fault she can't handle it.* Bella groaned at the thought of losing half an hour walking home, time that could be better spent doing literally anything else.

Bella pulled her phone from her pocket and flipped through various apps as she walked, looking up often enough to avoid veering into traffic or a street lamp. About halfway into the journey, a high-pitched purring sound drew her attention.

It came from a front yard. It could have been a kitten, but it didn't sound right. It was too high pitched, more like a loud insect. And it was incessant.

Bella followed the sound to a patch of low brush surrounding a mailbox. Pulling back the branches, she peered into the shadow. The purring grew louder, and big, shiny eyes stared at her.

"What the hell?" Bella settled onto her knees and leaned forward, reaching for the creature. It squeaked and backed away but then inched toward her fingers, purring the whole time. When it stroked Bella's fingertip with its tiny foot, Bella carefully scooped it up.

Out in the sunlight, the creature, which fit comfortably in her palm, buried its head against her hand. Its wrinkled, speckled gray skin and fin-like ears surrounding short horns reminded Bella of a weird fish she'd seen at the aquarium. But that was definitely a fish. This thing had four stubby legs, fat toes, and eyes as big as a Disney princess's.

"What are you?" She stroked its back, and the purring sped up for a second. The creature didn't lift its head. "You must not like the light." Gently, Bella placed it into her jacket pocket, then she doubled her pace toward home.

Locked in her room, Bella lowered the window shade and sat on her bed. Reaching into her pocket, she wrapped her fingers around the creature and removed it, setting it on her comforter. It uncurled, purring loudly again, and looked up at her with its huge, shiny eyes. It smiled at her.

Bella couldn't help but laugh.

It scurried to her, climbed onto her leg and up to her belly, where it chewed on a button to her jacket. A rapid tapping sound followed.

"I think I'll call you Button."

Button nibbled away, not breaking the button but leaving small nicks in it.

"You must be hungry." Bella opened her desk drawer and took out a cereal bar. "I hope you like apple." She tore off a small piece as set it on the bed, then moved Button next to it.

Button gobbled the snack, his purr going like a motor. She put down another piece, and another, until only crumbs remained.

"Wow. Where did you put that? It was bigger than you."

Button whined and ran over her legs, leaping off her and onto the desk. He crawled down the front of the drawer and clung to the knob.

"More? Really?" Bella maneuvered her fingers around Button to open the drawer, retrieving another cereal bar. Button leapt back onto the bed, where Bella fed him again.

Satisfied, Button curled up and went to sleep.

Bella took the opportunity to research. She entered Button's features into a search engine, but the results only showed fish and prehistoric lizards. Button was one of a kind. How did he end up in a bush? And what if his mother or something was looking for him? Should she put him back?

Maybe his species was one that required their young to survive from the outset, like sea turtles. If that was the case, Button wasn't doing so hot. He was obviously starving.

Bella decided to keep him a while, at least until she could figure out what he was and where he came from.

Button slept all day, and when it was time for Bella to turn in, she moved him to the small space between her pillow and the wall. He breathed rapidly, a little purr accompanying each exhalation. Bella dozed, comforted by his contentment.

A loud shriek jerked Bella awake. Button sat on the window sill, where he'd chewed a hole in the shade, and with his mouth open as wide as his head, was piercing the night with his yell.

"Shhh! What are you doing?" Bella hurried to him and grabbed him. He sank his teeth into her hand, sending a searing pain through it and up her arm. She dropped him. In no time, Button had returned to the hole in the shade and resumed screeching.

Bella cupped her bleeding hand. I have to get him out of here!

The door flew open and her mother ran in with her hands covering her ears. She yelled, "What is that?" over the noise, but Bella could barely hear her.

A crash came from the window, and the shade flung to the ceiling long enough to reveal what Button was calling. Another creature, this one as big as a truck, snatched Button and disappeared just as quickly.

Bella hurried to the window and peered out, expecting to see the large creature shrinking down the street.

Instead, there was only darkness.

"What was that?" Bella's mother asked.

Bella swallowed. There was no way to explain Button. "Something I found on my walk home."

Bella's mother took Bella's hand, assessing the wound. "Well . . . maybe it's time to get you a car."

Doll's Play
Bonnie Lyons
New Iberia, LA, USA
Copyright © 2018 by Bonnie Lyons. All rights reserved.
bonnielyons1@cox.net

Her name is NOLA. She is old, but she is beautiful. She is sinfully rich, but mired in poverty. Her rhythms are primordial and will pursue you, long after you have gone. But on that day, she was charmingly exotic.

New Orleans, Louisiana aka the Crescent City aka The Big Easy is an easy place to lose yourself. So Josh and Peter followed their wives at a distance, wandering down broken sidewalks and under the looming Spanish lacework of balcony railings, feeling as though they were on a movie set, perhaps for a Stephen King tome.

Peter talked and Josh watched. After 10 years of marriage and two children, Josh and Caroline were experiencing the best sex of their lives. Josh studied the gentle sway of his wife's saunter, the lively bounce of her long, honey blonde curls, the way her face came alight with the smile that she tossed back at him. Josh was contemplating getting lost in the curves of her body when Peter's voice broke through.

"Check this out, man!" Peter had stopped before a sign labeled, 'Marie's Back Door' and chuckled. "You a back door kind of guy, buddy? Seems you can't take your eyes off of Caroline's."

Josh smiled at his long-time friend and briefly considered telling him about the truly remarkable levels of intimacy they had discovered, but stopped. In his experience, others really did not want to hear about it. Whether it was discomfort, jealousy or disbelief, the subject was still best kept between them. So, Josh just smiled lasciviously in return.

The small, dark entrance to 'Marie's Back Door' might have gone unnoticed, had it not contrasted so sharply with the sunny, crisp November day.

"Go on ahead," Josh called to Caroline and her friend, Georgia. "Just going to pop in here for a minute. We'll join you shortly."

"'Maybe I can find something to bring back to the girls," Josh explained to Peter. "Allie has become fascinated with all of this paranormal business. I wonder if I should let a 10-year-old read all that scary stuff, but I like that she's reading so much."

"I wouldn't worry too much about it," Peter replied. "I think most kids are interested in that sort of thing at some point. I was. It fuels the imagination. But, wow, look at these prices! They think an awful lot of this. $500 for something that smells like.... Whew! Don't know how to describe that!" They joked and laughed, while scanning shelves of herbs, potions, relics.

"Many things in life are not what they seem to be." The voice from a back doorway was rich and lyrical. She was petite in stature, but powerful in presence and beautiful in a severe sort of way. Her skin was the color of café au lait and her hazel eyes jumped out under the framework of a bright yellow scarf wound around her head.

"That may appear to be a small bottle of essential oil or one of those white folks' potions." She said it with a chuckle. "But what that REALLY is…" she pointed a finger and moved around to the back of a counter, "… is salvation … salvation from a spell that is meant to do grievous harm. Taking that into account, it's a bargain."

Her eyes shone when she saw the amusement on their faces and she lowered her head to gaze at them pointedly.

"Come on, Josh. The girls will wonder what we're up to," said Peter, pulling on his friend's arm. They stepped out into the bright, autumn light.

"That place gives me the creeps," said Peter.

But Josh held back and waved his friend on. "You go ahead. I'll be out in just a minute. Just want to ask her something."

Peter was shaking his head, as he headed toward the restaurant.

When Josh peeked back inside, the woman was still standing behind the counter, waiting. "Look, I was really just looking for a souvenir. Something to take home to my little girl. She's fascinated with all this stuff. Got anything like that? Something perhaps in a souvenir price range?"

With hooded eyes, she smiled at him. "Not really, cher."

She almost left it at that, but then she said, "But wait. I can give you an experience that you can tell her about for a special price. Only $10. How about if I tell your fortune?" As though reading his mind, she added, "It will only take a minute."

She took a candle from a shelf, lit and placed it right under his face. "Now hold it with both hands and breath deeply." Josh complied and inhaled the sweet, musky smoke. She placed her hands over his. "Now close your eyes," she admonished, as she bent her own head down.

Allie would, in fact, be thrilled with this tale of adventure.

The aromatic wisps from the candle were pleasant, but made him light-headed and a bit nauseous and he was about to disengage when a flash of light disturbed his reverie. An image floated before him like a scene change from a movie, where a newspaper is tossed, spinning before you.

In big, bold caps the headline read, "Atlanta Man Charged With Murder of Family." His own image stared back at him from underneath the bold type.

Josh jerked backward so violently that the candle dropped to the floor and he almost fell backward. The look of fright on his face distorted it into a mask and his entire body pulsed with emotion. "What was that?!" he asked accusatorially. "How did you do that?!"

*****

The party was underway when Josh walked into the great, white room at the front of Antoine's Restaurant. Happy voices, punctuated by laughter and the clinks of spoons on glasses gave the place a festive atmosphere and he felt a sense of relief for the normalcy of it.

Peter and Georgia greeted Josh with smiles, but Caroline inclined her head at him and, reached for him, asking, "Are you okay? " She read him like a book.

He managed a wry grin and replied, "Fine. Fine," before taking a chair and ordering a double, Crown and water. Again, her expression told him that she took note. His eyes widened and he smiled fully. "Well, that was interesting."

"What happened?" asked Caroline.

"Nothing much. Really." Josh replied. "Just a local, eager to make a sale." Josh thought it best to keep the details to himself.

"Well, did you find something for Allie that didn't cost you your first born child?" Peter asked. "You should have seen this place. What a rip! Man, there's no other place quite like New Orleans."

Josh nodded. He reached into his pocket and brought out a tiny, but intricate doll. It fit neatly into the cup of his hand, as the shopkeeper had urged him to discover. It was a gift, she had told him, for being such a good sport.

"Just a little token," she'd explained. "We sell dreams here, Mister. Not everyone knows how to take that." Her smiling face embedded itself into his brain, as he stumbled out the door into the dimming day. He had been there longer than he'd realized.

*****

"What is it?" Caroline asked simply.

"It's some sort of voodoo doll, I guess."

This one was ringed with various colors, white, red, green, black, purple, yellow and blue, as though someone had carefully wrapped each limb with embroidery threads. Its face was a blank white ball with yellow threads for hair.

"And you got this for Allison?" Caroline asked pointedly. "I don't think so, honey. It's one thing for her to read about this stuff. I don't think I want her experimenting. Sorry."

"Yeah, you're probably right. Didn't think of it that way," he answered, with a grin. He stuffed the doll back into his pocket and determined to file it all away under 'Vacation Oddities'.

*****

Back in Atlanta, the doll was forgotten until Josh ran across it, while emptying the pockets of his good khakis. He tossed the

91

trinket into the dish on his nightstand where all of his loose change, matchbooks and stray buttons went for keeping.

The spell of the episode had faded and Josh had consigned the entire experience to stress and the power of suggestion.

A week in New Orleans to celebrate his new job with one of the South's top firms had been a welcome respite, but it was time to get some rest and prepare for a tough week. He already knew who his first client would be.

*****

"Josh, I'd like you to meet Charles Burton of Burton Industries." Richard Powers was the youngest partner in the prestigious firm of Lowell, Redding and Powers and had talked the others into recruiting Josh.

When Josh shook hands with Burton, he noticed the hand was cold and limp. Burton smiled, but the expression stopped short of his eyes, understandable for a man in his position.

"Charlie, Josh's career has been flawless. He is the only prosecutor for Georgia's Fifth Judicial District with a 100% record of success. We've watched him for a long time and think he's the man to handle your particular problem."

Powers turned back toward Josh. "As you know, Josh, Charles has been charged with the sexual assault of a 16-year-old girl. Of course, men in his position often have a target on their backs. People looking for a payday. But the under-aged aspect of the accuser makes it more delicate than usual."

Briefly, Josh wondered about 'more delicate than usual'. How many times had this occurred?

When the offer of employment at one of the South's most important law firms had been extended, Josh had agonized over the decision. In the end, however, he had taken the opportunity that could propel his career and give his wife and two girls what he had never had; a stable and prosperous family.

As he drifted off to sleep that night, doubt and anticipation picked away at his subconscious and he fell into a fitful sleep. He awoke with a start and the unsettling feeling that he and his wife were not alone.

Josh sat up and used the light on his phone to carefully scan the room, finding nothing until his eyes settled on Caroline sleeping peacefully beside him. She was his everything and his heart still jumped at the sight of her and the two girls she had given him

He smiled, rolled over and sighed, eyes flickering before catching a ray of moonlight on the doll, sitting in the nightstand dish, gazing down on him.

*****

Jessie was the baby and hated being called that. At six, she was in her first year of 'real school, not baby school', and feeling very full of herself. It was the worst time she could have chosen to insist her Daddy listen to the rhyme she was rehearsing for a class performance.

Josh was standing in front of his bathroom mirror getting himself and his own speech ready for his meeting with Burton, for which he was running late. It had not been going well.

Burton was holding back and lying to him. He didn't seem to grasp or care that he was handicapping his own defense. It was puzzling. He had to give Burton an ultimatum and it could end up costing him his job, the house they were planning to build and the very expensive private school tuition for the girls.

"Not now, Jessie. I'm in a hurry."

"Daddy, listen," Jessie implored with increasing urgency. While Allie was quiet and studious, Jessie was boisterous, uncontained and somewhat spoiled. "Daddy, Daddy, Daddy, listen, listen… "

As he tried to make his escape, she grabbed and twisted the fabric of his best gabardine pants with her small fist. In a pique, Josh swatted at her hand and caught her on her face instead, sending the small girl into a heap on the floor and summoning Caroline at the sound of her caterwauling child.

"Daddy hit me!" she cried, more heartbroken than hurt, as Caroline looked up at Josh in disbelief. It was a bad start to a bad day.

*****

Nothing was going right. The partners were pressing for a report on the case and his strategy. Burton wanted him to push for a dismissal, as though he had grounds. He was smug and contemptuous and Josh was feeling as though he was caught up in something unsavory.

Lying in bed that night, Josh and Caroline talked calmly.

"I know the stress you've been under and we want to support you," she told him. "It's one thing to get mad at me," she told him. "But you have to control yourself around the girls, Josh." It was becoming a familiar mantra.

She was right, of course. His temper had been short a lot lately and it was so unlike him.

Josh had grown up in a family populated by the dysfunctional. He had learned drive from a man who respected work, but nothing and no one else. It was an atmosphere powered by fear, anger and alcoholism. Josh had worked hard to be everything his father was not, a kind and loving man, a good husband and father, a success. Why was this happening to him?

He gulped down an Ambien to force the sleep he needed and rolled over to let it take effect. As he did, his eye caught the doll on his nightstand. He squinted at the odd little figure, briefly caught up in the impression that it seemed larger than he'd thought. He was just tired, very tired. Then he drifted off into a deep, dark sleep.

*****

In tone, if not topic, the images that began to flit and flicker across his subconscious were reminiscent of those from his experience in the shop in New Orleans. A bright flash lit his psyche and then the blurred image of a face, distorted in rage. A face and then a complete figure were hovering over him.

"Get up boy! I'm not finished with you! That old dog that you're always hanging on is smarter than you, you worthless son of a bitch! You'll never amount to NOTHING!" Spittle sprayed when he spoke. Then the man reared back and swung the stick in a vicious and swift motion and Josh jerked upright in bed. He was sweating and his heart raced as though it would leap from his chest.

Josh swung his legs over the side of the bed and held his head in one hand and his chest with the other. When the pounding finally subsided, Josh raised his head and found himself looking squarely at the figure on his nightstand. With head cocked, he picked it up and placed it in the palm of his hand. He could not close his hand over it.

*****

Reclining on his couch, Josh drifted in a state of semi-consciousness with an Astros/Cardinals game softly providing the white noise and a Sunday meal with an excellent pinot grigio providing the anesthetic. What a needed break this was!

After months of struggling with the Burton case and a truckload of other cases that had him working 7 days a week, he had finally sneaked in a day of rest with his family. He needed it so badly. They all did.

His anxiety had evaporated and he was floating when a tittering sound from the end of the couch prompted him to gently lift one eyelid. One little cap of blonde curls popped up and then quickly down again and the tittering continued.

Then a small hand cloaked in a sock and held in the puppet-position popped up and said, "My name is Sally. What's yours?"

Josh grinned sleepily. He had missed this. "My name is Josh. Do you know what happened to my daughter, Allison?"

"Oh, she's around here somewhere." The sock puppet appeared to look around and then look down, where there was more tittering. "Have you seen Allie?" asked Sally, the Sock to the titterer.

"No, but my name is Henry," was the response, as up popped the multi-colored voodoo doll.

Josh was shocked, disoriented. More shocking was that the doll was about the size of Josh's full hand. And on the face of the plain, white head with yellow hair two black beads stared at him.

Frissons crawled up Josh's spine and panic descended upon him. It was a panic he had not felt in a long time and it produced an aggression born of helplessness.

He snatched the doll from Allie's hand with a harshness that left the girl white-faced. He stared at the doll manically. "What are you doing with this?" he demanded. "And what did you DO to it?!"

Allie was shaken and spoke meekly. "I'm sorry. I got it in your bedroom. I know what it is. I thought it was for me."

95

"Well, it's not! You don't go into other people's private rooms! You can't take things that aren't yours, Allie!" He was aware that he was yelling and couldn't seem to stop. "Go to your room! Get out of my sight!" he demanded.

When Caroline returned from walking their dog, the girls were huddled together in Allie's bedroom and Josh had retreated to his, a bottle of Crown in tow.

*****

That night the flash was longer and it stuttered like the flickering of an old film reel. The scene was dark, in some sort of frail shack, the only shaft of light illuminating a golden liquid and the hand around the bottle that contained it.

Josh felt more than saw him. The weight of his malevolence was crushing. And he heard him cursing softly.

"I'd rather DIE than have a thief in my family." The voice was slurred and gravelly. He put the bottle down on a workbench and picked up a bat with one hand, tapping its head into the palm of his other.

Outside, a dog was clawing at the door, whimpering and barking. "Please don't hurt Missy," was the only thought Josh could muster.

"On the other hand…" there was a long pause, "…I didn't steal anything." And with a motion that belied the man's condition, he hit a home run.

The cries from Josh's bed woke the house.

*****

Caroline showed no mercy the following morning. When the alarm erupted, she was already up, dressed and throwing back the heavy curtains to allow bright light to crash onto his face. She slammed the empty Crown bottle on his nightstand and as she walked out the room, she threw the voodoo doll onto the bedcovers. "Here," she said gruffly. "Is this what you wanted? It's all yours! I never wanted Allie to have it anyway!"

Glare from the sun lit up the room, his hangover and his conscience. He scowled down at the doll. Then he picked it up and placed it in his hand, where it measured past his wrist. A red slash where a mouth should be, scowled back at him.

Allie had called the doll Henry. Henry was his father's name. Henry was the man in his nightmares. And his nightmares were just his memories. He couldn't shake the thought. Maybe he was his father's son.

*****

Peter recognized his friend from his back as he walked briskly, if unevenly through the aisles of Academy.

"Hey, buddy! Josh!" he called out. "Wait up, man. What's your hurry? Damn, it's been so long."

Josh stopped and half-turned toward Peter. Josh's eyes were red and puffy, his hair mussed, tie loosed, the well-put-together-man gone.

"Hey, what's up, man? You okay?" asked Peter.

"Oh. Yeah. I guess." Then he looked down and up again at his friend. "Actually, no. I got fired today."

"What? What happened? Why?"

"Long story. But you know what Peter? I'm not going to let it get me down. I'm going to show them. Been working my ass off and for what? Nobody appreciates anything!"

"Aw, man, that's awful. I can't believe it. Hey, you know what? Let's pop in to Rudy's and have a couple. You can tell me about it and we can catch up. What do you say?"

Josh's face brightened. "Great idea, Pete. Hell, let's have a bottle. Yeah. I just have an errand to run here. How about if I meet you out front. Do you mind driving? I've already had one or two."

"Sure thing."

When Josh climbed into Peter's Denali, he was carrying a large, plastic Academy bag with a baseball bat sticking out. Josh reached for his seatbelt and Peter noticed some sort of colorful toy poking out of Josh's jacket pocket and thought about what a great dad Josh was.

"Is Allie taking up baseball?" Peter asked.

Josh flashed his smile toward his friend. "No. The bat's for me. Come on. Let's get shit-faced."

97

Spirit Lake
Sharon K. Connell
Houston, Texas, USA
Copyright © 2018 by Sharon K. Connell. All rights reserved.
http://sharonkconnell.com/

Everyone says it's just a legend. I know better.

My name is Patrick Nahmana. I'm a mystery writer. My Uncle Jelmer had recently died and left his old log cabin on Spirit Lake to me. For weeks, my wife Jen had insisted on a two-week vacation away from the bustle of Chicago life. Probably so I'd pay more attention to her than my computer. So, peace and quiet beckoned as we set off for Menagha, Minnesota.

It had been years since I'd visited the cabin on Spirit Lake. It stood on the shore with a magnificent view over the water from its rough timber porch. Interlocking logs with hand-hewn notches made the mid-eighteen hundreds structure look like something out of a movie. A stone foundation, firm as the Rockies, had the letter "P" carved into one white-colored stone at the base of the back porch stairs. I had carved the "P" when my uncle first told me the cabin would someday be mine. Branded.

Midafternoon, after I parked our old red truck at the cabin, Jen got out and gazed at the wooden structure. "It's such a big place, Patrick. Wide and sprawling."

We strolled around to the back. At the porch steps, I fingered the carved initial. "Yep. This place has been in our family unchanged from its birth." I grinned at her. "I have plans to update it." We took the short stone path that meandered its way down a slope to the water.

***

Early the next morning, I sat on the porch in a lawn chair, coffee in hand, listening to the call of blue jays. A resident heron few across the water and landed in the top of a tall pine.

Wrapped in a wool Indian blanket and carrying a huge cup of coffee, my wife stepped from the cabin onto the porch. "Patrick, we're making a jaunt into the town of Brainerd for some early Christmas shopping, today."

To distract her from the subject, I pointed to the large windows on either side of the rustic back door. "Why do you suppose there aren't any windows on the sides of this cabin? And the windows in the front are only half the size of these?"

She smirked. "Maybe the big windows in the back have something to do with that old lake legend." She walked away, snickering.

Strategy hadn't worked. I grimaced. Christmas shopping in town still on the agenda.

After breakfast, we jumped into the truck. A surprise overnight snowfall had turned the countryside into an early winter wonderland, like a fluffy white blanket covering the trees and cabin.

As I drove, Jen and I discussed gifts for family members. Actually, she suggested. I agreed. She made notes, and I traversed the blacktopped highway during the lull in our conversation. I glanced over to her. "You know, when you teased about the Spirit Lake legend this morning, it made me—"

"Don't start with that spooky story again. You know it gives me the creeps! I'm sorry I mentioned it." Her voice had a nervous quiver in it. We drove on in silence.

***

After we'd navigated the packed stores and endless trinkets in specialty shops well into the afternoon, Jen suggested a late lunch in a quaint cafe. We sat back having coffee at the end of our meal. "Jen, what I wanted to tell you on the way here was—"

"Can we talk about it later? That dark sky tells me we need to get back to the cabin."

She was right. It wouldn't be good to be caught in a snowstorm, not in a truck with no snow tires.

As we drove out of town, the snow began. "Jen, we'll eventually have a family. We'll want more rooms when we vacation at the lake. We could pull the cabin down and rebuild once my next book is on the market. What do you think?" Jen didn't answer. Was she more interested in the scenery? Or she disagreed and didn't want to start an argument.

Her head turned to the direction from where we'd come, then straight ahead. "This road isn't right, Patrick. Did you take a different way back?"

After I brought the truck to a stop, I turned and scanned the area for a familiar landmark. Nothing. And no other vehicles on the road. "You're right. I must have made a wrong turn. We'll go back."

A prickly sensation snaked its way up the back of my neck. The paved road had narrowed to one lane, making a turnaround impossible. When had that happened? Had I been that lost in thought? Ahead on the left was a small dirt road. I pulled into it, but it descended at a sharp angle. We slid down the incline at an alarming speed. I pumped the brake pedal until we finally stopped with a jerk.

Ditches on either side still made a U-turn impossible. We'd have to drive farther on the snow-covered road, or back out. Since we couldn't see the end of the road, I decided backing out was the better of the two options.

Jen's eyes were huge as she peered out the back window. She braced herself with her hands on the dashboard. I stuck my head out the window and backed up. The incline seemed steeper than before. The wheels slipped from side to side in the ruts. A whooshing sound came from out the open window.

She grabbed my shoulder. "What was that?"

"That, my dear, was a flat tire." I hoped that was all.

Pitch dark, stuck in a thick stand of trees. Great! From the glove compartment, I retrieved my long-handled flashlight and slid out of the truck. The rim of the rear wheel had sunk deep into dirty brown snow.

The forest was silent and dark, except for the glimmer of huge falling white flakes. No yard lights anywhere. I lowered the tailgate. No spare tire. Strange. How long had it been missing?

"Now what do I do?" I whispered as the hair on my neck bristled again.

Jen's half-smiling face showed through the back window. She was scared, but then, she wasn't alone. I got back in the cab. She punched in 911 on her cell. No signal.

We couldn't just sit there. I got back in the cab. "Jen, I'll walk back toward town. There must be a house along the way."

"Oh no! You're not leaving me alone in these woods." She had that end-of-conversation expression on her face.

She opened the passenger door, stepped out, and screamed as she disappeared. My heart jumped to my throat. I pushed the driver's door open and rushed to her. She'd fallen into the ditch.

When she tried to stand, she fell again with another cry. I picked her up in my arms and managed to get her back in the passenger seat. Her ankle had already begun to swell.

From the back seat, I retrieved an old t-shirt and wrapped it tightly around her foot. "Murphy's Laws have decided to take over my life." At least the comment brought a smile to her face. I hoofed it around the back end and hopped into the driver's side. "Okay. Here's the plan. I walk down this dirt road to see if any houses are nearby. You stay here and lock the doors. Keep trying your cell."

Jen latched onto my arm. "Please don't go too far. We could just stay here and wait for help."

After a quick look around us, I knew no one would be coming. The muscles in my neck and shoulders tightened. Even my stomach had turned to rock. "Don't worry. I won't be long."

***

Past the bend in the dirt road, I caught a glimpse of sky overhead between the trees. A ring circled the full moon. My Irish mother's words came to mind.

Be wary when a ring circles the moon. It's then the magic starts. Spirits roam about.

A chill slithered up my spine. I'd never believed her superstitions back then. But the thoughts unsettled me. I quickened my pace.

After a stretch of thick, silent woods, little sparks of light appeared through the trees, as though hundreds of eyes watched me. Goosebumps ran over my arms and back. I began to jog.

At the end of the road, a log cabin stood barely visible in the encroaching woods. No light came from the windows. Not too far away, a wolf howled. My scalp prickled, and I scrambled up the steps to the porch. The structure of the cabin was the same as ours on Spirit Lake, except—it looked brand new.

No one answered my knock on the door. I crept around the raised porch to the other side of the house. At the back, two large windows with closed wooden shutters faced a dark lake. Stairs descended from the porch, and a stone footpath led to the lake. Again, it stuck me. Everything exactly like our cabin. An eerie sense of dread engulfed me. What was happening here? Our cabin would have looked like this over a hundred years ago. This timber smelled fresh.

The air hung still and damp. Not even a cricket chirped. I continued on the path to the water's edge. No hoots or screeches from owls, no rustling from small night animals in the brush came to my ears. Only the slow, soft lap of waves on pebbles and sand.

I stared out over the small lake. The same size and shape as Spirit Lake but surrounded by dense woods instead of an occasional house with lights shining in the evening hour. The snow had stopped and only moonglow lit the night. The eerie sensation filled me again as I let my gaze run across the darkness to the far side of the water. Something moved on the distant shore. A light floated on the surface and came straight toward me.

The Indian chief's daughter gasped when she saw the knife stuck into the chest of the brave whom she loved. She ran to the lake and cried that she would avenge him someday. The water splashed as she dove in. Her father watched as his daughter slipped beneath the surface before he could reach her. And that, Patrick, is how Spirit Lake got its name.

Uncle Jelmer's voice was as clear as when he'd first told the legend.

They never found her. People say they've seen her walking across the water. Searching for the killer to avenge the death of her beloved. They hear her moan.

I shuddered at the thought. Why had I ever listened to his stories?

The strange light came closer. The hair rose on my arms and neck. What looked like a knife blade flashed in the moonlight.

As the wolf howled once more, I turned and ran.

***

When I climbed into the driver's seat, Jen gaped at me. I closed and locked the door.

She touched my arm. "What's wrong? Why did you run back right away? You're trembling."

"Didn't you hear that wolf?"

"What wolf?"

Her words sank in. "What do you mean, I ran right back?"

"I mean, why did you stop at the bend, turn around, and run back like something was after you?"

"I didn't stop. I walked to the end of the road."

She tilted her head and glared at me. "I kept my eyes on you the whole time, Patrick. You never went around the bend. Quit! This is no time for teasing."

"I'm not. There's a cabin at the end of this road. No one answered the door. When I went down to the water, a small light glittered on the surface in the distance. A wolf howled—"

Jen's eyes were like saucers. "Stop it! That's not funny."

When I glanced at my watch, it indicated that I'd been gone for little more than ten minutes. How could that be? It had to be at least half an hour. My hands shook.

I slid my arm around her. "It's too dark to walk through the woods, and even if there is a house down there—my imagination must have worked overtime in this dark crop of trees. That's all."

After a couple of minutes, I turned the ignition key. The engine started but stalled. I tried again. Same result. My head dropped to the steering wheel, and I took a deep breath. Then I tried once more. The engine started. I let out the breath I held and yanked the shifter into reverse. Slowly we moved backwards up the incline.

Jen grabbed the dashboard. "What about the flat tire?"

"Maybe it'll keep us from sliding. I'd rather ruin the rims than stay here."

An hour later, moving backward inch by inch, we made it to paved road. Still deserted. At the sound of the wheel on blacktop, I cringed. The rims would be ruined for sure. Tiny specks of lights in the darkness shone through the woods and came closer. I shoved the gearshift into first and started forward.

We hadn't gone far when Jen yelled, "Stop!"

I slammed on the brakes. "What?"

She pointed to an unpaved road a few yards behind us. Beyond the trees were bright lights. Why hadn't we noticed it before?

I backed up and turned onto the road. An old service station with a strange gas pump came into view on the right. A light was on in the weathered building. Clanging filled the air and then stopped as I turned off the engine. An old man stepped out of the garage and wiped his hands on a red bandana. He approached the truck.

"What are you folks doing out so late?"

He thought eight o'clock was late? "We had a flat tire and no spare."

"No problem. I can fix that in a jiffy."

We got the wheel off, the man giving it strange looks the entire time, and he took it to the garage.

"Jen, stay in the cab. Lock the door."

Fear flashed in her eyes.

***

"Shore do have a newfangled truck there, boy. And here's yer problem. Ya got no inner tube in that tire. Never seen a tire like this one before."

I stared at the man, openmouthed. What kind of place was this?

"Don't know if I got one that'll fit." He walked out the back door, and returned a few seconds later, shaking his head. "Nope, don't have anything that will fit this here wheel."

Nothing the guy said made sense.

The old man searched through his tools. "I might could make a repair, of sorts." He began working on the tire.

A thought struck. I rushed to the truck where I found Jen frantically trying her phone again without success. Behind the driver's seat, I found a can of tire seal and ran back to the garage before Jen could ask anything.

The man had managed to patch the tire. I used the tire seal to reinforce the repair.

When we put the wheel back on the vehicle, I peered in at Jen. She still hadn't spoken a word, and her face had grown whiter than before.

I paid the man in cash. His brows furrowed as he looked at the bills. I climbed into the cab and rolled down the window. "Thanks for your help, sir."

"Say, you never answered why yer out so late."

Strange man. Something Uncle Jelmer used to say popped up again. *People used to roll up the sidewalks around here after five o'clock in days gone by.* I snickered to myself. "We took a wrong turn, and wound up on an old rutted road leading to a lake and cabin."

"Where was this lake and cabin?"

I pointed in the direction, told him about the light I'd seen on the water, and about the Legend of Spirit Lake. His eyes grew large.

He came closer and whispered. "The man who stabbed that Indian was my great-grandfather. You'd best be gettin' outta here."

Was he trying to scare us? Probably good advice though. I glanced at Jen who bit her lip.

"What did he say, Patrick?"

"Tell you later." I started the engine and made a hasty turn.

***

Several miles down the road, everything appeared normal again. We sped back to our cabin. When we arrived, I checked my watch. It was only a few minutes after eight o'clock.

As we unloaded our packages from the truck, I told Jen what the old man had said.

She shook her head. "Stop trying to scare me. This trip did a good enough job." She ran up the stairs and disappeared inside. I decided it was best to let the whole subject drop.

***

The next day, I drove into Menagha to buy a new tire and a spare. As I paid for the tires, the middle-aged man behind the counter talked about the snow.

I nodded. "Yeah, we drove through it last night. It wasn't that bad until we got lost."

"You must have gotten on a nasty dirt road, judging by the mud on that bad tire."

"We wound up on a pitch-black dirt-road that led to a cabin and lake." I told him the legend.

The blood drained from the man's face. "Everyone around here knows that story. The brave had won the heart of the princess, and his brother killed him out of jealousy. Word has it that the murderer's family still lives in the woods and keeps everyone out. No one's ever seen them…before maybe last night." His eyes narrowed.

"The family of the Indian princess built and still owns that old cabin on Spirit Lake. Supposed to be a sentinel of sorts to make sure the lake will always be there for the princess and her brave. Heard tell they're never supposed to sell the property, or do anything to change it. Some kind of—Indian curse involved.

"It's only when the princess walks without her brave you need fear her."

***

No one ever told me that Nahmana was an Indian name. I thought Dad was Scandinavian.

We still visit Spirit Lake and still own the old cabin. Guess we always will, considering. But—we make sure not to travel unfamiliar roads up there anymore and always keep an eye out on the lake.

Never have seen any sign of the princess again. Occasionally, we'll hear someone say they saw her walking in the woods with her brave. I'm *really* happy about that.

Ice Cream
Geoff Le Pard
London, England
Copyright © 2018 by Geoff Le Pard. All rights reserved.
https://geofflepard.com

'Arnold, will you stop that racket?'

Arnold Crump rocked back on his heels, his lips forming a tight line. He had barely started trying to remove the rust from the side of his ice cream van and already his mother was moaning. He placed the wire-brush carefully on the ground and stood up, squeezing his free hand so tightly that his knuckles went white. How hard would he have to squeeze her to stop her whines, he wondered? He began to turn with the intention of shutting out the complaints.

'What's got into her?'

Arnold jumped, caught unawares by his neighbour, quickly unclenching his fist before she could see.

Doris Lethridge approached the fence between their properties, putting down the basket of laundry she had been holding. She folded her arms tightly across her ample bosoms as if trying to stop them escaping. 'You're a ruddy saint, Arnie, to put up with her moans.' She wiped her nose on her sleeve, causing Arnold to pull a sour face. 'How's the van? Holding together? You should get a new one.'

His mother's querulous voice floated out of the still-open back door. 'My sinuses are bleedin' awful and all you can do is make more bloody dust...'

Arnold moved quickly to close the door before turning back to Doris. 'Oh, she can't help it. It's the weather...' He picked up the brush and turned away, once again considering the side panel of his van.

'Her bloody sinuses are a law unto themselves. She…'

Arnold wished he could shut a door on Doris as well. 'I must get on.' If he gave her any sort of opening, he'd never finish and he needed the van ready for his next shift that afternoon. The rust that had begun to stain the ice cream logo seemed never ending. He tuned out Doris's final suggestion and began to scrape at the metal paneling. After a few moments, he heard a door click; Doris had taken the hint.

He studied the battered old van and sighed deeply. He knew only too well that however may coats of paint he applied, it would only be a temporary fix. Doris was right; he really did need a new van and soon if he wasn't going to lose business. The customers in the park weren't going to accept an ice cream from some tatty old rust bucket. If the outside looked dirty, all those posh mummies would assume the insides were the same and boycott him. And if they stopped buying, then he'd be trapped here forever.

'Arnold.' Viola's voice penetrated the solid door. 'What have you done with my tissues? You know I need my tissues. If I don't have my tissues…'

Arnold covered his ears and released a silent scream, straining his jaw muscles until they ached. The tissues were where they always were, as well she knew. As he pushed himself to his feet, knowing that it would be quicker if he 'found' them for her, rather than ignoring her accusations, he began to calculate the quantity of tissue it would take to block her mouth and stop the noise.

As it turned out it was twenty-seven.

If rendering his mother mute removed the most immediate of Arnold's problems, it didn't pass unnoticed.

'Your mum's feeling better, is she?' Millicent Jackson, who lived at number 37 and whose lazy eye had seemed, since Arnold's childhood, to be able to read his mind, paused on her way to the bus stop. 'She's been so quiet these last few days. Hope that's a good sign.

Arnold felt trapped, but managed to say, 'She's visiting…
her sister.'

'Oh?' Millicent's expression suggested surprise, but then
she smiled. 'I didn't know she had a sister. Well, I'm sure she'll
enjoy the break. Does she live far away?'

Arnold nodded, well understanding the hope that lay
behind her question. Everyone would benefit from a few days
without his mother around. Before he could answer, Millicent
spied her bus. Moving surprisingly swiftly for one built more for
comfort rather than speed, she left him pondering what he should
do next.

Over the next few days, Arnold developed a plan. He
needed to deflect his neighbours' attention, so he invited them to a
barbecue. They all asked after his mother, some solicitous, some
just plain nosey. He explained how she would be away
indefinitely, due to his aunt's sudden illness.

'You're looking peaky, Arnold. Are you getting enough
greens? With your mother away?' asked Harriet Stromboli from
number 33, her permanent scowl suggesting she knew who to
blame for Arnold's neglect.

He nodded. 'Oh yes. Mother trained me well.'

'Stop fussing, Harry,' interjected Martin Paddock from The
Coach House, his tweed cap titled at a jaunty angle. He sniffed at
the plate he had been handed, his fat lips moistening. 'You must
give me the recipe, Arnie. This chicken is fabulous.'

Arnold looked away. 'It's a family secret. Mother always
said she's take it to her grave.'

'Well, I'd better enjoy it while I can, then,' said Martin, as
he bit gingerly into the lightly grilled escalope. 'There's something
familiar about this,' he said, chewing slowly. 'Garlic? Tarragon?
You really do need to say.'

Arnold watched as Martin swallowed a sliver his mother's
buttock. He knew the questions would keep coming; he needed to
find an alternative method of disposal. Eating his mother was not
going to be the whole answer, even seasoned with rosemary and
ground cardamom. And he had to disagree with Martin on one
point; his mother tasted nothing like chicken.

It was obvious, when you thought about it, Arnold said to himself as he sat in the basement the next day. Becoming a cannibal was fine, so far as it went, but it was never going completely to remove his mother from his life. Beyond the mountain of flesh that now inhabited one of his chest freezers, normally home to ice lollies and cornettos, there were the bones, the blood, and the inedible-looking viscera. Arnold wasn't given to panic. He knew that, given time, inspiration would come.

It was a hot Tuesday just after the schools finished for the day and Arnold sat in his van, watching the queue of mewling infants and their fractious parents grow, while he pondered this dilemma. Absently he handed a cone topped with whipped ice cream to the next customer, a sticky-faced girl of about seven with an eye patch.

'Mum, why doesn't he have strawberry sauce? I want strawberry sauce.'

Arnold smiled at the gobby little madam, imagining how her complexion would itself turn strawberry if only he could ram the cone into her yapping mouth. She'd become a small, monocular version of his mother if someone didn't stop her soon.

He drove home that evening, trying to ignore the clanking transmission and the unsettling rattle from the front bearings. He had the beginnings of a plan.

Arnold did things with a deliberation borne of years of having his patience tried. When Doris asked after his mother, he told her, with a shy confidence that she was being well taken care of. Using the hot weather as an excuse, he retired to the basement to 'work on a little project'.

He pooled his scant savings and the money his mother had hidden in her sock drawer, which he used as a deposit to buy a new van on hire purchase. Carefully he drew a new logo and script on the side panels.

'You come into money, Arnie?' Doris stood by the fence, her folded arms apparently restraining her chest, as if she was fighting two small mammals, trapped underneath her cardigan.

He smiled. 'Been meaning to do this for ages.'

'Your mum would be proud. She'd like the new logo.'

He managed a small nod and went back to his preparations.

A week later and Arnold was nervous, but also strangely euphoric. He drove to the park and set up, waiting for his first customers. It was another hot day, perfect for selling ice cream.

His first customer was the gobby girl with the eye patch. Perfect. Arnold didn't usually engage in conversation, but this was to be the new him. He pulled his thin lips back across his teeth, hoping he didn't look like the big bad wolf. 'I've a new topping, dearie,' he intoned. 'Just for you.'

In Arnold's limited experience, seven-year-olds were naturally suspicious creatures, but when he held out the cone the girl's eyes widened. Whether it was the sight of the thick ice cream or the dripping red sauce, or perhaps the the sticky sweet scent that hinted at vanilla with a tinge of burger, he couldn't be sure. While her mother fiddled with her phone, pleased, no doubt, to be free of the constant whining for a moment, the girl tested red sauce with a pointy little tongue that made Arnold think of snakes and chimeras.

A wide smile broke across her usually disgruntled countenance. 'This is yum!'

Word spread and the queues curved into the distance. People came from miles around. The mother of the little girl – a banker with a famous company - congratulated him on his entrepreneurial approach to ice cream. 'You have a winning formula, Arnold. What inspired you?'

Arnold smiled knowingly and tapped the picture on the side of the van. It was an image of his mother emerging from a cone.

He gave himself a moment to recall the toil of the last few weeks, closing his eyes as he did so. How he had ground the bones in an industrial-sized pestle, having drained the marrow into vats which, together with the contents of the spleen and lower intestines, he had whipped into a frothing cream; how he had then flavoured this confection, half with vanilla and the remainder with a variety of banana, cinnamon, nutmeg and lemon; how he then thickened the blood, to which he added his own concoction of spices and sugars, assisting its natural tendency to clot with the setting agent, pectin; and finally the most gratifying of his culinary achievements: how he had taken his mother's skin, grateful for her ingrained indolence and the resulting cellulite which he had stretched and dried, baking it until he had the consistency just as he

111

wanted it, before moistening it and creating a range of uniquely dimpled waffle cones.

'I owe all this,' Arnold said slowly, a sigh of real satisfaction escaping as he spoke, 'to my mother.'

'She must be some woman.'

'Indeed. She just keeps on giving.' As he spoke, his attention was caught by a wave. Doris, Millicent, Harriet and Martin were approaching the van.

The banker held Arnold's gaze. 'You should think about expanding. If you need help…?'

He smiled that thin-lipped smile. 'Oh I've already given that a lot of thought. If you'd excuse me these are my friends. I'm very much hoping that, over time, I will be able to involve them directly in this business. Knowing them I'm sure they'll throw themselves, body and spirit into this venture.'

A Glimpse Of The Monster

Anne Marie Andrus

New Jersey, USA

Copyright © 2018 by Anne Marie Andrus. All rights reserved.

www.AnneMarieAndrus.com

Seven straight days of rain, two tornados and one collapsed wall. After months of painstaking renovation, the little house still wasn't complete, but tonight's dinner had been set for weeks—and Raimond couldn't put Emily off any longer. He paced back and forth across the patio, adjusting tables and fluffing pillows.

What a mess. I'm a doctor, not a decorator.

All the original furniture had been moved out of his living room during construction.

These antiques might save the night. They ooze elegance, like the parlors of old Paris.

When the cottage was on the market, he had no trouble entering, as if it were free territory. Now, a wistful look through the dark windows was the closest he'd come to seeing the project since the house had secretly become Emily's property.

I need to figure out a way for her to invite me into a house she thinks I own.

Raimond struck a match, ignited a taper and went to work coaxing a sea of candles to life.

Emily will love the ambiance. Unless, of course, this whole date is a colossal mistake.

Raimond first lit hurricane lamps hanging from the trellis.

What if I hurt her?

He hadn't lain with a woman since his days as a Commander.

This will be Emily's first time. Mine too in a way, since on the last occasion, I was still human.

He moved on to candles in mismatched urns along the walkway.

We could just drink wine and I'd keep my promise to explain everything.

He blew out the taper and grunted at the tangle of curtains.

Supposed to be a luxury tent. Resembles the dressmaker's remnant section...or a whorehouse.

He wrestled to tie back fabric he'd draped across the low wooden structure.

Emily. Raimond pounded both fists into his forehead. *Emily.*

Scores of tiny flames cast dancing prisms of color through the lush garden hideaway.

It's been years. If I keep dragging my feet, I might lose her. His mind wandered back to the head nurse in Savannah and her counsel to choose his ladies well. *Emily did kiss me first. An angel with a touch of the devil.*

Raimond stood back and admired his handiwork. The delicate fragrance of night blossoms cruised on a breeze that toyed with hidden wind chimes. The setting whispered romance from the flower beds, but shouted seduction from the rooftop.

She's special.

He slouched onto an oversize chaise and rested his head in his hands.

But, she's innocent. And, I'm a monster.

Black veins exploded down his neck like ribbons of fire.

What if I can't control myself?

Heavy hoofbeats pounded the gravel road outside, growing louder and slower until they drew to a stop in front of the cottage. The creak of carriage doors was followed by muffled voices. One floated on the air like a feather.

"Raimond?"

"Back here, Emily." Raimond slammed the demon away and flashed under the portico. He threw his arms out. *"Bienvenue!"*

"You look so different away from the hospital." Emily planted a kiss on each cheek. She stood back and smiled at his unbuttoned charcoal vest and black shirt, with rolled up sleeves. "So dangerous."

"You must have raided the brandy stash in my carriage." Raimond returned the greeting and brushed back green fronds of the side yard. "This is my casual attire."

"Wait—there's a stash? Never mind, I'm dying to see your new house." She peered under the low-slung porch draped with purple blooms. "Those vines look like they're dragging everything down."

"Yes, well, sadly the repairs are a bit more complicated than I expected."

"I love the twin chimneys."

"They're a unique element." Raimond pointed to the front door. "You may take a step inside. A cautious one."

"Oh dear." A gentle nudge swung the door open. She lifted her skirts and crept over the threshold. "Quite the disarray. Come, Raimond." She held out her hand. "Show me your vision."

"It's supposed to be a surprise, you know?" Raimond smiled with relief as he glided through the doorframe. He found the architect's drawings on the stairs, unrolled them in the fading light and explained what still needed to be done.

"Will the kitchen be part of the main house?"

"Of course, but it needed expansion." Raimond pointed around the fireplace. "In the back, overlooking the garden."

"I can't wait to see it finished." Emily slipped back to the porch, plucked a flower from a wilting vine and rolled it in her fingers. "You won't tear these down, I hope?"

"I'll have my craftsmen prop them up." Raimond placed his hand on the small of her back. "Come darling, your celebration awaits."

"What's the occasion? Not my birthday." Emily tiptoed along the slate footpath and stopped short. She knelt and threaded her fingers through long grass. "So soft." Her shoes were off in seconds and she was ankle deep in green. "So cool. Feels like heaven."

Raimond followed her example and twirled her in a pirouette on the dark lawn. Two barefoot dancers in sparkling moonlight.

"You might be the most romantic man I've ever met." Emily tucked her head under his chin and swayed to imaginary music.

Raimond nodded toward the backyard and whispered in her ear. "There's more to see."

Ahead, a whitewashed garden shed gleamed in the clearing's corner. Framework over the door was draped with pastel colored linens and gauze. Lamps flickered in the rafters and candles painted designs on the patio.

Emily's jaw dropped as she crawled onto a huge sofa and sunk into the cloud of pillows. "You did all this?"

"To honor your job promotion." He uncorked a wine bottle and poured. "And new apartment."

"I was already scheduling the surgeries, you know? Only now, I have to order the supplies. It's soooo…not complicated."

"Still, all that work with no raise in pay." Raimond sat down, balancing the glasses. "But you're a master negotiator."

"Life in that convent was crushing me. Crushing us." Emily accepted the glass with both hands. "Don't want to spill."

"Won't matter." Raimond picked up a tasseled pillow. "My upholstery is the same color as your wine."

"The furnishings in my new home are sparse." Emily caressed the plush cushions. "Drab is a better word."

"What if that apartment was your official residence?" Raimond slid closer and pointed to the dark bungalow behind him. "And this was your true home? With me."

"That's positively scandalous." Emily sipped and grinned. "I did convince the nuns to allow me to move out, but they have spies all over town. Like my creepy landlord."

"Forget him." Raimond nudged the glass closer to her lips. "He'll be convinced you sleep in your own bed every night."

Emily closed her eyes and drained the glass. "I've not yet slept in yours, Raimond."

"Lack of privacy was an obstacle. But, that's all changed." He took the empty glass and set it on a low table. Slipping his hands around her waist, he eased her onto his lap. "You're afraid?"

"Not at all."

"You're trembling."

"Okay, maybe." Emily tipped her hand side to side. "I know I've been pushing for this next step, but I feel a bit like a hypocrite."

"Because it isn't proper?"

"That's not…hardly. You know me better by now."

"If you aren't ready, just say the word. Your place is here with me and since I've graduated—"

"About that." Emily leaned in and brushed butterfly kisses from one side of his mouth to the other. "We should be—" She let out a long, low breath. "Celebrating you."

"I meant, as a legitimate doctor, I have a bit more stature to go with my long coat." Raimond locked his lips onto hers and pulled back to meet her eyes. "We could make it legal."

"Tonight?" Emily popped open one of his shirt buttons. "Right now?"

"It's a bit late for a man of the cloth. How about a judge?"

"Not necessary." Emily rolled her eyes and undid two more buttons.

"Or a ship's captain?"

"In Augusta?" Her fingers trailed up his sculpted chest and rested under his chin.

"From a riverboat?"

"The last thing we need is some salty sailor in our bed." Emily pulled one pin from her hair and sent waves cascading around her face. "What does a piece of paper prove anyway?"

Raimond's knuckles skimmed her cheek. "That I love you, Emily Gastrell."

Emily melted into his burning eyes. "Those words are proof enough for me."

"I never thought I would…" Raimond locked onto her gaze. "My heart belongs to you, *mademoiselle*."

"And mine to you, *monsieur.* How does one say 'I love you' in French?"

"*Je t'aime.*"

"*Zhe temm*, Raimond Banitierre."

"Perfect."

"No judgy riverboat priest needs to grant us permission."
Emily sat back and bit her lip. "I know you're a man of the world.
If I disappoint you—"

"Beautiful lady, that's impossible."

"To be clear, I'm not saying no. I just don't want your
proposal to be rushed."

"I'll make it perfect."

"Unexpected and magical?"

"A spectacular surprise." Raimond pulled the ribbon on
her collar.

"Such a tease." The neckline of her blouse loosened with
each deep breath.

Raimond twirled the ribbon to the three-beat tempo of a
silent waltz. "And I've not been a man of that world you spoke of
in a very, very long time."

"I've taken your advice." She reached back to search for
laces. "And started wearing this silly thing looser."

"So, your lungs aren't crushed." Raimond chuckled.
"Medicine trumps fashion."

"Still, I'm always ready to have this corset off."

"Why wear one at all?" Raimond removed his own vest and
flung it away.

"Ooh, the gossip." Emily tossed the garment over her
shoulder. "The outrage." She fumbled with her skirts while
Raimond slid behind her and groaned at the caress of his fingers on
her bare arms.

"Breathe. Listen to the birds sing."

"Those pretty, colorful ones?" She looked up. "They make
the trees glow."

Raimond watched her shoulders relax as the bird's melody
bathed her in tranquility. Emerald and silver fabric fell to her feet
in waves, leaving her in a knee length chemise of pure white lace.
"Only one petticoat?" A single move swept her into his arms.
"Now, that's shameful."

Slow steps brought them to the edge of the cushions.
Raimond raised his lips and brushed them lightly across to hers.
Emily winked and dove into his mouth with a searching kiss. They
wound up tangled on the sofa in each other's arms.

"Is there nothing under this?" He pulled the loose chemise off her shoulder.

"The heat, remember?" Emily slid back, began lifting the thin cotton over her head and stopped. "Does this very charming tent close, at all?" She pointed at curtains hanging around the trellis. "Or do the neighbors get a free show?"

"The neighbors are a mile away, but I planned ahead."

Raimond forced himself to walk and not flash to the drawstrings. Heavy fabric tumbled free, turning the extravagant setting into a private love nest. *Control, control, control.* With the long curtains closed and fluttering in the late-night breeze, he drank straight from the wine bottle and slid out of his shirt.

"Come here." Emily knelt on the sofa and motioned with her fingers. "Undressing you is my job."

Raimond watched her pull a long drink of wine and wiggle out of her chemise. His chest trembled where his heart had pounded, long ago.

Emily pulled him close, until the bare skin of her breasts brushed his chest. She gently slipped a hand free and her fingertips wandered to his belt buckle.

Raimond's muscles quivered and a breath caught in his throat.

In one motion, Emily unclasped the metal and loosened the laces of his trousers until they drooped on his hips. She undid a singular button at his waist and inched the silk lower. Her eyes flicked below the deep V-shape of his waist and slowly climbed to meet his gaze.

"It's okay to look." Raimond swept a finger through her curls.

"Most girls do this in the dark the first time."

Raimond puffed out the brightest flame over their heads. He lingered while Emily's eyes burned a tantalizing path across his back. He returned to find her lying on her side, hugging a pillow. His fingers traced the back of her arm to the flare of her hips. "We'll take everything slow."

Emily discarded the pillow and pressed her soft curves against the length of his body. "Your skin is always so cool."

"I guess the heat doesn't affect me." Raimond shifted underneath her and skimmed the full length of her spine. "Maybe it's my French blood."

Emily's gasp was sweet melody in Raimond's ears as he cupped one breast in his hand and trailed kisses down the center of her belly. Her skin rippled as he drew circles behind her knees. "I promise not to hurt you."

"I trust you."

Raimond groaned and shivered as Emily's delicate fingers drifted below his waist. He slipped a hand behind her head and lifted a tangle of curls. "Why are you still so tense?"

"I know it'll be better for me the next time." Emily bit her lip. "I told you, nurses talk. They say the first time is always awful, but it makes the man happy. Eventually, I'll enjoy it too."

"Okay, hold everything." Raimond stood and unraveled a long piece of satin from the trellis. "Stand up. I won't peek."

"What in the world?" Emily giggled as Raimond wrapped the long train of fabric around her shoulders and spun her until she was draped in pink.

"Now." He sat down and pulled her onto his lap. "Be still in my arms."

"My dream is to make you happy, Raimond."

"You make me happy sitting on that swing in the hospital's courtyard. Pretend you're in that swing." Raimond rested his hand on her neck. "The birds are singing." He kissed her cheek, her nose and her other cheek. "Every flower in Augusta is blooming, and the scent reaches your pretty nose, one petal at a time."

"More than anything else, I want to be close to you." Emily closed her eyes and exhaled. She let Raimond lift her hand in the air and pressed her soft palm against his.

He alternated the pressure of each fingertip and smiled as she mirrored his rhythm. The back of his knuckles trailed up her arm, swirling inside her elbow and wandering across her flawless skin.

Emily explored his muscled arms and slipped her arm around the curves of his shoulders.

He loosened the end of the pink wrap and lowered her into a mountain of pillows.

This time, when Emily's fingers landed below his waist, she closed her eyes and pushed the silk shorts over his hips.

Raimond slid free of his last piece of clothing and kissed Emily's neck, inhaling the sweet scent of her flesh. His lips drifted under her breasts and around the sweep of her hips. She moaned as he kept going, until she was gasping for breath with shredded pink satin in her fists.

Emily twined her fingers into Raimond's hair and pulled him up until he was hovering over her. "I had no idea it could feel so..."

Raimond coaxed her knee to the side and rested his hips against hers. "Roll with me."

Emily's nails dug into his back and she muffled her cry against his chest. Her body struggled to match his slow pace and then sped up with pure instinct, to meet his energy.

Softly. Raimond forced himself to concentrate on small movements. *Gently.* As Emily quaked and melded into his flesh for the second time that night, he relaxed and let go.

"Raimond!" She saw his face at the same moment he saw the gash in her neck. "What did I do wrong?"

"Damn it!" Raimond clamped a hand over his mouth, hiding razor-sharp fangs.

"Your eyes..." Emily clawed at his arms. "Skin—black!"

"Sleep!" He grabbed her chin and dominated her gaze. "Sleep, until I wake you."

Raimond waited for Emily's eyelids to fall, then lunged to put pressure on her neck and the two holes spurting blood from under her ear. He bit into his own wrist and rubbed black blood on her wound.

Emily's breathing faltered and her pulse skipped a beat.

"Em, stay with me!" He ripped his arm open again and forced blood down her throat. With her face pressed against his chest, an old French prayer ran through Raimond's head.

Emily drew a deep, human breath and let her hand drift over newly healed skin.

He raised his eyes to the sky. *Thank you, thank you.*

Her eyelashes fluttered but stayed closed while a smile and frown battled across her lips. She sighed as Raimond laid her back.

Raimond grabbed his pants and staggered toward the garden shed. He hurled a blood-stained pillow over the cottage's roof and searched for towels to erase any splatters of evidence. Party lights around the edge of the patio flickered and barely clung to life until he ripped a few ruined inches from the pink gauze and tossed it into one of the sputtering candles. The rest of the fabric was tucked around Emily's limp body while the miniature blaze illuminated her peaceful face.

I ruined your fantasy, sweet girl.

Raimond picked up her delicate wrist and felt a strong pulse.

My monster's blood is in your veins.

He swept damp blonde locks away from her face. The lump in his throat felt like a boulder.

And now, I need to make you forget things from a night that you should remember forever.

Minutes ticked by while Raimond wrestled with excruciating decisions.

Who the hell was I praying to? What a nightmare.

He lifted her as if she were fine china until she was cradled in his lap. "Wake up, Em."

Her eyes flew open. She recoiled with a shriek that slashed the heavy night air.

"Shhh, shhh." Raimond grabbed both sides of her head and forced her to focus on him. "I'm sorry, I broke my promise." He loosened his grip. "I'm sorry, I hurt you."

Emily stared through the hazy air, her lips forming silent protests.

"I'll explain it all. But, for now, I need you to forget what you saw."

"No." Emily's head shake became a reluctant nod. "But . . ."

"We made love. It was beautiful, right?"

"Amazing." Emily smiled and tried to break his lock on her eyes. "Raimond, please."

"Forget the blood, my face turning dark . . . forget my fangs. You were never scared." He swallowed hard. "*Oui?*"

122

"We had a lovely night." Emily's face melted into a pure smile. "Now I'm yours."

"And you're mine." Raimond released her mind.

Emily flopped on her back and let the late summer breeze cool her skin. "Fireflies."

"What's that, dear?" Raimond nestled her in the crook of his arm.

"I didn't see them before. But look, now they're everywhere, twinkling brighter than the stars. Like they're cheering for us." Emily caressed the strong line of his jaw. "*Je t'aime.*"

"I'm amazed by you. *Mon amour.*" Raimond laced his fingers into hers, kissed her hand and wrestled with the nagging voice in his head. *An angel, in bed with a demon.*

A Best Selling Lie
Christine Valentor
Chicago, Illinois, USA
Copyright © 2018 by Christine Valentor. All rights reserved.
https://witchlike.wordpress.com/

I carry them. They are the diseased, the comatose, the crippled, the murdered, the suicides and the missing-in-action. I carry those that struggle and grope, hanging on to a last breath, frightened and desperate, as well as those that come willingly. Some call me the Grim Reaper, some call me the Angel of Death, but my true name is Charon the Ferryman. With my faithful dog Cerberus by my side, I transport my ghostly passengers across the River Styx to the left bank where my master Hades and his wife Persephone gleefully await their arrival. This is my occupation and I would have no other.

As you might imagine, I am overworked and underpaid, receiving a mere danake for each corpse I transport. It is with much effort I perform my tasks, lifting their bodies, heavy as brick, sometimes nearly sinking my boat. All the while I myself am the sole oarsman, no help from another. I am old but strong. In the sweltering summer heat, in the dead of winter, I move decrepit flesh, withered limbs and wasted organs. All go to the kingdom. How the Lord and Lady love this, the game of new souls.

On some days, Cerberus and I have literally thousands of passengers. In seasons of plague and famine my job is hectic, but the busiest of all is wartime. I am then given an endless shipment, the wounded, the maimed, the disfigured; all senseless deaths. Yet humankind persist in foolishly killing one another. Wartime is their biggest failure.

Upon the planet Earth, it is ALWAYS wartime.

Like a magician of stealth, I enter hospital rooms. There I reduce patients to no more than a flat-lined blip on a computer screen. I am the stopping of hearts, the strangling of lungs, the malfunction of digestive tracts. I am the ethereal glove that pulls a soul from a coma.

I do it all in the name of mercy.

I am circumspect in my choices. Discreet and selective. Yet even I, an all-knowing eye, am not perfect. Sometimes I make a mistake, choosing one who is not quite ready.

Today there is one such as this. A child, not more than seven years old. She lies on a hospital bed, the civilian victim of war's crossfire. I am reluctant to take her, but her body suffers so. The doctors speak of amputation; her little legs have been mangled, injected with a strain of gangrene. Her heart beats weakly. I cannot tolerate the sight of it. And so, in my kindness, I take her.

As my ferry boat shoves off from the harbor, already I sense that the child wavers. She squirms, stirs in her sleep, flutters her eyelids open. She cannot speak but she sees us, Cerberus and I as we hover above her. Cerberus watches with soulful eyes. He whimpers, pleading to me. "This one cannot be taken. Not yet."

It is always wise to rely upon the judgment of a dog. You have, no doubt, read about Cerberus. The books will claim he has three heads and that he is a vicious howling thing. The books lie. Cerberus is a magnificent animal, sensitive and loyal, the best companion any captain could wish for. What's more, Cerberus is never wrong. I know instantly I have made a mistake with this young cherub.

Before we have reached the third bend in the river, as we approach a glistening waterfall, I give the child a vision. I show her a dark tunnel of which she is flying through, ever so slowly. At the end of the tunnel is a white light. Often-times in a case such as this, I will provide the deceased with the vision of a deity, one they have been taught to venerate. This may be a Christ or an Allah, a Mother or a Buddha, or a loved one previously passed. It makes no difference, for all are the same. But the child I now charm is an innocent. She has been taught nothing of religion, has no preconceived notions. I provide her with only the vision of light, blazing in shades of silver and ivory, too bright for the human eye. Beyond this point all choice will be hers.

The child has a family. Parents and siblings that love her dearly. She is the youngest of five children. The family, Cerberus tells me, would be devastated to lose her.

We reach the left bank. Hades and Persephone greet us, the master and mistress of darkness, draped in robes of black velvet, holding their scepters of skull and orb. With a gesture they beckon us into their gardens. Here, moonflowers bloom in shades of deep purple. Black roses the size of lettuce heads climb high as the castle turrets. It is a spectrum of color and shadow, black-gold, metallic copper and dove-gray, invisible to the human eye. With her dead vision, the girl sees it all. In this place, time has stopped.

My Lord and Lady watch closely as Cerberus presides over the child. She sits up, runs her small hand across his mane. She cannot speak. Hades and Persephone already adore the girl, would love to have her as part of their kingdom. Here, she would never know war again. However, as always, they leave the choice to the human. Cerberus then barks, a definitive yelp. He lays his head upon the child's chest. The decision has been made.

* * * * *

Upon the flat, sterile operating table of the M10 Aleppo Children's Memorial Hospital, a little girl flutters her eyes open. She is now semi-conscious, emerging from a twenty-four-hour coma. The child is hearty and strong and although she has sustained a multitude of injuries, she will be healthy in time. The doctors determine she will need no amputations. Miraculously, although she has been deprived of oxygen, there will be no brain damage.

Once fully conscious, the child will tell a tale: There was a boat, she will say, a journey on a river with an old captain, decrepit and bent at his oar. There was a playful dog who guarded her and gave the most safety. She will tell of a tunnel with a white light at the end, a blaze so dazzling she could almost not look upon it. At the shoreline a lovely woman and a handsome man greeted her. The flowers, the trees, the air itself grew in colors she cannot describe, colors she had never seen before in the waking world. It was the dog, the child will claim, who brought her back to life.

The adults of the community will dismiss her story. A dream. A child's imaginings. Some experts of paranormal studies will take seriously only the part about the tunnel and the white light. It is easy, you see, for humankind to understand a metaphor. *The light at the end of the tunnel.* I, Charon the Ferryman, invented that very metaphor!

In time, a journalist will contact her parents. A book will be written. It shall be titled: *"The Afterlife: A Collection of True Near-Death Experiences."* (Or something similar. Dozens of such books have been written.) The book, however, will not be entirely true. It will be contorted and distorted to fit the needs of media moguls and the quasi-spiritual public. This book will become a best seller. A best selling lie.

None of humankind will ever know of myself or Cerberus. None will know the beauty of the Underworld, for this cannot be described in words. The facts will remain forever distorted, relegated to mythology, a dim memory. The truth shall be known only to the girl, myself, and all who enter the Land of the Dead.

Normal Things
Barbara Anne Helberg
Napoleon, Ohio, USA
Copyright © 2018 by Barbara Anne Helberg. All rights reserved.
<u>mywritinglifexposed</u>

I could envision the locals surrounding the cabin in the Vermont woods. They used the usual perfunctory call-outs: "Police!" -- "Open up!" -- "Come out with your hands high!" -- "No weapons!"

It made me chuckle. There was no one at the cabin.

I had come back to the old Ohio Penneynickel Canals instead, bringing Mother as my -- shall I say, captive audience? She was tied to the bow seat of my ouboarded rowboat, immobilized, terrified, captively readied to pay for stealing Thomas away from me. Mothers shouldn't steal from their daughters. I'd told her that.

I knew Stonebreaker and Thadberry, the FBI twins on my trail the last three days, were likely to show up to make things interesting at the end. Unlike the local authorities, Stonebreaker and Thadberry had considered a few different angles to my plan even if they hadn't identified me. They had decided I wasn't in Vermont, and the Ohio canals chase was on, which served to delight me.

But I really hadn't expected them quite so soon.

Mother screamed again. "She's going to kill me!"

Stonebreaker drew his Starfighter craft confidently close to my prepared rowboat.

I glanced at my watch, then at Mother, whose panic at this moment of crisis disappointed me. It lowered her level of dangerous significance. Lessened the triumph I deserved to feel in this final snuff-out.

By now, though, the FBI twins probably had figured out there had been some sort of family love triangle involving Mother, my sister Mira, and I with our beloved psychiatrist, Thomas Poppopolis, and that I was the one who had written of it in Mother's journal. They might even have realized I had already eliminated the others, and Mother was to be the last to join them.

Gently, the disturbed water lapped rhythmically between our boats as Stonebreaker eyed my boat, from bow to stern. Had he guessed a bomb was ticking?

He asked with force, but calm: "Are you having some difficulty? Can we come aboard?" And he reached to pull the rowboat's sideboards next to the Starfighter's rail. At the same time, he gestured in the general direction of my Mother and back to Thadberry, giving his partner an eye roll.

Trouble, I thought. He's got it. "I've a better idea," I said, leveling a sharp smile at Mariano Stonebreaker. I got up, checked the time. Nearly gone. "I'll come to you."

The other agent grabbed the rowboat's rim while Stonebreaker clasped my wrist to help me aboard the Starfighter. As I stretched across the boats, I showed as much distracting leg as possible -- one of Mother's old tricks I usefully remembered -- to buy the last minute of time.

Mother screamed. "There's a bomb under me!"

I slipped Stonebreaker's releasing hand and bolted for the Starfighter's wheel. Reaching it in a tumbling rush, I plunged the boat into breakaway speed. It lurched up and forward in one motion and skipped off, quickly putting distance between the boats.

Stonebreaker fell onto one and a half knees to the deck. Water sprayed over him. I saw only a portion of the other agent -- flailing legs, one arm reaching for the sky -- as he flipped in an awkward half-arc into the Muddy Penney off the stern of the Starfighter.

Mother's scream began but fell incomplete, choked off like captured and strangled prey, as a watery whoosh leaped forward accompanied by ear-splitting cracks and a deafening earthquake boom. It deliciously astounded me.

The detonating bomb sent billows of wet lethal terror upward in the form of ripped and smashed plastic and aluminum, wood, metal, and human parts, then toppled them back down piece by piece in a disconnected circular waterfall. It made my heart shudder and shake with triumph.

The blast buffeted the Starfighter without damaging effect, and I kept it speeding forward in high gear.

"Tha-a-ad!" Stonebreaker shouted. Unhurt, apparently, the FBI agent clamored wet and slipping to his feet and shielded his face from raining, landing debris.

I glanced a look off the stern. The outboarded rowboat was gone.

Stonebreaker lowered his arms, and I saw him looking frantically across the swirling, muddy water, breathing heavily as he took in the disappearing scene of the explosion. "Thad!" he shouted, cupping his hands around his mouth. He swayed with the Starfighter's swift, bouncing retreat. "Thad!" Water splashed and slapped loudly against the speeding Starfighter's slick sides.

Replanting one foot, Stonebreaker rushed toward me and the wheel. He looked ahead further, through the shatterproof windbreak. I followed his look and saw two white boats approaching, skidding urgently and shallowly on the water's surface, running toward us fast. Police boats.

Stonebreaker heaved himself at me.

I heard him, already had drawn out the pocket knife from my waist-band. His hand clutched my right shoulder as his body rammed mine in hard challenge, and I wrenched around bodily with the sharp pocket knife opened, deadly ready, in my left hand. It was an awkward thrust, across my own body, into his. My right hand left the wheel. The Starfighter twisted and slowed in the river, rudderless and bouncing wildly.

Stonebreaker seemed not to see the glistening blade before it was in him. It cut into his side, but was partially obstructed by his leather trouser belt. My position was too awkward to beat his bulk. And my weapon was too weak for a fatal body thrust against an active defender, especially one the size of Stonebreaker. He was

130

well over six feet tall and two-hundred pounds of muscle. The cut under his rib cage was a minimal slit. Wrapping his arms tightly around me, he got his larger hand over my hand clamping the knife for an outward tug, bent my wrist and kept bending even as my screech of pain pierced the air. The knife came free. It dropped to the polished, wet deck between us, as unruddered as the wobbling, drifting Starfighter.

"It's over, Lira." Stonebreaker shifted his weight off me. "Just relax. We'll have you out of here in a minute, or two."

I didn't struggle. That was useless. He was as strong as a brick building surrounding me. I felt frail, the adrenaline gone, the destructive, homicidal rush spent, the killing done. I sagged against him. He held me from crumbling onto the deck.

The police cruisers churned alongside the Starfighter, spitting bubbles of water hull to hull, sputtering noisily. The thump of my loudly beating heart was drowned out. I was only disconnectedly aware of other hands, handcuffs, the transfer to the waiting police boat. Later, I thought. No point now in resisting.

I watched as Stonebreaker reversed and sprinted back to the wheel and rocketed the Starfighter toward the explosion site. A third police cruiser was circling the scattering bomb debris.

Thad, I observed, sat wrapped in a blanket among the cruiser's stern cushions.

I heard Stonebreaker call out, "I always knew you were all wet, but it's good to see you're okay!"

"Oh, yeah," Thad yelled back. "Just normal things of the day!"

My mind still throbbed with those 'normal things of the day'. The FBI twins had known my name. They hadn't been thrown off at all. Didn't matter. It was all done. I smiled.

Roadkill
Ernesto San Giacomo
Mountain Home, Idaho, USA
Copyright © 2018 by Ernesto San Giacomo. All rights reserved.
https://ernsangia.wordpress.com/

Men with busy hands perched around an old folding table. Their chairs nestled in the shade between two semi-trucks with long trailers. Grim gazes pressed upon the man in black, *El Grimorio*. Four truckers, each holding five cards, waited for his next move. Would he raise the bet? Was he bluffing? All eyes scrutinized him for a sign – an opportunity for him to stoke the flames of passionate anger.

El Grimorio enjoyed bringing out the worst in people. A dark aura hovered around him and leeched into any soul he encountered, like a predator anticipating the perfect moment to pounce. In mere minutes, malicious emotions surfaced from the gentlest people and grabbed the spotlight, as if summoned by the deadly ringmaster of an evil circus.

His long black hair matched every article of clothing. From his hat and vest, down to his snakeskin boots, it gave the impression of a three-dimensional shadow. He grabbed some cash from his pile and reached out over the grimy table. Fingerless leather gloves showed off his unkempt nails and the dirt underneath them. His fingers spread like a claw, and the money dropped into the pot. "I'll see your twenty and raise ten."

With sideways glances and huffs, Bill, Steve, and Mortimer folded, but Tom held steadfast. With his gaze locked on the man in black, he grinned. "You're bluffing."

El Grimorio stared back at Tom. "Then hurry up and put your money where your mouth is." He smirked, enjoying himself immensely, cultivating Tom's anger.

Tom matched the bet. "Call." His knowing-half-smile disappeared and his eyes narrowed. "Only one thing's worse than a sore loser, and that's a sore winner."

"You should know all about being a loser." The man in black showed his cards with the ace of spades on top. "Full house. Aces over eights."

Steve gave a short whistle. "Lucky stiff."

Tom grunted and flung his cards down. His eyes flared. "Take it," he said with a dismissive wave of his hand.

El Grimorio leaned over the table to take the cash. A pendant of the grim reaper slipped free from beneath his shirt and swung back and forth like a pendulum. With fingers sporting gothic-style rings, he scooped the money toward himself. His hand clutched the small piles of crumpled bills and stuffed them into different pockets, like a homeless man hoarding food from a buffet table. *El Grimorio* sprung to his feet and picked up his guitar case.

Tom's glare fixed upon the man in black's every motion, and he arched a single brow. "Hey, pal, where the hell do you think you're going?"

A perfect moment to add some fuel to the fire. He dropped the guitar, placed two fists on the table, and leaned in toward Tom. "I'm not your pal, and I don't take orders from you."

With flaring nostrils, Tom said, "Six hands in a row and you're just gonna walk away?"

A sinister grin spread across *El Grimorio's* face. "Sucks to be you. Doesn't it?"

Tom leaped up. His chair tipped over backwards and he lunged at the man, but the other truckers grabbed him and held him back.

"Take it easy. This guy's not worth the trouble," Mortimer grunted.

"I'll bet anything he cheated us!" Tom said.

El Grimorio laughed. "You lost enough bets today, moron."

"Moron! Why you lousy…" Tom struggled to move, but the others had a good grip on him. *El Grimorio* almost wished they would let him go. He flexed a fist. It had been too long since he'd had drawn some blood.

Bill let go and stepped between the would-be combatants. He pointed a finger at the man in black. "I think you've worn out your welcome, you freak. Get lost or we're gonna let him go."

Tempting. But he deigned to let them live. With a last smirk, the man turned, picked up his guitar, and swaggered away.

"I'd like to run that guy over with all eighteen wheels and send his sorry ass straight to hell," Tom said, dusting himself off.

"Don't say things like that. It's just two day's pay," Mortimer said.

"Maybe it's not much to you. But I worked hard for it."

Mortimer opened a small portable cooler and handed Tom a beer. "Guys like him always get what's coming to them in the end."

Tom forced himself to relax, and the group settled down for some banter. Some time later, Mortimer stood to go. "Got places to go and people to see. Don't wanna be late for my next date." They shook hands all around.

"It's been a pleasure, Mort. I hope we meet again," Steve said.

Mortimer smiled. "I'm sure we will."

***

El Grimorio strolled along the shoulder of the interstate. A buzzard roosting on a guardrail stared at him with beady, lifeless eyes.

The scent of coal tar drifted up from the baking asphalt. Heat shimmers danced in the distance. A vast expanse stretched all around him, windless and full of silence. As if his footsteps were the lone sound in the world, a reminder of his physical presence on Earth.

When a mouse crossed his path, he stomped on it with the heel of his boot. Blood splattered outward from the tiny body. He kicked the little gray corpse back toward the buzzard.

The roar of an engine approached from behind, making him turn. He lowered his guitar case, held out his thumb, and waited for the distant vehicle to come closer. Would he accept a ride or slit the driver's throat and take the vehicle?

Air brakes squealed as the semi came to a halt. A sharp shooting pain flashed through his body and dissipated as quickly as it had appeared. Worry and weariness were for the weak. He shook off a light-headed dizzying sensation. *El Grimorio* stumbled up to the cab, opened the door, and hopped up into the passenger seat.

"Well, well, well. First you take our money and now you're looking for a favor," came a voice from the driver's side.

A sideways glance at the driver revealed it was Mortimer. After he curled a lip, he reached for the door handle. "I'll walk." He deigned to spare the lives of Tom and the others. Now, he regretted leaving them alive.

"No. It's okay. Tom has a bit of a short temper sometimes. But we settled him down." He shifted the truck into gear. "Where you heading?"

"Hoping to get to Las Cruces by tomorrow."

"Perfect, I have to go right by it. You might have to walk a few miles." The truck picked up speed, and the hum of the immense engine resonated through the cab. "I'm Mortimer D'Angelo, by the way, but most people just call me Mort." He offered his hand. "I don't recall catching your name."

"My real name or what everyone calls me?"

"Whatever." Mortimer said with a quick rise of a shoulder.

"In Las Cruces, they call me *El Grimorio*, the grim reaper."

"Because of the bad ass goth stuff thing you've got going on?"

"Maybe they sense my true vibes." He took a deep breath and straightened his shoulders.

"What's so important about Las Cruces? I mean…pardon me, but you don't look like the type who keeps office hours and appointments."

"Tomorrow is the last day of *El día de los muertos*. Big celebration." He tapped his guitar case. "Me and my friend here take in a shitload of bills from the crowd."

"Oh, yeah, that's the, um…that day of the dead thing, right?"

"Yep. I usually get a case full of bills and some free brews."

"Popular with the folks there?"

"They're afraid of me. They drop cash in my case like they're appeasing me or something." One corner of his mouth moved, making a sinister half-grin. "Maybe they are."

Mort let out a quick snort. "Halloween was yesterday. You don't need to keep up the act anymore."

That's what most people thought—until it was too late for them. "Halloween is child's play. I'm a real grim reaper. And there's a long line of bodies to prove it." He pressed a switch next to the base of his thumb. With a click, a blade jumped out from under his sleeve. "See? You saved your friend's life back there. Another click and the blade retracted. "He didn't know who he was messing with."

The truck lurched around a sharp curve. Mort kept his eyes fixed on the road. "I don't scare easily. If that's what you're trying to do." *Shhhhick.* The sound of the blade didn't even get so much as a flinch from Mort.

El Grimorio reached across the cab and pressed the blade against Mort's cheek. "Suppose I take this truck and drive into Las Cruces proper and save myself from walking those last few miles."

Mort lifted his left hand and gave one quick snap of his fingers.

***

Dazed, the man in black stood on the shoulder of the highway where Mort had picked him up before. He stared at the rest stop in the far distance where he had won six straight hands of poker. Mort stood just feet away; his semi parked a dozen yards behind. With a shaking hand, *El Grimorio* pointed his blade at Mort. "How did you do that? How did we get back here?"

Mort stepped closer to him. His irises bled into the whites of his eyes, like ink spreading through paper. In seconds his eyes turned black and void of expression, like the dead eyes of a shark. He tore the chain from the man's neck, examined the grim reaper pendant and dangled it in front of him. "I'm flattered, but this doesn't look anything like me."

"Give it back. That's mine!" He thrust the blade at Mort and got him in the chest. There was no resistance. No blood, no wound, as if the blade slashed through air. A cold chill surged through his core.

"*Car forty-five, check in.*" The disembodied voice made the man spin around. A police car with a flashing light bar idled on the roadside. Near the front of the car, a sheet lay neatly draped over a body. Blood seeped through the cloth. The stained shroud covered the head, but black snakeskin boots protruded from the other end, gleaming in the sun.

One of the officers keyed his mic. "Gonna be a while. There's a few pieces of this guy missing. What's the ETA on that ambulance?"

The eerie squawk of a buzzard rang out. With a mighty flap of its wings, it left the earth with a bloody chunk of flesh dangling from its beak.

The man spun back toward the trucker. "What did you do to me?"

Mort leaned his head back and scanned the sky. "Ran you over. A split second of pain and a disoriented feeling, remember?" His gaze shifted from horizon to horizon, examining the sky.

The man in black searched the sky as well. "What are you looking at? There's nothing there."

With a flick of his wrist, Mort tossed the pendant back. "Hmm. No choir of angels coming to carry your ugly ass home. I guess the others will be here soon. For sure there'll be hell to pay." With a snap of his fingers, he disappeared, along with his truck.

"You can't leave me here! Come back!" he screamed in vain at the empty sky.

"*Car forty-five. That ambulance is at mile marker one-two-nine. Figure about fifteen minutes.*"

El Grimorio ran up to the cop and waved his hand in front of his face. "Hey! I'm right here." But the officer did not react, scribbling diligently in his notebook.

Another officer walked around the car to his partner's side. "No ID. But then again, does he look like the type to have any friends or family?"

The first cop glanced over his shoulder at the corpse. "Just another sorry-ass loser."

"Loser! Nobody calls me that. You're not the first pig I've slaughtered." He growled and swung his blade in wide, wild strokes. It passed through the cop like he wasn't even there. Nothing. No effect.

From behind, a hand pressed on his shoulder. Slowly, the man in black shifted his gaze. A hand of dark orange skin, red blotches, and long unkempt black nails, lengthy enough to be claws, gripped him. Thick black hairs sprouted from two knuckles. The warm touch stiffened his soul; he was unable to budge. Searing heat from the hand penetrated his essence. The sizzling soul-pain forced a bloodcurdling scream from *El Grimorio*, the former man in black.

A deep, gravelly voice whispered, "Time to add more fuel to the fire."

Behind The Leather Apron
Alana Turner

Daytona Beach, Florida, USA
Copyright © 2018 by Alana Turner. All rights reserved.
Alana Turner Facebook Author Page

The streets were darker this particular night. Perhaps that is the reason they were also much quieter, maybe the darkness was simply devouring whatever sounds anyone dared make. It was most certainly feasting on the fear that was all but palpable in the air, gorging itself on such a glorious meal. For the dark had not been the main source of fear for many people the past few weeks. No, the darkness merely reaped the benefits of what I had caused. I could not hold any ill will against it either for its willingness to take advantage over such circumstance, for it benefited me quite nicely during my dark deeds.

While the people of the Whitechapel district went about their night lives, some in delicious fear and others in blissful ignorance, the darkness shielded me from their view. One could argue that in some ways we weren't so different, they and I. After all, we're all out tonight to have some fun. That is what the night is for anyway. The dark hours are always for the best experiences in life. In the dark, we hide from God our dark and sinful deeds, freeing us to do what we will, free of consequences. This is wrong of course, but I have found that I no longer care. Perhaps I never cared.

From the beginning I knew that my kind of fun was more than frowned upon. That fact never bothered me, except when I was young and my mother caught me. She never did appreciate having to clean the animal blood out of my clothes. She would

139

complain that it cost too much to replace them and that the stains never fully came out. You would think the wife, and eventually mother, of a butcher would not hold such hateful feeling toward blood. To be fair I did butcher more than just animals. Mother dear was always on my mind though, no matter my prey.

Especially the last one. I believe she called herself Mary, Mary Kelly. She was a fine specimen, and an even better plaything. I always loved the moment when they realized that they were in peril. That truly was the moment they became my toy. She struggled and squirmed more than the rest had. She put up a fight. She had even managed to land a solid enough hit to my jaw to make me spit out blood. I never would have guessed that my blood would be the first to stain her shawl that night. It was most certainly not the last. My knife penetrated her quite a few times before I could get her still enough to quiet her completely. She could no longer let loose her awfully shrill screams once I cut her throat, my knife snagging on bone at some points. Still the stains kept coming for her poor shawl; my mother would have disapproved highly I think. It almost mirrored her, for as I kept defacing and disgracing her body, the shawl grew equally as unrecognizable. I took her apart, piece by dripping, bloody piece. When I was finished with her, I stood back and admired my work.

She was ravishing now, well to me at least. With her legs now a brilliant red, and her innards splayed about her like wings, she looked more like an angel than any living woman ever could. I positioned her legs to make her more inviting to those who found her and tucked some of her hair behind her ear. She was so very stunning. I could only hope that I could create another angel such as her. An angel that might even make mother proud.

I snapped out of my reverie with a pleasant tingle crawling down my spine. Yes, she had been wonderful, and I most certainly hoped the police thought so as well. I often wondered what they appreciated more, my gifts or my letters. Despite what many may think, I do truly hope they appreciate them. After all, everyone should appreciate a challenge. This is especially true of challenges that you still have a hope of overcoming, or in this case, catching. I suppose that was the cruelest thing I was guilty of, giving the police false hope that they'd ever manage to find such a grand prize as myself. No, I would be immortal in my semi-anonymity, they would only know me by the nicknames they gave me, and the one I gave myself in the letters. Perhaps I would send another with my next kill.

That was when I saw her. Oh yes, she would indeed make a marvelous plaything. The illumination of the streetlamp gave her an unearthly glow. She was obviously waiting for someone as she was scanning the sidewalk on both ends, this cast shadows on her face at several different angles making her appear even more ethereal. Her corset hugged and emphasized every curve in vivid detail, leaving painfully little to the imagination. The matching navy blue skirt exaggerated her backside, as is the fashion these days, but came to a graceful hem at the bottom which would caress the ground when she moved. It was revealing even for the women that practiced such an old occupation as I'm sure she did. She herself had the most majestic ebony hair I have ever had the pleasure of laying eyes on. It was so black it probably made the feasting darkness quite envious. In the illumination of the streetlamp, she was as pale as a porcelain doll, with unnaturally blue eyes. Oh yes, she would most assuredly be mine.

I allowed myself to be seen as I strolled up to her, causing her to smile sweetly in greeting. "May I ask why an astonishingly beautiful woman such as yourself is out at such a late hour on a rough street?" I returned her smile with one of my own, the one reserved only for my playthings.

She giggled and looked away momentarily before responding, "Well maybe I was waiting for someone interesting to give my time to." She tucked one of her ebony locks behind her hair and bit her lip before continuing, "I don't just give my time away after all."

With how well this was going, luring her to her tomb would be far easier than it had been since I started my dark endeavors. I chuckled, "Well, one has to respect that, thankfully I don't like anything that's cheap."

"Well, I can't imagine anyone else will be as wonderfully kind to me tonight, so why don't you escort me somewhere more interesting, hmm?" I offered my arm, which she graciously accepted. Everything was painfully normal about the walk, making idle conversation with sexual undertones and playful flirting, that is until we passed an alley. I'm not normally taken by surprise as I am usually the one giving them. When she dragged me into it however, I was most certainly shocked. The effect was even more so when her mouth attacked mine.

I played along with the charade, kissing her passionately as she moaned and pushed me harder into the wall. All my thoughts were really concerned with was how delightful it would be to thrust my knife into her repeatedly until the blood ran dry from her body. I found that the more confident and strong-willed they were, the more I loved tearing them to pieces. I was so engrossed in my thoughts that I didn't notice when one of her hands left me. I was not aware of it at all in fact until I felt a sharp pain in the side of my neck.

Groping my neck in agony, I crumpled to the ground. I felt the hilt of a knife and the sting of cruel irony. In a vain attempt to live I tried to crawl away. I was halted rather quickly by her heeled boot striking the middle of my back. She graceful, cruelly, maliciously brought herself down onto her knee, lodging it right between my shoulder blades.

She put her lips to my ear and started whispering to me, "All of you men, all the same," She took the knife out of my neck, causing me to groan deeply. She then plunged it into my back with a ferocity that shouldn't have been capable for a woman her size, "All so easily deceived, all so easy killed," she dragged the knife from its current position to the original cut. It felt as though it snagged on something several times. My entire body numb except for my neck. *That* I could feel with intense clarity as ruby fluid gushed into my view. I was torn between whether it was beautiful or terrifying. She grabbed my hair and pulled me closer to her so she could easily whisper to me once more, "Goodbye, you bastard." She let my head hit the pavement with a solid thump. If I were not already in agony it probably would have hurt. As it was, I could do nothing but watch as she walked away, never looking back. I closed my eyes and let the darkness take me. I vaguely wondered if mother would be cross.

Clicking and Clacking, an Eldritch Twins Mystery
Nick Vossen
Sittard, The Netherlands
Copyright © 2018 by Nick Vossen. All rights reserved.
nickcronomicon

"Clicking and clacking, you say?" Quincy handed the trembling old lady her cup of tea.

"Exactly that." She nodded. "Clicking and clacking."

Quincy looked at his sister as she leaned against the hood of their humble grey Ford Fiesta. His twin sister Lilly raised an eyebrow at him and a gust of wind blowing down from atop the pine trees swept up a bit of her messy brown hair.

"There's always been tales of strange things, old haunts and the like around here." The old lady continued. "But the past few weeks have been absolutely terrifying. Hasn't been this bad ever since what happened a few years ago…"

"Let's not go into that now." Quincy straightened his tweed jacket and readjusted his glasses. He smiled weakly at the little lady. "When was the first sighting reported?" He asked. "Do you know?"

"Not really." She looked away, her voice trailing off. "I first learned about it just after the night everyone reported hearing that terrible noise."

"Thank you, Mrs. Mills." he smiled. "Don't worry we'll get to the bottom of this."

Quincy gently shook the old lady's hand, turned around and headed for the car.

"So." Lilly smiled. "What d'ya think?"

"Same as the last few witnesses we talked to; it all sounds like one hell of a curse." Quincy took out his notepad and started reading the clues aloud. "We got an abandoned theater from which ghostly orchestra music is sounding nightly, accompanied by the living dead coming out of the ground in the nearby cemetery. The clicking and clacking thing was new though."

"Yeah, what was that about?"

"I don't know but it sounds bizarre. Never heard anything like it before. First thing that popped into my head was that maybe a mischievous fairy is running around in a white sheet and on stilts."

Lilly laughed. "C'mon you can't be serious!"

"Stranger things have happened." Quincy fondled the car keys. "And besides, the way she described it... how it meandered about and walked so unnaturally. It sounds really creepy."

"Hmm. We'll just have to wait and see."

"Yup."

"By the way, listen up!" Lilly rapped her knuckles on the dashboard enthusiastically. "I've been checking up on maps and we're like just a mile off of Clinton Road."

"*The* Clinton Road? The *Most Haunted* stretch of highway in the United States?"

"Yes! Little boy ghosts, Satanic rituals, hellhounds and shadow figures. So, have you stacked up on your knowledge of Weird NJ magazine, lately?" Lilly giggled.

"Ever since we heard about this job." He laughed.

Lilly tapped on the car navigation screen a few times and made sure it recalculated the route towards the old theater. Then she started the car and they drove off.

It was a little after 6 P.M. when the twins rode up towards an overgrown patch of land with the massive theater building looming eerily in the light of the setting sun. It was a very old building and the distinct American colonial architecture revealed that it must've gone through a series of uses before it was discarded and left to rot, to be taken back by nature. Rotten wood had collapsed under its own weight while sturdy green and yellowed vines crept along the outer edges, into every nook and cranny of the dilapidated walls.

144

Lilly put her weight against the door to push it open while Quincy clicked on his flashlight. The beam illuminated the entry hall and Lilly marveled at the remnants of the once beautiful building. The ceiling and the walls were high and adorned with dirt, graffiti and plant life, but throughout you could see flashes of the old theater's art-deco grandeur. They silently moved on and listened to the creaks and other residual noises old buildings are known for. However, Quincy and Lilly were listening for something else; something out of the ordinary. They wandered slowly towards the end of the grand entry hall and turned around the corner into a smaller lounge area.

"A penny a coat? Preposterous!" The woman's voice came out of nowhere, it whispered softly.

Quincy jumped up and nearly dropped his flashlight, Lilly's eyes darted around, trying to pinpoint where the voice came from.

"Please, Karen," a man's voice groaned. "Don't embarrass me with these trifling matters about pocket change."

After catching their breath and feeling slightly embarrassed, the twins followed the voices from the coat area towards the stairs leading up to the balcony, where they disappeared.

"Residual haunting," Lilly whispered.

"Uh-huh." Her brother answered. "Harmless. Definitely not what we're looking for."

Lilly made a start up the stairs and waved Quincy over.

"Come on!" she whispered. "We'll have the best seats in the house from up here I bet!"

Quincy held up his hand and opened his mouth to reply. Loud applause burst forth from the theater hall. He grabbed Lilly's outstretched hand and they hopped up the stairs as fast as they could. After sliding through a very dusty curtain, the twins reached the balcony and took in the unnerving view before them.

The grand theater was in ruins. The nearly-set sun shone dazzlingly through a huge crack in the sealing and revealed the littered staircases, broken seats with ripped fabric and heavily rusted balustrades. All in all, it was not a pretty sight, yet it was completely overshadowed by the fact that the place sounded as if it was packed to the brim with patrons. It was not, for the record. Yet the applause, clapping and yelling was nearly deafening. Lilly crept over the railing to get a better look at the scene. She winced back.

"What?" Quincy whispered.

"Come, take a look."

From the left-hand side of the stage came the ghostly, distorted apparition of a music conductor. He wore period clothing, nearly all black but with a traditional white shirt and a spectacular bowtie. He was completely transparent, but his features were pretty clear, despite the fact that he appeared to flicker in and out of existence on short intervals. The invisible, ghostly crowd quickly sat back down and after the last soft hushes of disembodied murmuring died off only the periodical creaking of the theaters age-old wooden frame could still be heard. The conductor took center stage and bowed. Quincy couldn't take his eyes off the spectacle, he was holding his breath in awe and anticipation.

"Hey!" Lilly shouted at the top her lungs. "Can you see me?"

Quincy jumped up from the railing, then immediately ducked.

"What do you think you're doing?" He whispered, aghast. "It didn't know we were here!"

Quincy looked up at his sister, a few specks of dust, illuminated by the flashlight, disappeared behind her messy curls. She was looking intently down towards the stage.

"Well?" Quincy went on.

"It still doesn't know." She responded. "It's another residual haunt, I suspected as much."

"Well you might want to fill me in next time. I hate it when you do that." He sighed.

Lilly smirked at him.

"So, let me think." Quincy changed the subject. "We're probably not dealing with an intelligent specter, at least not here."

"Do you think it's the building that's cursed?" His sister asked.

"Hmm no. Wouldn't explain the dead rising from their graves outside. Though it may be linked somehow."

146

"Don't forget the clicky-clacky thing."

"And yes, we still have the clicking and clacking to consider. Cursed object maybe?"

"Could be. Say, we could go ahead and see what's up at…"

From the depths of the grand theater hall, flowing all the way to the top came the ear-splittingly loud music of a bombastic orchestra. Violins screeched over into each other, accompanied by the shrill noises of a brass ensemble. The deep tones of the contrabasses droned heavily and shook the building on its foundations and percussion-groups rumbled on endlessly. The music, lightly put, had a distinct wrongness to it. It was *off*, but not in a way that it was off-key or out of tune. It did not seem to follow any known style or rhythm, it was just a wall of horrible noise, primordial and savage. Lilly yelled and fell back in pain. She couldn't even hear herself screaming over the terrible onslaught. Both her and Quincy's ears started bleeding heavily and she felt herself falling into a trance. She saw visions of terrifying alien landscapes, where giant mushrooms grow and pitfalls with rows of razor-sharp teeth lie in wait of unfortunate travelers. She closed her eyes and fought back, but the noise became too unbearable

Lilly snapped back into reality and opened her eyes. Something was fumbling near her face. Quincy was rolling up cheap ear plugs and stuffing them into his sister's bloodied ears. He also had a pair for himself. Lilly was still dazed but she managed to find her brother's hand, who led her out of the theater as fast as they both could manage and into the fresh air outside. After taking some time to calm down, Lilly was the first to break the silence.

"Where did you get earplugs from?" she asked.

"Bought them down at the gas-station right before we got here. Listen I… I respect classical music, right? But, man, I can't stand it. So, I bought these to prepare myself."

"Probably saved my life in the process, too." Lilly grinned.

"That was entirely coincidental." Quincy smiled back wickedly. "So, got any idea what to do next?"

"Well, what I was going to say, before *Satan* turned his *mix-tape* on, was that we'd go and check out the cemetery. That one guy we talked to swore he saw the dead all swarming around a rather specific crypt."

"Probably the only solid lead we got now, yeah." Quincy agreed and started the car.

A thick fog had rolled into the cemetery once the sun had set. The twins parked their car just outside of the rusty crooked iron fence and wandered over to the front gates, which were half-open and creaked eerily in the cool breeze. Right away they could hear the sorrowed moans of the dearly departed resounding from somewhere in the hanging mists. Beyond the gate was a pathway leading into several directions, yet it was clear based on the sounds alone that the risen dead were congregating somewhere in the western part of the cemetery. The twins snuck around the tombstones as silently as they could, but Quincy barely contained a scream when one of the walking corpses brushed right beside him and nearly tripped.

"Quiet!" Lilly hissed and looked away from the shambling corpse. "Don't move... you know the drill."

"Lilly."

"Shhh! What did I just say?" She rolled her eyes in annoyance. "It hasn't caught our scent yet."

"Lilly..."

"What?"

"It's taking off. I don't think it's interested in us." Quincy pointed off in the distance. "Hey, look at its clothes!"

Lilly caught a quick glance at the torn and rotten fabric that clung grossly to the undead's skin. It was, or rather, used to be black formal attire.

"There's another one! A top hat! Quince, these are clothes you'd wear to..."

"The theater." They both said in unison.

"Follow that hat!" Lilly got up quickly.

The crypt seemed out of place in the relatively new and well-kept burial ground. It was really old and looked as if it was hewn out of solid rock. It was adorned with Christian symbolism; crucifixes, statuettes of the holy virgin Mary, doves and much more decorated its moss-covered outer walls. The undead, freshly risen from their eternal slumber were meandering about in the little grassy perk around the crypt door. They paid absolutely no heed to the twins, which in turn they did not mind at all. Then, in a moment's notice, it got very quiet. The shambling corpses hushed and shuffled about nervously. Quincy shot a look at Lilly, who was shaking her head. They both tried to listen for sounds, any sound at all. And then it came.

Click... Clack...

Lilly opened her eyes wide and held up her hand when her brother wanted to speak.

Click...

Quincy glanced around, it seemed as if the noises came from all around them.

Clack...

The twins clenched their fists nervously.

Clickclackclickclackclickclack!

A bloodcurdling, inhumane scream filled the silent void and at once packs of ravens previously nestled in the cemetery trees shot up into the sky and flew around in alarming confusion. A white haze darted out of the bushes and into the twins' direct path. Lilly blinked, it moved so fast it almost couldn't be seen with the naked eye.

"Where is it?" Quincy spoke frantically.

"There! Over by that bench!"

When Quincy turned around, it was already gone. Lilly moved towards her brother slowly and precariously.

"Quince..." she whispered as soft as she could. "It's right beside you. I... I don't think it's possible to see it directly, just from the corner of our eyes." Despite their fair share of encounters with paranormal phenomena, Lilly's voice trembled with fear.

Quincy glanced sideways slightly, but wished he hadn't. A white thing was standing just inches away from him. It jittered around on crooked, messed up white legs. It huffed and moaned incoherently, almost sounding like ancient guttural speech. But it was a twisted and despoiled language. It was mocking them with low distorted laughter. The thing jittered again and paced forward slowly. With each step came the clicking and clacking sounds which the twins could now barely make out were human bones tied to the thing's waist with old rope. Lilly peeped in fear as she caught a glimpse of a child's vertebrae. The thing screamed again as loud as it could and in the distance terrible orchestra music began drifting from the theater, louder than ever. Then it lunged at them.

"Run!" Lilly screamed and pulled her brother's arm. Another scream came from right behind them as they bolted for the crypt door. The twins threw themselves in the darkness of the stone chamber, turned around and pushed it closed as fast as they could. Lilly fumbled around in the dark and found a latch, effectively locking themselves in. Outside the dead cried mournfully over the wicked noise, but something far worse was now prowling about. The door shook heavily. The thing howled, it wanted in.

"Do you think we'll make it until daylight?" Quincy clicked on the flashlight and looked around.

"What makes you think it'll disappear during the day?" Lilly's eyes followed the beam of light around the crypt.

"Touché."

The crypt was laden with cobwebs, dirt and tightly sealed wooden coffins. More peculiar was the abundance of religious items such as chalices, a bible, crucifixes and a stack of liturgical vestments.

"Seems like a priest and his family are buried here, or at least some high members of the local parish." Quincy shuffled over to the corner on his knees. "Wait, what's this…"

He got up from the floor and dusted off a small wooden chest which was resting in the darkness of the corner. He opened it and pulled out an old moldy journal and a stack of yellowed and faded pieces of sheet music. Lilly sat down next to him. He opened the journal and skimmed through it. Meanwhile the door rattled loudly and started cracking. Restless howling came from right outside.

"Answers. Solutions. Anything." Lilly yelped. "Just do it fast okay?"

"Check this out!" Quincy traced his finger along a passage in the moldy journal and tapped it. "In 1893 this local reverend forbade the theater's conductor to play a new music piece he bought somewhere in town. The reverend claimed the piece was evil and should never be heard."

150

"Well let's agree on that!" The door was shaking violently and one of the planks gave way. A near-invisible strangely angled claw reached inside. Lilly jolted up. "Quince... we're sinking here!"

"The orchestra performed the piece anyway and that same night they nailed the conductor to a tree and burned him alive as punishment, right here in this graveyard." Quincy gulped.

"Good grief! Well, there's your curse." Lilly shook her head. "What now?"

Quincy reached into his coat-pocket and pulled out a bag of salt and a lighter. He proceeded to rub the salt all over the sheet-music.

"I've got an idea!" He yelled, the loud music was now thundering across the cemetery and even louder was the screaming monster hammering on the nearly broken-down door.

"Make it quick!" Lilly yelled back, clutching her hands over her ears.

"I hope this works!"

Quincy took the lighter and set the stack of yellowed paper ablaze.

"You've made your point!" He hollered to no one in particular. "This has gone on long enough!"

In the meantime, Lilly got up and was now actively pushing back the splintered door with everything she had. She was groaning in pain. Between the brute force and dodging the sickly white claw she knew she could not hold out for long.

"Be gone!" Quincy yelled and the door suddenly felt as light as air as Lilly crashed through onto the other side. The white thing was gone, the air was quiet and even the walking dead collapsed back onto the floor like good zombies should.

Quincy fell against the wall of the crypt in exhaustion. His sister, panting, stood in the doorway on top of the scattered splintered planks that once were a door.

"So." She plucked a splinter from her hair. "Sheet music was the cursed object. The reverend killing the music conductor sparked the curse which made the ghosts of the orchestra perform for all eternity. Why it suddenly started *now?* Don't know, don't care!"

She stopped, caught her breath and then continued.

"The occult nature of the music, and I use that term lightly, itself made the dead rise from their grave and eventually even summoned... *Whatever the hell that thing was*." She coughed loudly. "Am I missing something?"

"Seems about right." Quincy scraped himself up from the floor. "All in a night's work, am I right?"

"Screw you, Quince." She laughed in relief. "Now that I think about it though, how did you know lifting the curse would rid us of that thing?"

"I didn't. Pure guesswork."

"I hate it when you do that. But let's call it even." She laughed.

Quincy threw the flashlight towards Lilly and stretched his arms and legs. Together they made their way back across the cemetery towards the car. They were happy to note that even the fog was clearing up now.

"Oh, can I still add one last thing?" Quincy asked.

"Figure something else out?"

"No. Just wanted to say I really *hate* classical music."

The Haunting Of William
Robbie Cheadle
South Africa
Copyright © 2018 by Robbie Cheadle. All rights reserved.
robbiesinspiration

Something was different. Her body felt light and airy as she got to her feet. She glanced around. The familiar shape of the manner house stood in the distance, its turrets tall and proud.

"Why am I outside?"

A large, bright moon bathed everything in a cold, silvery glow. Tendrils of mist rose from the ground, shimmering in the moonlight. The lingering dampness in her clothes and hair did not chill her. The icy wind that blew across the fields did not sting her exposed skin, numbing her nose and fingers like it usually did.

How strange. I can't feel the wind blowing. I'm not cold but I am also not warm. What's wrong with me?

As Matilda shook out her skirts, getting ready to walk back to the house, a dark stain on the front of her dress caught her eye. The large patch of darkness spread across her ribcage, creeping down her bodice and into the fabric of her skirt. Horror wrapped around her like a cloak.

It's sticky, like blood. How can that be? I have no pain.

She reached out a trembling hand to touch the stain. She could see her garments right through it. Her hand was transparent.

Matilda feared for her immortal soul.

***

The housekeeper, Mrs. Chadwick, terrified her. Tall, thin and impeccably dressed she was the undisputed head of the female household staff.

153

Completely in awe of this formidable woman, Matilda set about her duties as the newest member of the large staff. She had an endless list of tasks to complete every day, starting with the unpleasant job of emptying the chamber pots for each member of the family into a slop bucket.

She had applied for the job as chambermaid at Summerset House a few weeks before and her appointment felt like a blessing. Despite her pleasure at having a paying job, no matter how insubstantial the weekly wage was, she had quickly discovered that maintaining the fires in the bedchambers was the most pleasant of her various jobs. It provided a brief opportunity for Matilda to warm her hands and feet in between the long hours of dusting, washing windows and sweeping inside the cold manner house. Despite the fires, the stone walled chambers were drafty and chilly. Matilda's own attic room was so cold when she got out of bed in the morning that the water was frozen in the wash jugs and her breath came in vaporized clouds. It was an improvement on the overcrowded and noisy conditions of her earlier life so she didn't complain. Matilda harboured a secret dream of working her way up to lady's maid to Her Ladyship; helping her dress and caring for her vast wardrobe of beautiful clothes would be wonderful.

Mrs. Chadwick and the cook, Mrs. Harlow, were unkind and impatient with Matilda. Slapping her if they considered her work inferior or slow, her answers too pert or her manners too course. Matilda and the housemaid, Mable, were both lower order servants and they knew it. They were not as badly off as Ellen the scullery maid who spent her days scouring pots and pans, cleaning vegetables, plucking poultry and cleaning fish of their scales.

Thoughts of her family home enabled Matilda to face the other servants with fortitude. The memory of Mother in their tiny two bedroomed cottage and her eight younger siblings who all needed constant care did not appeal to Matilda. She relished having her own bed in the tiny room in the attic of the mansion which she shared with the two other girls.

***

He had arrived at Summerset House in late May. She watched him arrive from behind the thick curtains of an upstairs bed chamber. The new groom was handsome with thick dark hair and an easy smile.

It wasn't long before he had won over all the household staff. Even Mrs. Chadwick, who considered herself a cut above everyone else, looked kindly upon William, who bantered with her and made her giggle like a girl. Mr. Johnson, the butler, said His Lordship was delighted by William's skill as a horseman and competency as a groom.

Matilda was astonished when he befriended her, a lowly chambermaid, and started bringing her small gifts of wild flowers and berries that he gathered while out exercising the horses for His Lordship. She did not see herself though his eyes, did not see the delicate features and large, blue eyes beneath a mop of wavy, honey-coloured hair, and the budding womanly form beneath her simple muslin dress. Matilda was completely bewitched by this sophisticated cad.

As the weather warmed and the flowers bloomed in the fields and woodlands around the manor house, Matilda's life of endless toil and drudgery improved. The brilliant patches of warm sunshine that made their way in at the small windows coupled with the delicate fragrances of the greenery and flowers carried in on the breezes, made Matilda cheerful and happy. As the season progressed, her friendship with William became inextricably linked in her mind with pleasurable moments and sunshine.

It was lovely to have someone to spend her half-day with on a Sunday afternoon. Matilda and William took long walks in the fields around the mansion, admiring the graceful bluebells that grew in abundance along the edges of the paths and in the thickets and woodlands. He was kind and courteous towards Matilda - even if he did tease her and beg for kisses which made her uncomfortable.

The attention William showered onto Matilda inflamed the sense of rivalry of her peers. Mabel and Ellen became frosty and unfriendly. Their unkind treatment of her, fueled by jealousy and spitefulness, made her more reliant on William as her sole source of company and friendship among the staff.

She recalled the day in the thicket. A carpet of yellow, orange and brown leaves covered the ground. William pulled off his jacket and spread it over them. It was late afternoon and the warmth of the September day was gradually dissipating into a chilly evening.

"Let us sit here," he said. "This will keep the damp away."

She remembered his kisses and the promises he made.

Anger, like bile, rose up in her as the memories flooded her mind.

***

Telling William about her pregnancy wasn't as hard as she thought. She found him at the stables, currying His Lordship's favourite horse. He listened without saying a word. When her tears overflowed and ran down her cheeks he wiped them away and told her not to worry.

"Everything will be fine," he said.

The next morning, she heard that he was gone. Fled during the night without a word to anyone. His Lordship was furious.

Devastation overwhelmed Matilda when she heard the news. She contained her anguish and shame all day as she went about her tasks. She daren't let her feelings show on her face or in her behaviour. The punishment for immoral behavior was instant dismissal. She had nowhere to go. Mother would not let her come home in her present condition.

How could he do this? He seemed pleased about the baby. We spoke about being together. He said he loved me.

The same thoughts went around and around in her mind.

He had left her all alone, an unmarried woman carrying a child. That night she silently cried herself to sleep. Mabel and Ellen couldn't see her pain. She was all alone.

***

Climbing the steep stone steps of the North turret and flinging herself from it seemed the only reasonable thing to do at the time.

She remembered the horrible feeling of vertigo as she fell. Recalled exactly the explosion of pain as her body hit a projecting gargoyle on the side of the mansion, ribs shattering and internal organs ripping lose as her chest tore apart.

Anger licked at her, its small flames fanned by the memories. She focused on the building ahead. *He would pay. They would all pay.*

She knew where he was; could see him in her mind's eye. He had returned to the mansion when he heard about her death. It was a good position, after all, and his trouble had taken care of itself. His Lordship had welcomed him back. He was very good with the horses and so what if he had been responsible for the death of some chit of a girl. In His Lordship's opinion, she had brought it on herself.

I'm coming for you, she thought, as she walked across the fields towards the mansion. *You are going to pay ten times over.*

A malevolent smile spread across her face. Her skin looked translucent in the soft light of the moon but her vicious expression made her look almost demonic.

***

William opened his eyes when the cock crowed. Time to get up and start the day's work. He smiled, he had his eye on Ellen, the pretty scullery maid. She was plump and rosy as well as young and innocent.

His clothes were neatly draped over the chair in his room. As he reached for them, they fell to pieces at his touch. Each article had been roughly hacked with a knife, his breeches, shirt and waistcoat. Nothing had been spared. His riding boots were full of tiny stones. They were impossible to get rid of entirely and as he walked they worked free from underneath the soles and stabbed his feet.

William's day did not improve. A strange and vicious animal attacked Sultan, His Lordship's best hunting horse, while William was exercising him in the woodlands. Sultan reared, his eyes rolling in his head, and took off at a gallop through the trees. William ducked down but stray branches tore at his exposed head and borrowed clothes.

Late in the evening, William returned to his room. As he opened the door he gasped in shock. The room had been turned upside down. His few belongings had been thrown out of the chest of drawers and the bedclothes had been ripped from the bed and scattered all over the room.

As he gathered the bed linen from the floor and remade the bed, he thought he heard the sound of female laughter echoing around the sparsely furnished room. It was a frightening sound; mirthless, pitiless and distinct.

He slept fitfully, every few hours some strange sensation or event dragged him from sleep. A cold wetness in each of his ears, a chilling draught from the door that was mysteriously open and bumping sounds from the darkness under the bed.

William was not superstitious, but the on-going low laughter and the eerie happenings sent a convulsive quiver down his spine.

***

Matilda continued to play with William all week. She watched gleefully as his handsome face grew weary and haggard from sleep deprivation. Dark circles stood out beneath his eyes, noticeable against his pale skin.

The other servants asked him if he was ill and he answered in the negative. He wasn't ill. Not in the usual sense of the word.

The strange happenings did not stop William from arranging an outing with Ellen on Sunday afternoon. Matilda listened as he spoke to Ellen, the lies flowing glibly, and she made her plans.

This is the most fun I've ever had. Now who's got the power?

Matilda felt drunk with power. Her concerns for her soul were long gone as she reveled in William's slow destruction

There's more to come, my friend. You haven't seen the worst of me yet.

***

Ellen and William sat in the hayloft on his outspread coat. William capitulated to the bitter day and biting wind and found a more suitable venue for them.

Matilda sat next to William, watching as he leaned over to kiss Ellen. Matilda deftly pushed her face between the pair and her pale, cold lips found William's. She chose that he could now see and feel her. At the touch of her lips, his eyes opened. A look of horror settled like a mask over his handsome features as

158

recognition dawned in his eyes. Matilda ran her long, claw-like nails down his cheek. They had grown since her death.

"Oh my God," the words screamed in William's mind.

Matilda whispered into his ear:

"Come on, William, touch me, run your hands all over me. Kiss me."

"I don't want to hear this". William jerked backward much to Ellen's anxiety. She was not a guest a Matilda's party and could only see William and his strange behavior.

William leaped to his feet and started towards the ladder down to the barn.

Matilda stayed with him.

"What's wrong, William," she whispered, grinning a dry, spitless grin. *"You liked it when you took me in the glade. You were thrilled to have your hands all over me."*

William leapt towards the trapdoor. As he landed, his feet tangled in the hay and he tripped, falling headfirst down the hole.

Ellen, who had been sitting on the jacket, looking confused, became suddenly animated. Jumping to her feet she ran to where William had disappeared through the floor. Her eyes widened at the sight of William lying in a crumpled heap. She could see that his head lay at an unnatural angle. Screams issued from her wretched body as she reacted to the shock.

A satisfied smile curled the corners of Matilda's mouth as she watched Ellen's confused panic and horror.

Serves the bitch right. I've done her a favour.

The few moments it took for the life to drain completely from William's body were accompanied by the siren song of maniacal laugher. The last sounds he heard were Matilda's whispered *"beware of the woman scorned"*. He did not prove himself courageous and strong-minded as he gazed into the mouth of Hell.

Where The Power Hides
Anne Marie Andrus
New Jersey, USA
Copyright © 2018 by Anne Marie Andrus. All rights reserved.
www.AnneMarieAndrus.com

The streets of the French Quarter didn't allow the limousine to invade their labyrinth without a vicious struggle. The engine roared over and over, until an invisible barrier split and the ghostly grey car landed on Rue Chartres with a thud. Steering wide around tight corners and slowing every time a pack of vibrant revelers danced in front of the grill, glossy tires finally crunched to a stop in a lot on the neighborhood's Esplanade border.

"Are you sure this is right?" Sorcha clicked the map icon on her phone and pounded on the window control until smoky glass disappeared into the door. "I said I missed the Quarter, but actually being here makes me—"

"Ill? For years, not a soul on earth could pry you out of this district." Draven tossed back his blond hair and squinted at a handwritten note. "Ivori is waiting in the lobby of Le...I don't know, some sordid hotel."

"Feels lonely." Sorcha gazed down the crooked alley at snapshots of a stray parade. "Or empty? Might just be me."

"It's positively hollow." Draven tossed the crumpled paper to the only other being in the car. "Have I deciphered that scribble correctly, Lock?"

"Indeed you have, Your Highness." Lock kicked the door open and grabbed for Sorcha's hand. "Leave that dreadful device here."

"It's brand new." Sorcha pulled her phone back from Lock, just to have it plucked away again. "Seriously, Draven?"

"Doesn't the incessant, social connection exhaust you?" Draven flung it to the farthest corner of the car. "I prefer ravens and wax-sealed parchment. Ominous and classy."

"Nothing feels like those old days, except the weather." Sorcha peeled off her sweater and glared into the dark limousine at the blinking phone, before tossing the garment on top of it. "But, what if?"

"Anyone you're looking for..." Lock tugged her across the gravel lot. "Has no need for that contraption."

The trio rounded a saltwater pool and stopped in the middle of a checkerboard tile floor. Ivori drummed her fingers on the concierge's desk. Without a word, she spun and motioned them to a hidden door.

"I hate tunnels." Sorcha swept the hair off her neck and twisted it into a loose knot. "It's a sauna down here."

"When you mentioned an Equinox reunion, Ivori, I assumed you meant something spectacular." Draven touched the muddy wall and cringed. "Or at least, sanitary."

"Nights of grand balls and one-of-a-kind dresses are history." Ivori forged into the pitch black. "Y'all took your sweet time getting here."

"We were on opposite corners of the earth." Lock frowned when Ivori struck a match and lit her torch. "I was hoping for an enchanted courtyard."

"Me." Sorcha raised her finger. "The cathedral bell tower."

"I've planned something way better." Ivori stopped so short, everyone crashed into her back. "None of your supernatural eyes saw the massive iron door?" She pulled chalk from her pocket and wrote on the rusty surface, waiting for each letter to disappear before she scripted the next. When the jumble was finished, the barrier creaked open.

"Marginally impressive." Draven grunted.

"The reigning king, a shifter prince and our own duchess." Ivori deliberately pointed at Draven, Lock and Sorcha, in order. "All that royalty and not one of you can crack a smile?"

"We're here because people we love are—" Sorcha lunged for Ivori's neck.

"Easy." Lock caught her arm. "She's messing with you."

"She has a damn personality disorder." Sorcha's hands shook like leaves in a hurricane. "Ivori, my husband has been missing since our first anniversary!"

"I apologize. And, if you repeat that to anyone, I'll turn y'all into toads." Ivori strutted past and snapped her fingers. "Step lively, my undead allies."

Draven growled as she disappeared into the maze of shadows. "Just lovely."

"Humor the witch." Lock jammed a wisp of dark hair behind his ear and urged them forward.

"Bar noise, coffee-shop racket." Draven pointed to the corridor's grimy ceiling. "Is that traffic?"

"We're under Decatur," Ivori said. "Clueless fool."

"Your bizarre friend has gotten nastier over the years."

"Draven, she is not my—" Sorcha howled and dropped to her knees.

"It's the railroad tracks." Ivori scampered back and yanked Sorcha to her feet. "Suck it up."

Sorcha took a deep breath and slammed across the barrier. She turned back to see Lock and Draven stroll past the same spot, unaffected. "What the hell?"

"That steel is the boundary of *your* city, girl. Not theirs." Ivori hauled her forward. "Now that we're on the fringe, maybe we can send some messages."

"If you don't stop touching me..." Sorcha clamped her hands over her ears. "What's the infernal drumming?"

"Even I can hear that." Draven clenched his jaw. "Can we get to the bloody point before we all go deaf?"

"The river. The giant, muddy, tourist attraction." Ivori sighed. "Just swallow to equalize the pressure—like in your private jet."

Their tunnel flared into a dry chamber with a polished floor. Carved benches surrounded a round fire pit.

"This is unexpected." Lock ran his fingers over glittering gems set at regular intervals in the stone walls.

"Sit down, it's nearly midnight. The currents are whispering." Ivori loomed over the fire pit and emptied her deep pockets. She arranged a display of sachets, vials and boxes onto a low altar. "Sorcha, center bench."

Draven whispered in Sorcha's ear. "Creepy enough?"

Sorcha choked back a giggle and Lock smacked her shoulder.

"Smiling now, is inappropriate." Ivori glared at them until the room dropped into silence. She tipped her head side to side and motioned to Sorcha's hair. "Take it down, glamour girl. It's where your power hides."

In the muggy cavern air, Sorcha's auburn curls puffed with freedom as if stirred by a devilish breeze.

"That's our cue to get started." Ivori rubbed her palms together. Her eyes flashed every color of the rainbow as she mumbled peculiar lyrics in a foreign tongue. Smokeless fire erupted in the circle of rocks.

"What, exactly, are we summoning here?" Lock asked.

"Not what. Who," Ivori answered. "All of us are searching for someone. Picture that person in your mind."

"My Gwyn, murdered and not avenged." Draven exhaled frost. "Not yet."

Sorcha brushed away a pink tear and slipped back to a night in Nepal, the eve of her own tragedy. "Vir."

"I can't say his—" Lock flashed his brilliant violet eyes. "Who did you lose, Ivori? Your pet snake?"

Sorcha squirmed and searched the floor around her feet.

"Never mind me. Memories equal pain." Ivori played an invisible piano with one hand while pouring the contents of a sachet in a perfect square with the other. White dust wafted around her head. "No need to speak names aloud."

"Is that—" Draven choked and held his nose. "Bone?"

"Teeth, actually." Ivori dumped a vial of black syrup in the center of the square. "From a shark, who is still very much alive."

"What a comfort." Lock watched Ivori's finger point to a metal box. "May I help?"

"Just with the latch." She waited while he jiggled the mechanism and sprung the lid open. Inside, a twisted, rusty arrow lay next to a perfectly polished dagger and a sapphire candle.

Sorcha rolled her eyes.

"Oh, it gets weirder even before I cut you...and myself." Ivori deflected angry stares. "First, everyone needs to clear their minds and recall the moment when you were strongest."

"My apologies—no." Draven bolted up. "This sounds preposterous."

"I want to hear her plan." Sorcha wrenched him back down. "We've had no luck doing this on our own."

"I'm shocked. Amateurs." Ivori dipped the blue candle's wick in the fire and set it on the altar. "If you can evoke your soul at its most powerful—the instant when you embodied the best of your dreams—that force, can summon anyone across all realms of the universe. I think."

Sorcha threw her hands in the air. "You think?"

"So," Lock said. "I just picture that occasion in my head?"

"Project the vision in front of you, like a widescreen television. Once you've got it, raise your hand." Ivori waved her candle over the puddle of syrup, directing liquid outward into the border of bone dust. The mixture ignited flames that crawled until the circuit was complete. Ivori looked up to see three raised hands.

"All ready." Draven faked a smile.

"Perfect." Ivori grabbed the dagger and raced around the fire pit. "This next part goes pretty quick. Don't do anything until I tell you to, but keep concentrating."

Draven and Lock each hissed when she sliced their palms. Sorcha didn't flinch when Ivori cut both her hands at once.

"Now." Ivori ran back behind the fire. "Men, squeeze a few drops into this square."

The moment Draven and Lock's blood mingled, they were knocked back onto the benches.

Ivori sliced her own flesh over the flames and snapped her eyes to Sorcha. "Your turn."

When Sorcha's blood touched the fire, the ground quaked violently.

"Be ready to join hands with her when this metal pierces wood." Ivori raised the twisted arrow over her head and drove it toward the altar. "Now!"

The three slammed their hands together and the blood of ancient dynasties filled the air with black and gold sparks.

Sorcha looked to the weapon in Ivori's hand and then into the girl's inky black eyes. "Uh-oh."

A low growl escaped Ivori's lips. Force leapt from her chest, rippled the air and plunged into the earth under their feet. Each vampire's perfect vision swirled overhead until their solid bodies flickered and distorted.

Draven's shift solidified first. His modern suit became a classic, midnight tuxedo. In his fingers, a velvet box sat open with a glittering ruby ring perched in the center.

Lock's appearance dissolved next. Instead of the black t-shirt and jeans he arrived in, he now wore his full military uniform. Royal insignias lined his shoulders and medals covered his broad chest.

Sorcha dropped her gaze and changed last. Her eyes blazed with blue fire and her long hair became a chin-length, bob. Her porcelain skin melted away, replaced by the snarling face of a tiger.

Ivori flung her arms out and threw her head back to a cacophony of drunken notes. "By the power of a lone trumpeter's call, the roar of a warrior's charge, and the murmurs of phantom saints that prowl our legendary streets—I summon all the lost souls home!"

Nightmare Man
Betty Valentine
Jersey, U.K Channel Islands
https://bettys-stories.com

It is dark and the little town sleeps peacefully under a big white moon.

Not everyone slumbers; the Nightmare Man is wide awake.

He sees you and he wants your dreams.

Old Ma Ferris isn't sleeping she will never wake again.

Pa Ferris snoozes on beside her.

He has no idea that he has just killed his wife, but the curtains are blowing in the breeze, the Nightmare Man has left his calling card.

Unease is all over town, people toss and turn in their beds.

He is the dream maker, the dream raper, he is the Nightmare Man.

A wisp of smoke, a shaft of moonlight cold and sharp.

Old Toby is awake, he sits in his chair and sips his coffee and he rocks and he rocks and he rocks!

He knows the Nightmare Man, they have met before, many times.

Now Toby is old but the Nightmare Man is strong, so he rocks, and he rocks and he rocks.

Beside him Long Jack blinks his one eye, he knows the Nightmare Man of old, they have a score to settle so he waits and he waits and he waits.

Dream feeder, dream seeder, he sews and a nightmare grows.

For he is the Nightmare Man, who lives on fear. He is the dripping tap, the gate in the wind and the squeaky tread on the stair, he's barely if ever there.

The Willow Tree
Robbie Cheadle
South Africa
Copyright © 2018 by Robbie Cheadle. All rights reserved.
robbiesinspiration

The man stood hidden in the deep shadows of the tall hedge, watching the young boy. Thick clouds hid the stars, making the darkness complete. The thick velvet curtains had not yet been drawn across the large window of the living room and the boy was clearly visible in the room's bright lighting.

The watcher knew the child's name was Philip and that he was four years old. He was playing with his toys, lining them up in order by size, starting with his biggest trucks and dump truck and ending with a long line of die-cast Thomas the Tank engines.

As the man watched, Philip leaned over the toys, shouting and flailing his arms. His small, perfect face suffusing with blood as he became more frenzied. The sound could not penetrate the thick glass of the window, but the man didn't need to hear the words. He knew they were meaningless. An outward expression of an internal anxiety. He understood Philip's symptoms well.

Philip's mother, Sarah, came into the room, drawn by his shouts. Her pretty face creased with concern as she assessed the scene; the toys in an orderly line and her son's intense and frantic shouts and actions.

Her anxiety for the well-being of her child touched the man.

They need help, he thought. *This situation can't continue.*

Sarah walked across the room and drew the heavy curtains. *That's it for tonight. Time to go home.*

168

The man slipped across the garden, staying close to the hedge, his movements careful and concise. As he reached his car, parked in the next road, memories flooded his mind.

"He is a good boy, Doctor. Extremely neat. His cupboard is immaculate with all his clothes, t-shirts, shorts and jerseys, folded and put away according to their colour and style. He displays his toys on his shelf in size and colour order too. I am lucky to have such a tidy son." Mother folded her hands on her lap and stared at the psychiatrist, defying him to challenge her views about her son's unusual behavior.

Dr Keller, the psychiatrist appointed by the state to treat her son, didn't respond to her unspoken challenge. He made a few notes on the pad on his clipboard.

"I'll see Ronan now."

Idiot, Ronan thought as he gazed at Dr Keller, his dislike evident in his dark eyes. He hated these sessions with this dry and unsympathetic man.

Dr Keller maintained that the mild disability Ronan had been born with, and which had evolved into such a traumatic and nearly deadly ailment for him, was the root cause of his post-traumatic stress disorder and the resultant obsessive-compulsive disorder. Ronan's symptoms were all related to a need for hygiene and cleanliness and a fear of germs and illness. Dr Keller was also of the opinion that Ronan did not want to get better. He had told Ronan's mother many times that he resisted the treatment.

I do try. It's hard. He doesn't understand how hard this is for me.

Ronan had been seeing Dr Keller since he was eleven years old. School had always made him anxious. Interacting with his peer group was immeasurably difficult for him as his more mature thought pattern and high intellect made him unable to join in their childish games or understand their simple ideas of pleasure. When he had won a computer by entering, and winning, an interschool mathematics competition, it was a God-send.

A gateway to the internet and learning; it wasn't long before he had mastered the art of research and could seek out answers to the things that troubled him. His interests included illnesses and diseases that had plagued the planet and resulted in mass deaths. He learned the symptoms of the black plague, Spanish flu and tuberculosis. His research did not help put his fears and anxieties to rest. On the contrary, they resulted in even more compulsions as he sought more and more different ways to control his obsessions and intrusive thoughts.

Living with Ronan became more and more difficult for his parents after he started high school. The stress of maintaining his scholarship at the conservative, all-boys grammar school he attended led to increasingly invasive compulsions that took up more and more of his time at home. The visits to Dr Keller were one of the steps his mother had taken to try and improve their home life.

"How is school?" Dr Keller asked. "Are the boys still teasing you?"

"School's good."

The teasing by his peers was relentless. They couldn't fail to notice his raw and reddened hands from all the hand washing, bald patches on his head where he had pulled out his hair, strand by strand, and bizarre aversions to touching library books and second hand stationary or clothing.

"Is the Zoloft helping you?"

"Yes, I feel much better on it."

The change in medication from Prozac to Zoloft had not helped control his symptoms, as Dr Keller had said it would. Nothing helped. Neither the steadily growing pile of prescriptions for medications and pills nor the cognitive behavior therapy used by the psychologists to treat his chronic obsessive-compulsive disorder gave him any relief. He didn't like the pills. They made him feel detached and unfocused. He didn't want the dosage to be increased. Upping the dosage or prescribing an additional pill was always Dr Keller's solution when told that the pills weren't working. Ronan said nothing.

"How is the cognitive behavioral therapy going? Do you feel you are making progress?"

"Yes, I haven't slammed a door for over a week."

This was true, he hadn't slammed a door since last week Monday after his session with the psychologist. Dr Keller didn't ask if Ronan has started any other rituals to substitute for the one he had given up and he didn't offer that information. The foot stamping didn't irritate his father nearly as much as the door slamming, so things were better at home.

The sessions with the psychologist were unbearable. The treatment required him to touch all the things he feared with a soft cloth, that was never washed, and then wipe all his treasures with the cloth. Just thinking about wiping his beloved computer equipment with that tainted, filthy cloth made him shudder with disgust.

"Here are your scripts," said Dr Keller, handing the paper to Ronan. "Do you have any questions you want to ask me?"

"No, nothing at all."

Ronan's symptoms did not improve. He did not embrace the treatment with a determination to get better.

When he was fifteen years old his mother suffered a nervous breakdown. The stress of staying up, night after night, to see him through his lengthily rituals, explaining to nosey neighbours about the repeated banging of doors and eventual frequent disintegration of the whole situation into shouting and screaming between father and son eroded her ability to cope. Unable to find any real help for him, her spirit eventually broke.

His mother died in a horrific accident after turning in front of an on-coming car. Ronan never knew whether her actions were deliberate or not. He could still remember the sharp agonizing pain of his loss that gradually became a dull ache that had never left him. His mother was the only person who cared enough to try and understand the reasons behind his rituals. His father thought his mother's death was a form of suicide. After her funeral the beatings started. These became worse and worse for Ronan as his father found solace at the bottom of a cheap whiskey bottle.

The man pulled his mind back from these unbearable thoughts. It was almost a forcible act of will; he needed to focus on the issue at hand. The problem of this boy, Philip. He needed a clear head to plan.

**

Sarah stood in the queue for the ice cream vendor. She was enjoying the warmer Spring weather and the fact that it was Saturday. As a working mother, a whole day to spend with her

small son was a thing to be treasured. She knew Philip would want
to bathe and wash his hands when they returned home. Back in his
own home, he would not tolerate the dirt and germs he imagined
covered his body after being in the playground. Right now, though,
he was happily playing on the park equipment.

Obessive compulsive disorder has no logic, Sarah thought
with a sigh.

Philip had joined in with a group of other small children
who were all climbing and crawling all over the huge plastic jungle
gym and Sarah had decided to treat them both to an ice cream.

"Here you go."

The ice cream vendor handed Sarah the two Soft Serve ice
creams.

"Thank you." She paid him and turned, walking swiftly
towards the play area. She smiled as she imagined Philip's delight
at this towering ice-cream, but it faded as she failed to spot her son
amongst the children near the jungle gym. She felt a mild tinge of
anxiety as she drew closer and Philip still did not materialize,
popping out of the tunnel slide's mouth, shouting with pleasure.
Her anxiety turned to dread as she walked slowly around the
outskirts of the play area and still saw no sign of her child.

The search for the boy went on well into the evening.
Willing volunteers had searched the entire park and the
surrounding wooded area. There was no sign of the child
anywhere; he had simply vanished. Sarah sat nearby with a friend,
her eyes were wide and glassy with shock and the strong sedative
that the doctor had administered to her. Her husband was in the
woods with a flashlight searching for any traces of anything
unusual amongst the bluebells and the thick green foliage. The
current thinking was that Philip must have wondered into the
woods and become lost. Death by exposure to the cold night air
was a huge concern for the searchers. The more sinister thought of
abduction was not yet the primary focus of the police.

Constable King was the first officer to arrive at the scene.
One of the mothers who had been sitting watching her children
playing, had reacted to Sarah's frantic screaming for her son and
called the police. He recalled her face vividly, a beautiful woman,
her eyes had been wild and red with sobbing and her fine blonde

hair was matted from dragging her fingers through it. She stood between two puddles of melted ice cream, each adorned with a broken sugar cone. The ice cream cones had slipped from her hands when she realized her son was no longer in the play area. None of the mothers had seen anything, they had not noticed anyone unusual in the play area or seen the child leave.

People are so unobservant.

He was worried about this disappearance. There was not a single sign of anything unusual, but the child was gone and was nowhere to be found.

***

The man sat at the small table in his immaculate kitchen, reading the evening paper. The thick recycled paper looked out of place against the heavily scrubbed background of the table. The headline splashed across the front page read "Missing four-year-old found dead." The front page also displayed the picture of a beautiful willow tree. The tree grew in a small patch of ground at the bottom of the parking lot of the local shopping center. Its slender green branches trailed to the ground.

He remembered how thick those branches were when he pushed his way through them one night three weeks ago. They swung closed behind him like a thick curtain. It was very black behind the green, with the lights from the shopping center being cut off most efficiently by the overhanging foliage. The earth was crumbly and smelled damp and musty when he laid the plastic bag containing the boy's dismembered body parts against the trunk.

The article said that an elderly lady out walking her dog had detected a foul smell like rotting meat as she passed the tree. Peering through the sheltering branches and into the gloom, she had spotted the large plastic bag and called the police to investigate further. The whole town had reacted with shock and horror when the remains of little Philip had been found inside the bag.

The man sat back in his chair with a sigh of satisfaction. He took a sip of his tea and thought how easily this problem had been resolved. The threat the boy, Philip, posed to his beautiful mother had been terminated and she could now continue her life undisturbed. He would never be discovered as his numerous cleansing rituals required a dedication and extreme focus on detail that was unmatched by anyone else. He had taken great pains to ensure the minimum mess when he killed and dismemberment the child with skill appropriate to his profession as a pediatric surgeon. He had tested his new surgical gloves for this procedure and they had proved to be perfect for the job, resilient and comfortable.

He finished the story and turned over the page of the newspaper.

The Changeling
Christine Valentor
Chicago, Illinois, USA

Copyright © 2018 by Christine Valentor. All rights reserved.
https://witchlike.wordpress.com/

My child is not frail at birth. Not in the least. He is a strong infant, fit and robust and bigger than most. I name him Gideon Tannersonne. He is not my first offspring, but he is the first to survive. Our village is fraught with plague and disease, babies delivered by the precarious tending of midwives. Before Gideon, I had borne three others.

My first baby, a girl, died before I had the chance to hold her. The umbilical cord had wrapped around her neck and she became a strangled corpse, a tiny bundle of translucent blue. The poor thing never cried, never breathed, never even had a chance at life. My second, a girl as well, became riddled with the sweating sickness and passed before her first year. And my third, a boy, was born with no hands nor feet. He had only withered stumps that protruded from his wrists and ankles like quivering worms. Yet I held him and loved him all the same.

"Mathilde!" my husband shrieked, as if the child's malformation were somehow my fault. "What have you wrought? A demon child! Lack of hands, lack to make a living!" My husband then snatched the infant from me and threw him in the fire.

Flames leaped and ash sizzled as the baby's flesh burnt like a blackened crust of bread. My heart wrenched and I covered my eyes. Smoke engulfed the house with the sickly smell of smoldering skin. Finally, I could bear it no longer. I fled from the cottage, my bedsheet wrapped around me like a cloak. I carried the afterbirth in my arms, a bloody sack of placenta that hung like raw meat. I did not want my husband to destroy *that* as well – the one thing left of my pregnancy that could be made useful. I'd take it to the forest, perhaps bury it for the fair folk. They'd look with favor upon me. I ran deep into the woods, trees closing around me. It was then I came upon the Blue Fairy.

This was not so strange a meeting as one might assume. Fairies, the fair folk, were a-plenty in our forest, if one only had Sight to see them. The Blue Fairy was tall with skin the color of turquoise and tangled sapphire hair that matted like seaweed across her face.

She did not ask what vexed me, for already she knew. "Fret not Mathilde," she told me, taking a bite of the placenta which melted like red butter beneath her sharp teeth. "Soon you will birth another boy-child. He shall be hale and healthy, and live to full adulthood. He shall wed and sire many children of his own."

I was overjoyed at this news, so much so that tears poured down my cheeks. The Blue Fairy dried my eyes with her long hair. She bit the placenta again. "Be aware, though," she cautioned, her mouth full of blood. "The survival of your son depends upon one condition."

Oh, the fairies! They are sneaky, evil things! Although they promise much they always ask much in return.

"Be not suspicious," she told me. The Blue Fairy knew my thoughts before I uttered them. This was a bothersome problem. One must always monitor thoughts and keep secrets when dealing with the fair folk. This, of course, was impossible.

"Alright," I sighed. "What then is the condition?"

"You must let this son do as he pleases. He shall be free to take any occupation, wed any lass he so chooses, live his life in a manner he *himself* sees fit. Do not impose upon him restrictions of any kind, for if you do, the consequences will be vile."

Now, one year after the Blue Fairy's promise, I deliver Gideon into the world. He is perfect and whole with clasping hands and a strong beating heart. His eyes are vivid blue, his skin smooth as a peach, unmarked save for one tiny mole upon his neck.

My son grows sturdy and tall, a child of the earth. He loves animals and all things in nature. He also loves to draw. With chalks and inks he sketches the likeness of everything he sees; the trees, the flowers, the cows, my own countenance and that of my husband.

When Gideon reaches his seventh name day, my husband decides to teach him the trade of tanning hides.

Gideon, however, cannot abide this. He weeps at the very thought of skinning an animal for profit. The cows, he claims, are his *family* as much as my husband and myself. The cows are perfection, never to be slaughtered. He runs to the fields with his chalks and begins sketching them.

"What you create is nonsense, boy!" my husband scolds. "Nothing but doodles and scribbles! What profit could possibly come of it?" With this he takes all Gideon's creations, his paints, his inks, and throws them in the river. "There will be no artistry in this family. Gideon, come the morrow you will go with me to the barnyard. There you will slay the beasts, skin their hides and learn the skill of soaking and liming."

My poor son cries all night.

In the morning I go to awaken him. Upon pulling his bed curtains, I am astonished at what I see. Gideon is pale and frail, a tiny wraith of a thing. He is no longer the picture of health I have raised for the past seven years. He looks at me with wide, placid eyes. In a stuttering gasp he coughs, green mucous spewing from his mouth.

"Gideon!" I cry. "What has happened?"

But already I know. The Blue Fairy's warning comes back to me, her voice a ringing bell in my head. "Do not impose upon him restrictions, for if you do, the consequences will be vile."

Of course. The Blue Fairy has taken Gideon and left in his place a changeling. The creature that now sits before me can barely lift its own head. Upon shuffling the bed sheets I look closer. This situation is worse than I thought. The changeling sprawls across the mattress, rolling naked. With chalk-white legs spread open, it reveals an even bigger woe. This is no boy-child, but a female!

I try to speak to her, but she only stares, her face vacant. The changeling does not even have command of a human language.

Just then my husband pounds upon the door. "Gideon! Get up lad, for there is work to be done!"

I panic. What to do? If my husband sees our "son" in this condition he will surely be outraged. He has already thrown one child in the fire. I put no act of violence past him! I creep to the door, cracking it open. There stands my husband, face ruddy with anger, an ax clutched in his hands. I whisper through the slivered doorway.

"The child is ill, my dear. I fear he may have the plague."

My husband drops his jaw in horror. "The plague!" he gasps. "The deadly, rutting plague! It is a curse upon our house."

"Yes, yes," I continue, for once I begin to spin a lie, I am quite good at it. "Get you gone from this room my dear," I plead. "For I have already been exposed, but you have not. Go to your duties. I will tend to the child."

"God's blood!" My husband quivers in terror as he backs away. Quickly he exits the cottage.

I lead the changeling back to the woods where the Blue Fairy again appears to me. She crosses her arms, eyes me sideways as though I am some disobedient child. "You are a foolish woman Mathilde," she says. "I had warned you of Gideon's upbringing, had I not?"

"Yes, but this is not my doing! It is my husband who imposes an unwanted trade upon the boy."

"And you stand by and watch? What kind of mother are you?"

"What am I to do?" I wring my hands. The changeling coughs, once again spouting mucous that trickles down her chin. She is but a whey faced imp, yet I feel a kindness, a tenderness toward her, as much as I did for the three babies I had lost. If only there were some way to nurse this changeling back to health…

"Very well then," they Blue Fairy says. "You shall have them both. The changeling and your son. But only according to conditions."

I sigh. Here it comes again! The fairy's impossible "conditions."

"Oh, Mathilde." The Blue Fairy crouches her long, lanky frame close to mine. "It will not be as bad as you think! Now listen closely. First, you must leave your husband, never to return again."

I cringe. Leave my husband? How would I survive? A woman alone in this world, no trade of my own, and worse yet, with a frail changeling in my care?

The Blue Fairy shakes her head. "Mathilde! For a clever woman you are certainly not very resourceful. Now listen further. I will give you a key to a cottage in the next village. Inside you will find a placenta. You must feed it to the changeling. But take care! Give her only one piece at a time, for she must ingest it slowly. Do not let her gobble. Then wait three days. During this time, you must not sleep. Never let the changeling out of your sight."

I do as the Blue Fairy asks. In my web of lies I convince my husband that I am to take Gideon to an apothecary, many miles away. There he will be treated with the best of care.

Once settled in my new cottage, I find the placenta in a washing tub. It is a noxious thing, a red slab of veins and membranes, quivering like raw liver. I try to feed it to the changeling but she refuses. Instead she sits in the corner, vacuous. She rocks back and forth, makes unintelligible noises. Sometimes, of a sudden, she screams, runs around the room until she exhausts herself. She then collapses and goes to sleep.

Two days pass. I finally persuade her to taste the placenta. Upon the first bite she turns ravenous. She grunts, digs her teeth into the blood strewn organ and chews through sinew and vessels. She stuffs her mouth like a pig in a trough. God's heart! Has the child never before been given a decent meal? Soon she finishes off the entire thing.

The next day I grow weary with exhaustion. Following the warning of the Blue Fairy, I have not slept. The changeling watches me, eyes full of sympathy. Color has bloomed in her cheeks, the shade of a rose.

"Mathilde, you are not well," she says in perfect English. "I will take care of you until you recover."

The next day I feel worse, burning with fever. My skull is a furnace of hot coals. The changeling brings damp cloths and places them on my forehead. "You should sleep, Mathilde," she tells me. She sings a lullaby and my heavy eyelids droop. I cannot fight it and drop into a deep sleep that seems to last years.

When I awake sunlight pours through the windows. The cottage has been polished from floor to ceiling. A young man enters through the doorway. Who is this stranger? I am slow to recognize him, but after a time I spot the mole upon his neck. It is my son Gideon, no other. He is much taller than I remember. Full grown in fact. He chats with the changeling, but I cannot understand all their words.

The next day I am weaker still. The kitchen is a blurred haze, walls reeling around me. Gideon pulls the changeling close, strokes her hair, kisses her lips. Together the two dance a waltz across the floor. How have they gotten so familiar? I try to speak but I cannot find my voice. "We are to be married, mother," Gideon says.

Married. What is married? And what is we? I had known it once, but now my mind deceives me.

The next day I am too tired to think. "Mathilde, will you have breakfast?" the changeling asks. I want to agree but how? The words of agreement escape me.

The changeling tries to comb my hair, props me up in bed. "Come now Mathilde, we must make you presentable." She holds a looking glass to my face. A pale waif with enormous sunken eyes stares back at me. Who is this imp, this simpleton? Surely she has a name, but now it eludes me.

The figure that approaches in the kitchen is tall, a great blur of wings and glitter. Her body is the color of the sky. Once I had known the word for that color.

"Pay a tithe. The price of a changeling. One piece at a time. Do not let her gobble! It takes time to ingest. Had I not warned you?" Mayhap these words have meaning. But no, to me only sounds. Some secret code. Some secret code of the humans? I am not one of them. Not a human. Humans are deceiving! Can't be trusted! But this one, the color of the sky, perhaps she…

"You must take her. Take her now! I'll not have her in this house, sniveling and staring at me all the livelong day, like a pathetic idiot! She will not eat. She will not speak." It is the voice of the changeling.

But what is the changeling? Once I had known. Once I had known many things…

"I am to marry her son. Now be rid of her, Blue Fairy! I'll have no more of your mischief!"

Finally, the winged creature takes me. Her hair flows around me like strands of an ocean wave. The ocean, I believe, was a thing I had once known.

Soon there is nothingness. I cannot. Yet something I hear. I cannot.

"Never underestimate the power of a changeling, Mathilde. They are deceitful. Once they commence feeding upon human energy they often cannot be stopped. It becomes a thing beyond their control. She did not mean to do it, you see. It is an addiction, an insidious urge. At least your son shall have a robust wife. I am sorry Mathilde. I did not intend it to end this way, but your health, your mind and body are irreparable."

Who is Mathilde? Of what does this creature speak? I want to ask but no sound comes from my lips. I am feeble, too feeble to hold up my own head. All is darkness.

* * *

In the room there are three children. One sits, straight backed, a doll of blue porcelain, umbilical cord wrapped around the sparrow bones of her neck. Another, more lifelike, is covered in sweat, bulbous drops pouring over her face, pink with heat. And the third, a boy with no hands nor feet, wiggles the wisps that extend from his wrists and ankles like slithering snakes.

We are here, we four. Incomplete in a limbo of unformed hope. Never, she had said. Never underestimate. The power. But whose?

Together we await the exchange. Somewhere, out in those vast shadows there are healthy humans. Soon, very soon, we changelings will trade places.

What If?
Geoff Le Pard
London, England
Copyright © 2018 by Geoff Le Pard. All rights reserved.
https://geofflepard.com

Jeremy sat back, staring at the final words. *What if?* Nicely ambiguous, he thought as he closed the document and made for the kitchen.

Mel looked up, a frown melting away from her forehead. "Well?"

"Yep, all done. First draft is complete."

She jumped up, hands flapping in a parody of a small girl's excitement. "Woo-hoo. The Booker next."

Jeremy allowed himself a smile. "Perhaps."

"What about the title? Are you sticking with *What If?*"

The smile began to dissolve. "Let's have a drink." As Mel poured two glasses, he added, "I had a great idea yesterday."

"Oh? You ready to share?"

"It's gone. I dreamt it, but when I woke… poof." He shrugged.

She laughed, "Poor lamb."

He nodded, his frown growing deeper. She didn't understand how it grated.

"What does the great author want to do? Champagne bar, or snuggles on the sofa?"

The evening passed quickly. As Mel chatted inconsequentially, his mind drifted back to his story, vivid images forming in his head.

He started as she asked, "You ok?"

"Yes, why?"

"You winced."

His laugh was forced. "Day-dreaming. One of my characters has just been injured. God, sometimes they seem so real."

"What happened? You're all flushed."

"Oh, nothing. It's all make-believe. I'll get us another glass."

Mel stood. "I'll go. You need spoiling."

As soon as she'd left the room, he began pacing. His stomach felt knotted. It had felt real enough, like he'd just had bad news. The scene that had come to him – which originally had involved killing off Arvand, but which he'd changed by allowing the sexy Daleen to save him – had troubled him from the beginning. He'd almost changed it, that afternoon, but the effort had been too much. Maybe he should look at it again.

As he turned for the door, Mel reappeared, holding up a bottle and grinning. "Early night, cowboy?"

Jeremy breathed deeply, feeling calm in the afterglow of sex. He felt Mel roll onto her side, giggling. "You up for having a go at a sequel?"

His body tensed. He wanted to, but the word made him feel nauseous. He stopped her hand as he felt it move. "Too much wine. Maybe tomorrow."

She sighed and rolled away.

He'd told her he'd write a sequel, but just now that felt impossibly hard. She'd think him weak if he didn't, wouldn't she? "You don't mind, do you?"

He heard her yawn, "It's your call," she said.

She had misunderstood him, as he knew she would but he didn't correct her.

Sleep took a long time coming; as he slipped from consciousness, he heard his name being called - a distant cry - in a familiar voice which he couldn't quite place. His dreams were troubled. At one point his eyes sprung open, and he sat bolt upright, his chest heaving, his T-shirt drenched in sweat; he was utterly convinced in that moment he had lost something so dear as to leave him completely bereft. The next thing he remembered Mel was waking him.

"Why did you call out?" Mel peered at him anxiously.

He massaged his jaw, which felt stiff. "Did I?" But he knew.

"You called out *Arvand*. More than once."

"Arvand?" Jeremy shivered convulsively, like a cold finger had run down his spine.

"It was definitely *Arvand*. Is that a place?"

"No idea." He stumbled as he hurried to the bathroom. "I need to get a move on. I promised Martin I'd be in early." Behind the locked door, he fought to suppress a rising sense of guilt. Why lie? It was just the name of a made-up character, though he'd not told her about the change to Arvand from Sebastian.

From the bedroom, Mel called, "Mum rang. She wants to stay. Maybe you can devote a chapter to sending her home quickly."

***

The next two days were hard; he couldn't concentrate and the urge to revisit his draft almost overwhelming. At night his febrile love-making satisfied neither of them. Sleep, too, was difficult, with shapeless dreams that he couldn't recall; all that remained were the wispy remnants of a sense of foreboding, of some impending violence, of people in fear for their lives. The face that stared back at him from the bathroom mirror was gaunt; he needed a break and soon.

On the third evening, Mel was cooking when he arrived home. He'd barely said hello, when she asked, "Someone called Daleen rang for you."

"Daleen?" He could barely stop from shaking.

"You left your mobile." Mel turned, but Jeremy couldn't meet her gaze. "She has the oddest voice, sort of cartoonish sexy, all deep and husky and come-hither. Who is she?"

"I... I don't know any Daleen."

Mel expression hardened. "Well, she knew you. She said she'd catch you at the gym tomorrow."

He knew she was staring, sure she could sense the lie and would assume his silence was just a cover, but what could he say?

184

The only Daleen he knew was dead; he'd taken his character's name from a grave. "Wrong number. Really. What's for dinner?"

He fully intended skipping the gym, but he couldn't. He had just parked and was digging out his sweats, telling himself to relax, when a voice behind him nearly stopped his heart.

"Hey sexy, good to see you."

He spun round, his face ashen as the shocked speaker jumped back. It took him a moment to recognise Maggie, one of the other regulars.

"You ok, Jem? You look dreadful. Have you seen a ghost?" Her frown betrayed her concern at his reaction.

"Why'd you put on that stupid voice?" he snapped. "Geez." He saw her expression begin to change from worry to annoyance. "Look, sorry. You made me jump. I shouldn't have snapped."

"Yes, well. I'm sorry, too." She turned away, clearly hurt.

He pulled back his hand before it touched her arm, growling to himself, "Get a grip, man."

After a ferocious session, Jeremy headed for the changing rooms. The endorphins kicked in, and he felt good for the first time in days. He stopped at the drinking fountain; the cold water was very welcome. His mind drifted, to the scene at the icy lake where Arvand left Daleen for dead. He grinned to himself. He should have let her die, then she'd not be ringing him.

As he straightened up, his attention was caught by a movement outside, by the pool. It took a moment to realise what he was seeing; a woman floated, face down, in the water, her blonde-streaked hair and blue patterned dress spreading out on the surface of the water. He gripped the fountain to stop his legs giving way: Daleen, exactly as he'd described that scene. Bile rose to his throat as he tried and failed to swallow.

He hesitated, his chest tightening, when two things happened. First, a young man leapt into the water, frantically swimming to the inert woman; then, from behind him another man, laughing, pushed past to the window. He rapped on the glass. "Look." The man beckoned two others. "Seb's doing his lifeguard test. I bet he lets her drown."

Jeremy backed away. He shook, his nerves in pieces. Instinct drew him to the Grand and its quiet bar. As the barman pushed the whiskey at him, he said, "You look done in, mate."

Jeremy grimaced as the spirit burned his throat. "I thought I saw someone drown, but it was just an exercise." He forced himself to smile, feeling stupid.

The barman grinned back at him. "That's Daleen, mate..."

Jeremy gawped, and nearly dropped the glass. "What did you say?"

The man jerked his head back, as if slapped. "I just said, 'That's some scene'. Geez." He wandered away, muttering.

Outside, Jeremy breathed deeply. He needed space to clear his head. He was late getting home but Mel wasn't there. No note, no message. He tried calling, suppressing a rising anxiety he knew to be irrational.

When, finally, he heard the front door, he squeezed his eyes shut before going to the hall. He found her sitting on the bottom stair, trying and failing to take off her boots.

She was drunk. His frustration turned to anger. "Where the hell have you been?"

By way of a response, she fumbled with her phone and held it up. A woman with blonde-streaked hair, startlingly turquoise eyes, a mole by the side of her nose and a scar from the corner of her mouth and wearing a blue patterned dress, smiled at the camera. "I've just spent the last two hours with your girlfriend."

Everything slowed. A ringing filled his ears, accompanying an insistent pulsing of blood as he fought to stay upright. "Who?" But he knew who; this was exactly how he'd first described Daleen.

"She called me, needed to talk. How could you?" Mel barely contained her sobs.

"What are you on about? I told you I don't know any Daleen."

Mel shook her head. "Stop lying. You recognised her right away." She snorted a laugh. "Who knew you liked them so tarty? Did you pay for those fake tits? She said you did."

"I didn't..." He stepped back, as if a force-field emanated from the picture and pressed on his chest. "It's not..." And then it

186

hit him and he laughed, starting deep down and coming out with a burst of air. Tears followed, so hard did he laugh. He pointed at the phone, at Mel and shook his head. He could see she looked, at first perplexed, and then furious, but the laughter just kept coming. "Oh Mel," he managed, gulping air in short breaths. "Christ, you had me going. That's what happened in chapter seven. Did you hack my laptop?" She was parroting his own words back at him. He shook his head in order to look serious. "Tell me. Was she wearing grey suede thigh boots? The photo doesn't show her legs."

"You bastard." The fury that had filled Mel's face a moment before was now partly masked by the cascading tears. "She told me you'd spent the afternoon together. Martin said you'd not been back, after the gym."

He felt colour drain from his face. "I went for a drink. And a walk."

Mel's shoulders sagged. "When do you ever just go for a walk?"

"I did today. It…" Sweat beaded his forehead. How could he explain?

"Here." She swiped a second photo. It was him entering the Grand, with the blonde close behind. He hadn't seen her. "She said you made love."

"I just had a frigging drink. This is crazy, a wind up. If it's not you, it's Martin. She's a character in my book…" He petered out as he saw her expression.

"A character in your bloody book? Oh please. And this 'character', when did you get her pregnant?"

"What?"

"She showed me the picture from the scan. You hit her, didn't you? In the stomach. How could you?" She spun away, apparently intent on going upstairs. He grabbed her arm, but she shook him off. "Get off me. Don't come near."

He held up his hands, defensively. "Honestly, love, it must be Martin. He's set this up. You know what he's like."

Mel's voice was harsh. "She described you. How does a 'character' know where you have a two inch scar?"

Jeremy took a step forward, his throat dry. "This has stopped being funny. We need to call Martin. Now."

Mel's eyes blazed. "You son of a bitch. For months you've said you were off to this café or that bar to write that bloody book. 'I need somewhere different,' you said. 'I'll get stale here.' That was your excuse, wasn't it?" She swallowed another sob. "But it was 'us' that was stale. Me. You were just shagging another woman. What a cliché. She knew all the details. I've seen where you hit her, Jeremy. God knows why she's not gone to the police.'

"She's fiction, Mel. Let's have a drink and I'll show you. We'll laugh about this in the morning."

"You're serious, aren't you? God, the nerve." She began to climb the stairs.

"Where are you going?"

"I'll get a bag and go to Mum's. That tells you how desperate this is."

He began to follow, but his head was spinning. How could Daleen be pregnant? He'd toyed with the idea, but eventually left it out, thinking it a neat twist for the sequel. If she was pregnant, then so much else needed changing. After a quick glance upstairs to check Mel wasn't leaving immediately, he rushed to the kitchen and his laptop.

A sound made him turn. Mel leant against the doorframe. "Our lives are falling apart and you're what? Writing?"

He didn't look up. "I didn't make her pregnant. That was Arvand's idea and I scotched it."

"Arvand? Isn't that the name you called out the other day? The one you said you didn't know? Who's Arvand?"

He glared at her. "Just a bloody character. Come here and I'll show you." He typed *pregnant* into the 'find' box. The response was seven hits. The first was on page 159: *Daleen knew what the sickness meant; she was pregnant. Her stupid fumble with Arvand had had consequences after all.*

Jeremy blinked. That wasn't how it happened. He clicked through the links. That wasn't why Arvand attacked her. It ruined the ending, it no longer made sense. He rolled the tension out of his shoulders and pulled a pad to him. As he did so the front door slammed shut.

"Shit." He ran to the window, just in time to see Mel reverse out of the drive and speed away.

He needed to talk to her, but first he needed to find out what had happened to his book. Only that way would he make sense of this nightmare. He returned to the table, surprised at how numb he felt.

His phone rang and instantly a weight felt as if it lifted off his shoulders; smiling he reached for the handset. "Hi Mel, I'm really…"

A male voice cut across him. "This isn't Mel, Jeremy."

His throat began to constrict as, with his hand shaking he looked at the screen. The phone clattered onto the table as he screamed. It fell face up and he goggled at the caller's name:

Arvand

It couldn't be. He, too, was a name from a grave. He didn't know any Arvand, so how could he have that name saved in his contacts? How could he be calling?

Swallowing hard, he picked up the phone. "Yes?"

The voice felt so familiar, one he had heard during his recent dreams, one he felt he had been hearing for years, a smooth voice with a slight lisp. "What are you doing, Jeremy?"

"I'm correcting the draft."

"We've told you before. That's not your job."

"I know this is really you, Martin. It's all very clever, but don't you think you've taken it far enough?" Jeremy felt something slip inside his head, wanting Martin to reveal himself and fearing for his sanity if he didn't.

"You know this isn't Martin, don't you, Jeremy?" Whoever it was didn't wait for an answer. "If you don't believe me, then have a look at what you changed just now."

Jeremy scrolled back up the page to where he had hastily deleted the first reference to Daleen's pregnancy. It had gone, the previous version restored. "How did you do that, Martin?"

"We explained how we wanted our story to come out. That's your job. Your only job."

Jeremy pulled his shoulders back. "That's enough. This has to stop now." He softened his voice; Martin loved his jokes. "Come on, mate. Why don't you pop round? We can run through the manuscript and tailor it so it's just how you want it."

"We're already here. Outside."

Jeremy wiped his hands on his trousers before reaching across his desk. He yanked back the left curtain. Looking up at his window, Arvand held the phone while Daleen cradled her stomach. Jeremy no longer felt connected to the scene in front of him. How had Martin managed to find two people to so accurately match his characters?

Then his blood turned to ice as Arvand's voice sounded in his ear. "We need to talk about the ending, Jeremy. It's time to let us in."

Jeremy gagged, a globule of greeny phlegm splattering the screen. His heart raced, beating so hard he wondered if anyone's heart had ever broken a rib. "I'm not letting you anywhere near this. It's my book and…"

As Jeremy watched, Arvand bent down and opened a bag by his feet. He knew exactly what he'd see: a short-handled axe. Enough. He needed to end this.

"What do you want?"

"What if you let us in and we'll tell you?"

What if? "What if I don't?"

"But that's not how *what ifs* work, is it? Not in a novel. You can't leave them unresolved. The readers will never forgive you for that. There always has to be a conclusion. You have to see this through."

Jeremy put the phone down and stared at the screen. He clicked on *Select All*. He just had to hit *delete* and this would be over. The sounds of wood splintering filled the air, accompanied by someone calling his name. As his finger brushed the key, something cold pressed against his throat.

A woman's hand, sporting a large emerald ring stretched past his shoulder and softly closed the laptop. A voice – husky, sexy and full of a mix of promise and foreboding that froze his blood, while it melted his heart – whispered next to his ear. "Oh darling, you couldn't do that to me, could you? After all, we've been through."

Jeremy forced himself to speak, tears squeezing out of his eyes. "What do you want?"

The man spoke next to his other ear. "Time to plot that sequel, don't you think?"

Swimming
Frank Parker
County Laois, Ireland
Copyright © 2018 by Frank Parker. All rights reserved.
https://franklparker.com

George bounces the old tennis ball on the sun-baked earth. Joining the line of boys waiting their turn to bowl at whoever is in batting position, he sees his friend Paul. There are two boys standing between them in the line. He speaks across them.

"Hey Paul. Are you coming swimming with us later?"

"I guess so."

Paul has not learned to swim properly yet. He hopes George won't hear the reluctance in his voice.

"You will be okay. Mr. Lewis is coming with us."

The sports teacher is an excellent swimmer and all the boys in Paul and George's class look up to him. With him in charge, the afternoon's swimming session at the lake will be fun for most of the boys. Paul is not so sure.

The line moves forward. One of the boys between Paul and George says, "Better make the most of this session. They're building a new accommodation block here after the summer hols. There won't be any 'bowling up' next summer."

'Bowling up' is a summer tradition in the school. Loosely based on the English game of cricket, it involves one boy taking the role of batsman, facing bowling from a series of other boys. No 'runs' are scored but the batsman remains in place until got 'out' by a bowler whose ball bypasses the bat and hits the 'wicket' – actually an old wire mesh waste basket. That bowler then takes up the role of batsman. The batsman 'out' now joins the line of waiting bowlers.

A handful of boys, neither of whom possesses an old tennis ball, wait on the fringes of the game hoping for an opportunity to catch a high ball. This will also result in the batsman being 'out' to be replaced by the successful bowler. The catcher will be permitted to keep the ball whilst its owner is batting.

"It's hard to imagine a new building on this plot," the boy in front of Paul says.

"You could if you had a time machine." Paul has been reading H.G.Wells and likes the futuristic ideas contained in some of his short stories.

"What, like that cartoon in the newspaper, '4-D Jones'? Preventing disasters by going back in time to stop a train before it hits a car on a level crossing and stuff?"

"You could take a tour of the new building and see yourself in a year or two from now."

"Might find out if you ever learned to swim," scoffs an older boy just before taking his run-up to bowl at the batsman.

Paul's face grows hot. "I'll learn this afternoon, just you see," he says to no-one in particular. It's his turn to bowl but the original batsman is out, beaten by a turning ball from the scoffer who now stands facing Paul, a big fat grin on his face.

Paul rubs the ball on his trouser leg. Unlike a cricket ball, you can't polish a tennis ball to improve its flight, but the gesture is one he has seen real cricketers make and he hopes it will intimidate the batsman.

He turns to walk away from the batsman, extending his run-up. Another ploy designed to worry his opponent. He does not turn to face the batsman until he reaches some rough ground at the edge of the plot. As he turns, his foot catches in a tree root and he stumbles and falls.

******

The first thing he notices is the smell of fresh paint. There is a lot of it on the walls and doors of the new building. Bright white on the doors and flat pale green on the walls. He is in one of the dormitories. Much smaller than the one he normally occupies, it has only four beds. They have wooden head boards like the ones at home, not the iron ones in the school dormitory.

He is not standing in the room. It's as though he is floating somewhere near the ceiling. The door is slightly ajar and outside in the corridor two people he cannot see are holding a conversation.

"I see the new swimming pool is very popular." Paul recognises Mr Lewis's voice with its Welsh accent.

"Yes. We had to do something after that tragedy two summer ago."

"You know I did my best, but he was under for too long. I administered CPR until the paramedics arrived, but it was hopeless."

"It must have been terrible for you. We all feel your pain. And the poor parents." He pauses, places a consoling hand on his colleague's shoulder. "The boy had such talent. Who knows where he might have ended up."

"Are the parents coming to the opening ceremony for the new pool?"

"I had a letter just this morning. They are pleased that the tragedy that took him from them will never happen to another boy in the school."

******

"Are you okay? You took quite a tumble."

Paul struggles to his feet. His ankle feels as though it is being stabbed by hot knives. He leans on George.

"Come on, let's get you to the first aid room. Get something done about that ankle. I guess you will not be coming swimming this afternoon after all."

Paul's ankle heals rapidly and two weeks after his tumble Mr Lewis announces another swimming party. "It's okay, if you don't feel like swimming, you don't have to," he tells Paul. "You can sit on the bank and just watch."

The party is small. Mr Lewis likes it that way. It's hard enough keeping his eye on six boys. Any more and he might not notice if one got into trouble. He's glad that Paul is content to watch the other five.

"No horse play, now." he admonishes as George jumps on the back of another boy causing him to inhale water and push

George in retaliation. George turns and swims quickly away using powerful strokes.

The other three appear to be well behaved. One has brought a snorkel, flippers and a face mask. He is swimming face down, the flippers churning water. After a while he stands and waddles towards the bank, the flippers making it awkward to wade.

"Give us a go," a tall blond boy pleads.

"No sharing of equipment," insists Mr Lewis. "You need to be taught how to use it safely."

Paul turns away from the argument and looks towards where he last saw George. The boy with whom George had been fighting is swimming back to join the rest of the party, but there is no sign of George. A strong swimmer, he is probably out of sight beyond a small promontory containing a willow whose lower branches caress the surface of the lake.

Paul stands and walks towards the promontory in an effort to see where his friend has gone. His ankle still hurts when he puts weight on it. There is still no sign of George.

"Sir, sir. It's George, sir."

"What about him?"

"I can't see him, sir."

"Right, you lot, out of the water, now. Where did you last see him, Paul?"

"After you told him off for wrestling with Sam, sir. He swam off in that direction." Paul points to the promontory.

"Okay. Wait here – no good you trying to run with that ankle. Billy, run to the phone box and call 999. Sam, grab that life belt and come with me." He sets off, running towards the promontory, Sam following with the life belt. Paul hobbles after them. Every jab of pain in his ankle reminds him of the dream he had the afternoon of the injury.

The Call
Juliet Nubel
France
Copyright © 2018 by Juliet Nubel. All rights reserved.
omgimfifty.com

They sat on each side of her pink princess bed. Sue stroked her daughter's sticky, tousled, blond head, watching intently as her beautiful rosebud mouth moved, making a series of strange, loud sounds – 'Ant, ant, ant.' Always the same noises, almost every night for the last six months.

'It's getting worse, Sue. It's much louder and she seems really perturbed now.' He took Emily's tiny hand, his brow creased deep with concern.

Short, quick gulps replaced his daughter's calm breathing.

'Ant, can you hear me? Ant, are you there?' This was no longer their little girl speaking. Antony's eyes flashed in recognition. Only one person had ever called him by this childish nickname.

'I'm here,' he replied gently. 'What's wrong?'

'You need to tell your dad that I hid it. It's in a nylon stocking taped to the back of the top drawer in my dresser. He must find it before he signs the papers for the house and all the furniture tomorrow. It's for Sue. He must give it to Sue. I can't get through to him, Ant. Call him now, please.' The voice faded to a low hum, and Emily returned to a deep, dreamless sleep.

'Mum, are you still there? Mum, I miss you so much!' Anthony bent over the pink and white checkered quilt and wept silent tears of pure, undistilled grief.

As Sue looked over at her husband, he lifted his head, slowly wiped away the tears, then dialed his father's number.

'Dad, sorry to wake you. I know where to look for Mum's diamond ring…'

La Garconniere
Excerpt, "Last Dance at the Blue Moon"
Bonnie Lyons
New Iberia, LA, USA
Copyright © 2018 by Bonnie Lyons. All rights reserved.
bonnielyons1@cox.net

Cora was the girl of the family, with all of the insignificance that the status can entail. She may not have been the heir to the family's extensive bookie business, but she was their keeper of numbers, their scribbler of long, precise columns.

Tonight she sat at her desk in the halo of an old banker's lamp, going through figures in a book that tracked bets, odds, debits and credits for a long list of customers of vague reference. With one final snap, she closed the book to reveal a tattered cover that read *The Adventures of Dick and Jane.*

In her flowered housecoat, fluffy, pink slippers, rollers in her hair, Cora shuffled quickly to the kitchen table to present her work to her father. This was one of two sets of books. One was contained in a conventional ledger, prepared for the potential inspection of the rare affiliate of consequence. The *Adventures* ledger was for her father's eyes alone.

"You're going to be late," Gloria Hulin warned Cora. "Eddie, please tell your daughter it can wait. It's Saturday night and Cora has a date for God's sake. Collections are not till Monday."

"Aww, she's just doing her job, Glo. Bobby Chauvin ain't going away for Christ's sake."

To her father, Cora was simply recording symbols, as a parrot mimics sounds, or a chimp apes its master. Good marks

197

were no more than a daughter's duty in Eddie Hulin's mind, but with little effort, Cora had finished third in her class and first in the science of sums. The significance of the figures and the two sets of books had not escaped her.

Cora's exasperated mother slipped an arm around her daughter and ushered her out of their kitchen and her father's reach. Gloria bit back what she had wanted to say to her husband, which was that young men were not so easy to come by during times of war. But that would have been cruel.

Eddie had not been the same man since the loss of their oldest in the fighting in North Africa. None of them had, but Walter's death had left a shell of a man, where Eddie had once resided.

*****

Two weeks earlier, the two women had been making dinner when the problem of Cora's love life got her mother's attention.

Regardless of her own misery, Gloria had been making a concerted effort to lead her family back to a normal existence after the loss of their oldest. Even though her heart wasn't fully into it, she knew she could not sacrifice her living daughter at the altar of her dead son.

"So, honey, how is it going with you and that Chauvin boy? Has he asked you out yet?"

From her place at the counter, where she was chopping onions, Cora grinned awkwardly. "Well, maybe. Does it count if they ask you if you'd like to see a movie and then say, 'I'll see you there?'"

Gloria laughed. "Well, in my limited experience," she said, "it's probably one of three things. One, he's shy; two, he's broke; or three, he's trying to leave his options open. Men are like that. Heroes in war, but cowards in love."

They shared a moment of light laughter, despite the reference that hit so close to their hearts. "The fact is," said Cora, "there's not much to choose from with the war on. I'll tell you the truth, Momma. It's downright depressing. Bea and I were walking over by her house the other day and saw some of those German boys on the back of an Army truck. They sure were cute …."

198

The sugar cane farms that populated their area had been crippled with labor shortages with most of their local boys off fighting. A prisoner of war camp housing mostly German soldiers had become a source of salvation and of worry for the community.

Cora's mother abruptly slammed down the knife she was using, strode over to her daughter, grabbing her roughly by the shoulders and shaking her to achieve her full attention. The look of alarm on her face was startling. "Cora Ann, are you out of your mind? Do you have any idea what your father would do to you if he caught you so much as looking sideways at one of those people? Why, there wouldn't be nothing left of either of you to scrape off the sidewalk!"

The exchange frightened both of them and Gloria took a breath, lowered her voice and released her daughter, but the urgency was still in her voice.

She was trembling now when the words came out. "Cora, how could you even think such a thing after what they did to your brother?"

Cora stepped away from her mother and looked down. "I know, Momma, I know. But I'm so tired of it all. The war. The sadness. The anger. Momma, I'm eighteen! I just want to go on with life."

A tear trickled from Gloria's blue eyes. "I know, Cora. Believe it or not, I know what it is to be young and to have everything in front of you. But swear to me, Cora! Swear to me that you will never let your father hear you say or do anything like that! I couldn't take it! I swear. I couldn't!"

Cora saw that her mother was on the verge of hysteria and she pulled her into her arms and held her, briefly exchanging roles.

"It's okay, momma. I won't. I promise, I won't. But momma, promise me something. We can't let Daddy do anything crazy."

*****

On the evening that was supposed to have been the last in her young life, Cora finally had that date with the boy who had been dropping hints for months. It was late when Bobby crunched his father's Ford on the long, gravel drive to the Hulin carport. The lone light that was typically left on until all family members were

199

home was not. Probably burned out was the thought that ran through Cora's mind. It was a good thing, since it was later than she had anticipated.

"That was fun, Cora. Next weekend *Sahara* is playing. Interested?"

War films were not of particular interest to Cora, but she didn't tell that to Bobby. "Sure," she answered with a bright smile, moving closer and waiting for Bobby to make his move.

But Bobby was careful. He knew all about Eddie Hulin and about the rumors that he was 'connected'. With a respectful kiss and handshake, Bobby saw Cora to her parent's door and bade her a good evening. He had no idea how bad it could be.

*****

Cora slipped her key into the side door and turned. The door squeaked open, as it always did, and she slipped through it as quickly as possible and stepped into the living room. She was out past her curfew, and so she stepped quietly over the creaky hardwood floors, testing for the best spots to step to avoid detection.

Then she realized there was something different. She couldn't quite put her finger on it, but her senses sharpened, in response. She felt a frisson run up into her hairline and stopped breathing, listening.

Her parents would be home, but should be in bed asleep at this hour. Normally, she would hear her father's loud snores cutting through the house, but there was none of that. Instead, from the back of the house, she heard what sounded like soft murmuring. Were her parents awake, waiting for her?

The sounds seemed solemn, as a priest in a confessional and strangely palliative, as a blessing bestowed on a penitent.

Cora began to inch quietly in the direction of the sound and was almost through the living room, aiming for the hallway on the other side of the kitchen when a sharp crack split the night open. She froze, in shock.

The first crack was followed quickly by a second, and then by her father bursting into the room and crashing into her, screaming frantically "Run, Cora! Run!" All color was gone from him and he pushed her back toward the door before the face appeared behind him.

It was a face, she'd seen before, more than once. It was a cliché of a face; one you would expect to see on a 'Most Wanted' sign in the post office. It was looming and closing in on her father with dead, black eyes, a heavy brow and a handlebar mustache, trimmed with a fringe of yesterday's growth. It was scruffy, with thick, dirty blond hair. It was unmistakable.

She saw her father turn to meet the man and she heard the scuffle behind her before she tore through the side door and fled on legs that pulsed with their desire to survive the night. In wild flight, she reached the edge of her father's property and was heading across a long pasture for the Crochet home when she heard the third crack and thought her legs would buckle beneath her.

In an instant, she measured the costs of knocking on the neighbors' door, waiting for the answer and the killer. Who would win the race? What payment would she impose on the Crochets for her rescue? Would it be a wasted effort, costing all their lives and her soul? She heaved, gasping for breath, wanting to turn around to spot her pursuer; afraid the motion would slow her.

She shot up the steps to the Crochet's front porch, her heart pounding in rhythm to the pounding of her feet. Impulsively, she chose the outdoor stairs leading to the deserted garconniere, once used as a boys' loft for the old, Acadian style house.

The door screeched unbearably, as she tried to slip through undetected and shut out the intruder. Cora fumbled desperately with the knob, unable to remember if there was a lock. Finding none, she slipped to the floor, leaning back on the door, terror crowding any reasonable thoughts from her brain.

Inside, the four corners of the room were dark, deeper in their blackness for the two shafts of grey light that protruded in from a pair of windows on either end of the gabled roof.

On hands and knees, she crawled as quietly as possible to the window that opened to the side of her parents' home, crouching down to hide herself beneath the windows ledge. Though her movements were quiet, her breath was ragged and wheezing and she felt it must be audible from outside. She sat at the window for a moment trying to bring it under control.

Then, very cautiously, she inched up and peered over the window ledge into the pasture that separated the two houses. A waning moon illuminated the open pasture and the dark figure following the trail she had left in the high grass toward her hiding place. He walked a bit tentatively, as though scenting her and he led with one hand pointed before him.

With morbid fascination, she watched him cross the pasture and approach the house. He started to make his way to the side of the house, working his way through bushes, running his hands through them. She saw him crawl under the raised porch and disappear briefly, before emerging a bit further down. While he made his way around the back of the house, she crawled with infinite care to the other window ready to pick up his image on the other side.

When he had almost reached the front of the house, he stopped. She watched his stout, muscular frame, as he turned, searching, hunting and she remembered the visits he had made to her house.

*****

"Eddie!" Gloria called to the back of the house. "Someone here to see you!"

Cora was working on a history assignment at the kitchen table that opened to the living room and the front door. Her father didn't introduce the man, but that wasn't odd. Many of his customers would just as soon remain unnoticed and unidentified at the Hulin home.

Eddie ushered the man outside, where they talked in animated fashion. Bored with her homework, Cora watched their heads bob and hands fly. She heard the occasional word or phrase from her chair near a window. "… New Orleans… Carolla … out of time… doing my job". The visit was brief, but her father had been brusque and agitated when the man left.

It was not unusual for Eddie Hulin to have such conversations with visitors to their home, but he was normally the aggressor in those conversations. This one had been different.

The second visit was quieter, subtler, more solemn. And when it was over, her father had taken a pint of whiskey from a kitchen cabinet and left the house abruptly.

*****

Now this nameless face was moving again and worked its way around to the front of the house and out of her line of sight. She moved quietly back into the darkness.

Then she heard it, a slow, heavy creak and then another, a pause and then another. She held her breath, feeling his presence making its way up the stairs. Her heart sent its pulse in audible beats through her brain and flipped her stomach, like the victim of a dropping roller coaster. By rote, she found herself saying a *Hail Mary,* trying to focus on the words.

"… Holy Mary, Mother of God, pray for us sinners, now and at the hour of our death … " But she was only able to listen to his approach.

She had closed her eyes, but swore she could feel when the light came on beneath her. It was followed by the distinct double clicking of a cartridge being sent into the chamber of a shotgun and then a booming voice cut through the night, sounding to her like God. "Who's there?" demanded the voice. A pause. Silence. Then, "I got a gun and you can bet I plan to use it!"

The standoff was broken by the quick hammering of feet, dashing down the stairs. Cora expelled a great breath of air, as her family's killer dashed away and back in the direction of her home. For good measure, Mr. Crochet flung open the front door and sent a series of shots into the night.

Cora began to shake and sob uncontrollably. She realized she was sitting in a wet pool of her own making, but seemed incapable of moving from it. When the Crochets searched their property to make sure it was secure, they found her that way.

Through her paralyzing fear, there was only one thing she knew for certain. She was the only witness to her family's murder. And there was only one place she felt secure; in the arms of those who had delivered her. It seemed incongruous, but the Crochets honored her request. She was sheltered quietly in their home until she recovered in mind and body sufficiently to face a world that had been split into pieces.

Lucifer's Revenge
Christine Valentor
Chicago, Illinois, USA
Copyright © 2018 by Christine Valentor. All rights reserved.
https://witchlike.wordpress.com/

I first met the Devil in a pub called the Boar's Head on Old Cork road. The night, as I recall, was All Hallows Eve. Having spent my last farthing on ale, I tried to barter the barkeep for one last drink. My mouth watered, but he refused me. "Go on home boy," he ordered. "Get you a good night's sleep. Come the morrow all the world will be brighter."

He was wrong. My world was darkness. I had no intention of retreating home to my bare and filthy hovel where paint peeled off the walls, rats basked in the waste bins and I had drained every ounce of my whiskey bottles dry. I knew not where I'd wander, yet the barkeep bid me leave. And so, it was to my great fortune that before exiting through the pub's swinging doors I encountered Lucifer himself.

There he stood, hands crossed at his chest, a blithe smile on his face. He was a hideous creature, with pocked, patchy skin not unlike a reptile. His thick brows knitted above ominous eyes and his chin was so pointy it could be used as a weapon. Yet he was oddly graceful, a strange dignity about him. I'd read my primers, knew he was a dangerous man, yet there was something appealing in him. I felt no fear.

"Your days are numbered, Jack," he told me. "A life of thieving, gambling, drinking and whoring. What have you to show for yourself? Well now! It seems your time has expired, and I've come to take you to the iron gates."

The Devil. He may think himself wise, but I, Sneaky Jack Skrumpington, was much wiser!

"You don't look like the Devil to me," I challenged. "If you are true, then prove it. You surely must possess the powers of a metaphysician or mage. Change yourself into a shilling!" One shilling, I reasoned, would buy me a fresh pitcher of ale.

Lucifer scowled. He laughed at my challenge, and yet, he could not resist a good dare. In an instant he transformed himself into a shiny silver coin which I did not hesitate to snatch. I quickly hid it in my pocket, right next to the cross of my rosary. These were prayer beads I carried with me always, though I was lack to utter even one Hail Mary.

Everyone knows the Devil cannot abide a cross. He was thus under my spell. Yet I was not entirely unmerciful. I made a bargain with him. In exchange for his freedom he would give me the sum of one million ducats and another ten years to live upon this earth. He agreed to my bargain. After all, he had no choice.

During my next ten years I lived a life of decadence, sparing no expense. I dined at the finest of inns, drank wine from crystal goblets, slept in silken sheets upon feathered beds. Beautiful women, those that could be bought, accompanied me at every turn. I constantly indulged my great passion of gambling, cheating mercilessly and winning every time. I cared not a fig for those I left in debt. The money I acquired could not be spent in a lifetime.

Finally, it all came to an end.

It was upon All Hallows Eve, ten years later when the Devil returned to claim my soul. He found me sprawled beneath an apple tree, sleeping off a long drunk.

"Skrumpington!" he barked. "Your time has expired." His lips formed a wide smile, green teeth reflecting the light of the moon. Although he attempted his best of horrifying theatrics, commanding streaks of lightning across the sky and claps of thunder, he did not scare me. I knew better.

"Lucifer," I pleaded, kneeling before him. "Can you not give a damned man one last request? Do it! Do it, so you prove yourself a creature of mercy, not the evil demon they paint you to be! Do it, so you prove yourself a being of justice, not the slithering snake they claim. Forget not, dear Lucifer, you were once a son of light!"

He stared at me. This remark had struck a chord within him. I moved my face close to his. "Aye," I whispered in his hairy ear. "Once there was a time when you sat at the right hand of the Father. You were his favorite, were you not? The brightest star in all the heavens, Luz the light. Oh, but that was long before your great sin of pride, wasn't it?" I murmured seductively, my voice a mesmerizing chant. "You banished yourself from the heavens, fell from grace into your own lonely cavern of hell. Surely you remember?"

I stroked his neck, moved my hand across the small of his back. He quivered at my touch. "Show me now that you have not lost all your goodness," I urged. "Grant me but one last request." I moved my lips to his cheek, kissed him gently and tasted the salt of a single tear that fell from his crusty eye.

He nodded, for even the Devil had some shred of decency. Besides, he knew that my soul, once pacified and docile, would be much more useful to him. He clutched my hand. "What then would you have from me, Jack Skrumpington?" he asked.

"Only a simple apple," I answered. "Ripe and sweet, picked from this very tree." I pointed to the top bough, heavy with fruit.

Lucifer nodded and like a lizard he shimmied up the bark, entrenching himself between the branches. He reached up to pick the largest, reddest apple the tree bore.

I wasted no time! In one instant I pulled my knife from its scabbard. Quickly I carved a cross in the trunk of the tree. Lucifer's eyes widened in terror. He was now stuck on the branch of the tree, unable to descend, for everyone knows the Devil can never approach a cross.

I grinned up at him. He spat down on me. "Skrumpington," he hissed. "You have deceived me again!"

"I will release you," I said. "If you make me but one single promise."

His body writhed and wriggled, now blending into the wood of the tree. He wheezed, struggling to breathe as the tree's tentacles closed in around him. His eyes were frightened, pupils lost in a sea of white iris. A knot in the tree bark swallowed him whole, then spat him out again and he hung like a folded fish on the branch.

"Very well Skrumpington!" he gasped. "What bid you this time?"

"This time…" I sighed a sigh of deep satisfaction, strolled grandly in a circle, my eyes fixed upon him. "This time you shall agree to never take my immortal soul, regardless of whatsoever evil deeds I may perform."

He nodded slowly, for even the bold Lucifer knew he had no other choice.

"Swear it!" I commanded.

"I swear it. Jack Skrumpington, I will never take your immortal soul."

He was a defeated thing, weak and gray, his body now sliding like a stretched lump of clay. I almost felt sorry for him. Almost.

For what remained of my life I continued my ways of debauchery, drinking and whoring myself into an inevitable grave. I was a liar, a user and a sycophant. I frequented gambling dens and houses of ill repute. I lived only for myself and my own gain. It would later be said of me "Jack Scrumpington never once performed a selfless act, nor did any kindness toward his fellow man."

Yet time waits for no one and even I was not immune. My body grew old. My back bent, my bones ached with arthritis. Finally, my unbridled exploits caught up with me and the syphilis pox set in. My hands shook. My walk became a staggered, struggling gait. Warts the size of marbles sprouted within every crevice and fold of my skin. My liver became diseased, bloated with cirrhosis, swollen from years of hard liquor. Yellow jaundice enmeshed my flesh. Death, when it finally came, was a mercy.

I then found myself at the pearly gates, tended faithfully by Saint Peter.

The Saint shuffled his feet, looked at me and shook his head. "I cannot take you, Jack," he said sadly, "for never in your life have you performed a single selfless act. Not once have you done any kindness toward your fellow man." Peter leafed through his book of souls, double checking as if there might be a chance he would still find my name. But no. He closed the book and shrugged. "Not once." He caught my eye with a look of genuine sympathy as he locked the white pearl of the deadbolt. "Sorry Jack. You are not welcome here."

The wind gusted. I felt a chill up my spine. Winter was coming, and it would be a long, merciless one. Ice formed on the pavement beneath me. I wore only the sack cloth I had been buried in. My teeth chattered.

What to do? What to do? I'd go to the Devil! Of course I would! At the very least, it should be warm in hell. True, it would be an eternity of misery, the lake of fire, but I'd embrace it, punishment for the damage I'd done in my waking life.

Lucifer peered through the gray mist that surrounded his iron gate. Upon recognizing me, he furrowed his brow and shook his head. "Oh no," he said. "I've no want for you here, Jack Scrumpington! I promised I'd never take your immortal soul and I'll NOT take it. A promise is a promise." He clasped his hands together, long hairy fingers and black talons fidgeting. He bowed his head. "I may be a lot of unsavory things; a deceiver and an arrogant fool. But Lucifer Luz is a man of his word!" He stomped a foot and pounded his own chest.

Not fit for heaven, not welcome in hell. I was the lowest of souls, left to wander on the brink of nothingness. I turned away from Lucifer's gate. The thick mist clouded my eyes. I stumbled like a blind man. The night was black as pitch. In the impossible darkness I could see nothing, not one outline, not one shadow.

Just then I felt Lucifer's warm touch upon my shoulder.

"You'll need something to light your way," he said, not unkindly. He then handed me a pumpkin. It had been hollowed through the middle, scraped of seeds and pulp. A lone candle burned within it, blackening the inside rind. The smell was rich and sweet.

"Take this lantern, Jack," the Devil said. "May it guide you through the darkness." He then handed me a knife. "You might want to carve some designs in it. Perhaps a circle, to allow extra light from the candle."

It was an act of unmerited kindness, considering what I'd done to him.

In that moment I felt guilt for the first time. I was sorry I had treated him so badly. For the first time I realized my hateful acts, my vanity, my many sins.

But alas, by then it was too late.

With Lucifer's knife I carved a face in the pumpkin; triangular eyes, a nose, even a smiling mouth with one lone tooth. The face, you see, was all the companionship I would ever have.

From that day on I was left to wander through the land of spirit. I am usually unseen but sometimes, upon All Hallows Eve you might find me. It is then the veils are lifted, and humankind may enter the realm of the other-worlds. Look for me in your alleyways, in your dark streets that spill with costumed trick-or-treaters, those innocents who try so precisely to resemble us ghouls. I am the ghostly figure who carries a lone pumpkin of candlelight to brighten my sad path.

They call me Jack of the Lantern.

The Nightmare
Lori Micken
Copyright © 2018 by Lori Micken. All rights reserved.

The dream's horror is still fresh in my mind. It seems as real as when it first awakened me: clear, chilling, and indelible. I'm driving north of Cut Bank, Montana, only a few miles from the Canadian border. The two-lane road shoots narrow and straight, roller-coaster style over ancient glacial moraines and drift. There is a tall projection of wind-worn sandstone called Headlight Butte up there, close to the road. It can be seen for 10 miles or more from all directions. It's been a landmark and guide for the traveler, no doubt for centuries: a natural beacon on this undulating landscape.

In the dream it is dark, and there is no traffic. As in all tales of terror, it is midnight. I drive within the 55 miles per hour speed limit. There is no moon, so the blackness is palpable. I'm at Headlight Butte. There is, as I top the hill, a glimpse of a shuffling form at roadside, a person in dark clothes. The impact is soft, considering the speed of the car. I stop, back up, and scramble out. The smell of spring confronts me: moist earth, ozone from the afternoon rain, and a few wildflower odors. Fear glues my tongue to the roof of my mouth. My headlights show a dead man lying where he rolled into the barrow pit. He is dark-haired, bearded, dressed poorly, entirely in black. His worn pants, shirt, and overcoat are heavy wool, his shoes old-fashioned, high topped, laced. His eyes are closed. Nothing stirs or makes a sound in the blackness except the moths and other insects attracted to the headlights. I realize I must bury him, so no one will find out. The field just beyond the barbwire fence is fresh-plowed. It had been

210

pastureland within all of my memory, and probably since the glaciers retreated 15,000 years ago.

Turning the car so the lights beam across the fence and field, I get a shovel out of the car's trunk, drag the man under the wire, and frantically dig a shallow grave in the newly turned land. I lay him face down. The light wavers and flickers from the flitting insects. I imagine this is what it would be like in a cave with bats fluttering about. My shadow bends and lifts with me as I fill the grave. My pulse beats in my ears. Although the night is cool, sweat trickles off my temples, back, and underarms. Still, there are no cars. I am alone now. He is covered. The stars that witness don't care. A bum, a tramp, trying to trudge across the Canadian line at night to avoid customs. Maybe he couldn't thumb a ride; maybe he had escaped from prison or the mental hospital at Warm Springs and didn't want a lift. No one will miss him; no one will care or search. I won't be found out! My breath is so shallow I'm suffocating.

That lack of oxygen wakened me. I started gulping air, then cried, and shook. My hands were clean. I was in my own bed, shuddering at the strange twisting convolutions of my brain

and wondering at my warped alter ego, mostly hidden, but sometimes released to stalk like a Norse troll in deep sleep times.

Dreams seldom bother me, most aren't remembered very clearly, but this one replayed several times that day. So much, that the next night the dream returned; only now it is daylight on the same road. The grasses are that magical spring green. Crops are coming up; the fallow fields contrast brown between the strips of new wheat or barley or oats. The smell of the earth, the wildflowers, the impounded water in glacial pothole ponds fill my senses. As I pass Headlight Butte in the dream, I slow, to look for clothes, or any sign that the other dream really happened. My heart skips, and I start shaking. A rancher is on his tractor, disking the plowed field, heading directly for the makeshift grave. I panic. Should I try to turn or stop him? What if he hits the body? His tractor passes by, followed by the discs, but he looks back and stops. The machine is dragging something black. I awoke, nearly paralyzed with fear, weeping, so weak I couldn't sit up. The rest of the night sleep was not an option for fear the dream would continue. Dawn brought some sensibility back. I couldn't let the rats and cobwebs of my brain destroy my favorite season.

I decided to go for a drive, enjoying the meadowlark songs floating in snatches through the open car window, marveling at the renewal of life, the warmth, the joy of being alive. A power like a magnet drew me north. It wouldn't hurt to drive out to Headlight Butte, maybe even climb it. My mother and uncles had cut their names in the soft grey stone fifty-some years ago. It would be fun to try to find those inscriptions again and take some pictures. The view is forever up there.

I let up on the gas to find a turnout on the crest of the moraine, jammed on the brakes and stopped in the middle of the road. I felt as though the glacier had returned, grinding, chilling, and destroying me. A rancher was disking his fallow field. He had stopped his tractor and walked back to check out the black thing dragged up on the far side of the disks.

Who Am I?
Chuck Jackson
Boynton Beach, FL. USA
Copyright © 2018 by Chuck Jackson. All rights reserved.
https://chuckjacksonknowme.com/

When you look fifteen and have the knowledge and experience of a man who has lived a century, life should be perfect. Why do I still grope through everyday life wondering what to do? All I want is for people to like me, but they call me a freak. *What's wrong with me?*

When I look at my naked image, it is of someone I should know, but he looks foreign in my eyes. He looks young and somewhat feminine. The blonde curly hair is to the shoulders, soft, and wispy to the breeze flowing from the open window. The hands are delicate and soft. Skin white as china only marked by the indigo veins running towards the pink nails.

As are the hands, the face is delicate in features, with soft arching eyebrows. A gentle sloping nose is upturning at the narrowed nostrils. The eyes crystal blue as a summer sky, look back at me pleading.

I'm mesmerized by the reflected person. Females would seek such beauty, yet this is definitely a male. No whiskers are visible only sparse fuzz almost invisible in this light. *Who is this person?*

I'm startled, finding someone has laid out clothes for me to wear. I slip on white jeans of a soft stretchy material. They are tight and revealing. The shirt is a bright ruby color of silk material. It opens at the neck with three buttons and when pulled over my head; the length ends at my hips. The sleeves are bell shaped and buttoned tight at the wrist. The jeans look modern, but the shirt is not of this century.

Even when the room appears foreign to my eyes, I don't falter in my movement. I walk out of the bedroom, across a living room, and I find the front door. *Is this Déjà vu?*

It is late at night; I suspect after midnight. As I walk across the grass towards the backyard, there is a hint of dew wetting my bare ankles. I look back towards the house. The style looks old, but the condition appears new. The white clapboards glisten in the light of a full moon. I see no light on within and the windows look of crystal from the lunar refraction. I have no fear even when this looks eerie.

I walk on towards the woods behind the home. I'm being pulled towards the dense trees and bushes. A small trail winding its way inward is my guide. Had it not been for the moon and the clear sky revealing a heaven of stars, my path wouldn't be visible. An unknown urgency makes me walk faster. My step is of lengthened strides and sure footedness as I move deeper into the woods.

Other than the sound of my swift movement along the trail, the woods are silent. An occasional snap of a limb from my feet echo through the night. I stop to listen for other sounds. In the distance is a call of the night owl. A moment later a reply from the opposite direction. Listening, crickets chirping are as soft as the sound of the wind blowing through the leaves. Now I hear a rustling of the grass from a quick moving rodent.

Sensing no fear, I resume my quick steps toward an unknown destination. My thoughts are empty other than the compulsion of the urgency. I hear no voice, but someone is calling. My breathing quickens, and my heart is pounding. Sweat forms on my upper lip and it trickles down my back.

It is as if someone raises a curtain; I find myself at the edge of a clearing. I'm looking at this location, but it doesn't seem real. *Is that a church?* I know no voice has spoken, yet I hear, "Hurry— hurry?"

My pace quickens to a run. Instead of the dirt trail I hear my feet echoing off the street. I look around expecting to see other

Dark Visions

people, but I'm alone. In my head I hear the voice again, "Hurry—come quickly."

At the end of the street is a church. No, it's not a church. It's bigger than a church. It has to be a cathedral. There are two spires in front that rise at least three hundred feet in the air. Between the spires is a huge stain glass window over the elevated entrance. The lighting within the cathedral was dim. The moon illuminates the magnificent neo-gothic style of what appears as white marble.

I've seen this cathedral somewhere before. Was it a movie, on TV, or have I been here before? It can't be, I think it's St. Patrick's in New York. But St. Patrick's has skyscrapers surrounding it. Rockefeller Center is across the street. Nothing is next to the cathedral and it appears the street ends at its doors.

I begin my run this time pushing my legs to their limit. The harder I run, it appears the cathedral gets no nearer. The voice in my head is more urgent. My heart is banging in my chest and I'm struggling to catch my breath.

It is unexplainable, one moment I'm running, the next I'm standing at the door of the cathedral. My breath and heart are normal. I'm not sweating as before. *What just happened? This can't be real.*

The doors have to be sixteen feet tall. They are beautifully sculptured replicas of St. Patrick and other saints. There is an image of the risen Christ in the archway above the doors. I want to stay and marvel at its beauty. The door opens, and I'm beckoned to come in. I see no one, yet the door opens and closes as I enter the narthex.

My mouth hangs open as I stare at the alluring sanctuary. Even when there is no visible light I see the ceiling rise to a height of two hundred feet. I stand mesmerized by the stained windows along the side. The moon illuminates each window even when it's night.

The voice again calls to hurry as I briskly walk towards the candle lit altar. I turn towards the side altar where there are rows of lit red votive candles. I think I see a shadow and move in this direction to investigate. That is when I see an open door to the left of the main altar. A strong light seems to be coming from

215

somewhere down a hallway. The unexplainable urgency pushes me down the hall to find another open door and a staircase going down.

The stairs are marble and my footsteps echo as I descend. There is no lighting and darkness covers my sight like a heavy veil. I make a turn and a faint light is visible at the bottom. Hallways lead in three directions from the stairs and I stop to consider my direction.

In my mind, only one way seems correct. I turn to my right and using my hands along the wall, I proceed down the passageway. I can't see my hand in front of my face. I stop and find something, but it's not a door. It is an opening, but it's sealed. My fingers sense something engraved on the opening. *This is not English. Is it Latin?*

I jump back when I hear a loud grating sound. The thick marble scrapes as it opens. It only retreats enough for me to enter a small tomb like room. Candles illuminate the area and I see a carved marble sarcophagus in its center. The lid is missing and lying within is a man. He is in formal attire, but it reminds me of something from the movies. The jacket has wide lapels made of silky material. Lace edges the cuffs of his white shirt and the front pleat of the shirt. His hair is a black as his suit and long hanging beyond his shoulders.

The voice in my head speaks again, "You arrive—why did you delay?"

Delay—what delay? Is he the one who has been speaking?

The man in the blackness opens his eyes, he stares straight at me as he sits up. His stare hypnotizes me, I can't escape. His voice now audible surprises me. "Yes, it is I who has been calling. I am the one who commanded your swiftness. You will listen and obey"

My mouth goes dry and my heart is pounding. I force my eyes to blink. My voice cracks when I speak. "Obey you? Why?"

His nostrils flared, and his eyes widened, "You will obey me. I command you." The eyes were black, and the pupils dilated. The whites of the eyes were bloodshot and the edges of the lids crimson. I couldn't avoid his stare. My body shakes and as my strength weakens.

His voice strong, yet raspy dominates my attention and I dared not look away. "Don't you recognize me? I am your maker. You will do as I command, or—or you will suffer."

Frozen in place, I felt my body continue to shake. It was if my insides shook in opposition to my legs and arms. A nausea began in my stomach and a sour taste invaded my mouth. The voice was familiar yet this creature before me was frightening. "My maker? I don't understand."

His eyes narrowed. and he pointed his finger at me. His voice boomed within the burial chamber. "You, impudent child. I gave you immortality rather than see you die. My blood runs in your veins."

His presence paralyses me and I fall to my knees. I dared not take my eyes off of him in anticipation I might anger him more. It's as if he floats out of the sarcophagus to stand over me. He reached out and tenderly stroked my cheek. I noticed the long nails and his alabaster like skin. There was no warmth to his touch.

In my heightened terror, he took my arm and pulled me upright. His voice softened, "You need not fear me. You are my child and I love you. I only demand your allegiance."

His mouth opened in a smile. My breath caught seeing his teeth. The incisors were lengthy and resembled an animal—the animal he was. His eyes demanded my attention and I couldn't look away. He ran a finger nail across my throat, breaking the skin. The warmth of what I know is blood runs down my neck. I convulsed when I felt his tongue lick the blood from my neck. As he raised his head, the diabolical smile returned.

He reached out and took my hand and we exited the tomb. In a movement faster than my eyes could focus, we traveled up the stairs, through the sanctuary, and out the front door. When we stopped the breeze from our rapid movement followed us out the door. Its intensity is warm against my skin and my hair blows in response. As my eyes focused, we weren't on the ground, we were floating next to the stained glass above the massive doors.

I wanted to cry out, but he put his deformed finger against my lips. "Quiet—my child. Do not be alarmed, I will protect you." Looking at me with his fiendish smile, he turned to toward the darkness of the night. He took me in his arms holding me as if I were a child and we took flight. The lights of the city below reflected as twinkling stars. The wind blew so powerful, I could hear nothing other than its roar at my ears, the swirl through my hair, and the press of my shirt against my chest.

How long we flew and to what was our destination, I could not grasp. With the same speed as we took off, we landed without a sound or sensation. We were on the roof of a skyscraper overlooking New York. This was Twenty-first century New York, the one that doesn't sleep. I could hear and see the traffic movement. The flow of humans were as if they were a river drifting between the buildings. The pulse of the city filled my ears and eyes.

I looked around and my escort in black was moving in the shadows of the roof top. One moment he was visible, the next he was out of view. *Oh my God—what just happened. Where did he go? How do I get down from here?*

The words had only left my thoughts when he was beside me again. "Oh, my child, I told you not to be alarmed." His voice was raspy and barely audible "I love you and want you near, so you can adore me."

I'm pulled me into his arms with one hand on my neck and the other at the small of my back. He leaned forward as if to kiss me, but his lips found my neck. The silky collar is pushed aside exposing the bulge of the carotid vessels. There was a sting as his teeth entered my neck and I sensed the sucking of his mouth as he drank of my blood. The longer he drank the weaker I became.

I woke in his arms as we both lay on the roof. He was staring into my eyes and I'm transfixed to his spell. He spoke no words, but as before, I understood him. "Oh—you sweet child. your blood runs through me and gives me strength. You must now share in this strength."

He took his left arm, pushed back his shirt sleeve exposing the area above the wrist. He brought it to his mouth and savagely tore at the skin and attacking the blood vessels. As soon as the blood spurted, he put the open wound to my mouth. "Drink—my child. Drink of my gift to you. Drink of the power I share."

I tasted the metallic of the liquid of life. It fills my mouth and runs down my throat. Excess was leaking from my lips. The more I drank, the more I thirsted for more. He gasped as I sucked harder and swallowed more.

"Enough, my beauty. You will feast more later."

He smiled at me with pleasure as the curtain of blackness drew over me and there was a loud ringing in my ears.

I woke in darkness and in a confined space. It surrounded me in a soft pillow material that filled the area in all directions. I pushed my hand into the material to find a firm surface below. As I pushed in all directions, I found the same firmness. The darkness so intense, I could not see my hand move in front of my eyes.

I gathered my strength and took both hands and pushed upward. Dim light crept in and the hard surface moved aside. This was a hinged lid. With the sparse light available, I took in my confinement. Suddenly I couldn't breathe. I gasped for air as my arms reached for the ceiling. I heard my scream, but it sounded more of a wail from a wounded animal. *NO—No, it can't be. This can't be a coffin.*

I lay stiff in my coffin, my eyes flashing in all directions. My heart throbbed uncontrollable and my breath came in short intervals. My mind raced trying to remember something familiar. My memory was blank.

Not knowing how I got here, I lay for a period trying to quiet my mind and body. When my breath and heart returned to normal, I surveyed the room viewable from my reclined position. The light source were several large pillar candles on sculptured holders rising above the height of the coffin resting on the floor. I easily sat up and climbed out to take notice of my surroundings. I had returned to the bedroom and I stood naked as before. My white jeans and ruby shirt lay neatly on the bed.

Over in the corner stood the full-length mirror on its decorative stand. I wanted to see the wound to my neck. My breath caught, and it frightened me by what I didn't see. There was no image of me reflected in the mirror. the room was visible, but my image was missing. I raised my hand and waved it toward the mirror, yet there was still no image.

With a second look, I noticed in the top corner of the mirror a reflected window of the bedroom. Within that mirrored image stood a naked boy with long blonde hair. There were no sounds other than my quickened breath and the echo of my heart pounding in my ears. In my head the familiar raspy voice, "Oh, my beauty—you rise."

The Documentary
Ellen Best
Hessett Bury Saint Edmunds, Suffolk England, UK
Copyright © 2018 by Ellen Best. All rights reserved.
https://ellenbest24.wordpress.com/

Twigs snapped, right then left. Feet pounded and thumped against the parched forest floor. Sounds ricochet as they bounced off trees, the echo distorting their direction. Crunch and snap, a rush of air squealed from twisted lips; lungs under pressure.

In my hide, I watched the bazaar event unfold. A whoosh of wind lifted dust in a raging swirl; obscuring my view. A flash of red appeared in the clearing. Bent over, the writhing snarling beast set to work. Claws poised, jaw extended, thrusting, slurping and gnawing under the scarlet cloth.

An abrupt silence filled my head. Only the sound of my recording equipment quietly whirled; silent enough to go undetected by the creatures I usually document. I knew in that four minutes, what the people of Pompeii must have felt. Stock still, afraid a flutter of my lashes would alert my presence.

It raised itself to its full height, turned with speed, the cloth fell leaving me shocked at the reveal. A crown of golden hair spilt free. It froze, cocked its head, alert, wired, ready to pounce.

It shockingly spat a mouthful of guts and pulled a blood-soaked forearm across its mouth. All the time its green glowing eyes seemed focused on my hide. I watched, holding my breath as the evil being shook, flicked its head, and changed into a female youth. At her feet, the remnants of a huge wolf.

I daren't move, my life depended on the skill of holding my breath. She wiped her face and hands on the fallen cloth, tied her hair back, and swept the red cloak across her shoulders—while kicking the remnants of her supper beneath the debris on the forest floor.

My heartbeat as ragged as my breath began to calm. She pulled up her hood and, humming a sweet tune, sauntered through the forest swinging her basket.

I shot an email to my producer, attached copyright and a clip of the recording.

It paid off! I caught the transformation. No doubts. Amazing footage. Meet me at the helipad four am British meantime.

The Doctor's Walk
Betty Valentine
Jersey, U.K Channel Islands
https://bettys-stories.com

The Doctor took his customary evening stroll. It was a pleasant walk and as usual the butterfly was behind him.

It landed on his hat and unsurprisingly it fell right through. He brushed it away with his hand, silly thing!

He had been dead for 160 years and so had the butterfly, but still it hadn't quite got the message. He strongly suspected that it had become trapped in his coffin when they screwed the lid down.

He remembered his last day so very clearly. It had been warm, and he had been very tired. The rank stink of sweating fevered flesh would remain with him always. The cries of those afflicted growing weaker as the hours passed. He felt powerless to help beyond giving a little comfort.

Cholera had ripped through his patients scything young and old like so much straw. Leaving withered husks where yesterday there had been vibrant life.

The grieving families had all been so grateful. Offers of tearful thanks were many but it did no good. One by one he stood with the relatives and watched their loved ones die.

A broken arm or a case of gout he could fix without trouble. But this creeping fetid blackness was beyond him.

His beloved Mary and his own boys had been among the first to go. He scarce had time to grieve for them before he was dealing with another case. It felt like a judgement, he had been weighed in the balance and found wanting.

They all had been there when he had returned in the morning for a clean shirt. The house was alive, bursting with the noise that children bring. It was an empty shell by the time the setting sun lit the parlour windows orange for a final time.

Could there be any greater punishment for a father than to carry his children through the darkened streets to the churchyard in a single box, while a cart brought his wife. The coffin had been so light, he remembered the weight in his arms. They had been sturdy boys of six, not infants.

Then he had carried on, and on until he just could not do any more. Working kept the pain at bay and there was plenty to do. Finally, when the worst seemed over he had allowed himself to rest.

Exhaustion they called it, some said a broken heart. He hadn't been able to hear them. A great black wave had broken over him as he sat in his chair and he moved no more.

He had been buried beside his wife, the wildflowers he had placed on her coffin still fresh.

But here he was, still carrying his bag and welcoming strangers who came to rest in his little patch. There were fewer these days, just the occasional one for a family vault.

Mainly it was the living that came. He found it curious. They studied the graves and wrote things down. Sometimes they took strong liquor and passed out on one of the stones.

The tomb of a man named Perkins, who had made his money in mattresses, was favourite. It was shaped like a double bed and surprisingly comfy.

Occasionally a couple would come seeking privacy, with no idea that their lustful actions were observed by the ever-watchful eyes of the dead. He wondered if this would have stopped them.

The Doctor nodded to a bony figure leaning on a spade. The old man tipped his cap, he knew everyone, and everyone knew him. As parish gravedigger for 60 years, he had put most of them into the ground. Someone else had to dig for him when his time came, but they gave him a lovely plot.

He continued his walk, waving to anyone he saw until he reached the end of the path.

They were arguing as usual. The three of them as animated and opinionated in death, as they had been in life.

The Colonel red-faced and blustering under his huge moustache was sitting astride his own tombstone. He had wanted to die a hero, at full charge on his horse with the guns blasting in his ears, but it hadn't happened.

He had departed peacefully in bed aged ninety-four, surrounded by his adoring grandchildren, a fact that never ceased to annoy him.

Mr. Chalmers dashing in his white suit sat cross legged on the grave next door. A big game hunter in life he had met his end falling down the stairs.

He had tripped over his wife's poodle, and in a final touch of irony he had speared himself on the preserved head of a large rhino he had shot. It was laying quietly in the hall awaiting a stepladder and a few big nails!

Finally, there was Eddie, Aldermaston Eddie the other ghosts called him. He had choked on a sandwich during a protest march, hot Bovril running down the front of his duffel coat. Eddie loved a fight as much as the others and they argued constantly.

"Evening lads, " the Doctor called, but they were far too busy to hear him.

He walked away with the words "and you can shut up as well, your lot shot all the tigers!" ringing in his ears!

Later it would degenerate into name calling and Eddie would probably say the phrase 'Imperialist oppressor of indigenous peoples' at least once.

Finally they would agree that the current lot were a shower of 'spoilt degenerate whingers' and that previous generations had got it right.

They enjoyed themselves enormously.

The Doctor walked off smiling. Mary and the children would be waiting for him back at the grave.

It occurred to him that people never really changed, in death they were just as stupid and bigoted as they had been in life.

Why should six feet of earth and a wooden box make any difference? People were still people when all was said and done, the dead ones and the living. They were what they were and that never really stopped.

The human spirit just carried on.

Silly to think that the sour-faced old biddy up the road, would be any less sour-faced in the next life than she had been in this one.

He reached home and made ready to turn in. All was right with his little family of souls. He cared for them as always and that was his own destiny.

He smiled as he saw movement behind a tree. He stuck his fingers into his mouth and whistled high and sharp.

Two small boys very obviously twins, appeared laughing from the tangled grass where they had been hiding and raced ahead of him.

Finally there was the butterfly.

It was said that they could change the world with one flap of their wings, but this one just fluttered and followed him into the tomb as always.

He took his place beside Mary and closed his eyes.

A butterfly life lived in just a few days, or a human span of a hundred years, it was all the same in the end. Great or small we all have our part to play and death takes everyone sooner or later.

He went to his rest peaceful in the knowledge that he had done his best and that all was well.

The sun went down and he dozed.

Outside, the lovers loved and the drunks finished their bottles and took a nap on Mrs. Perkins, who never seemed to mind that they preferred her side of the bed.

That was the thing about eternity he thought as he drifted off, there was always another day to get it right.

Excavation Murder
Victoria Clapton
USA
Copyright © 2018 by Victoria Clapton. All rights reserved.
victoriaclaptonauthor

Over a week ago, I'd received a call from Eugene Bryan requesting that my archaeological team join him immediately in America at some field site in rural Tennessee. Curiosity got the better of me. Eugene's request to pull my team out of Spain and rush them to some pasture in the States, well...it caught my attention. And being that he was a friend who had once pursued ancient ruins with my parents when they were younger, I now felt an obligation to honor his summons.

I arrived in the middle of the field and discovered Eugene pushing around what looked to be a fancy version of an old-fashioned mower with a computer attached. He clearly wasn't cutting the grass. It was an expensive ground penetrating radar system, and it could create a map of what rested beneath the surface.

"Dr. Whitcomb!" He offered one wave of his hand but did not pause in his slow walk across the field in his garish-patterned sweater and 1970s era corduroy pants.

I walked through the grass towards him. The countryside should have been bustling with life, but it felt lonely, like that of a crypt. I brushed away the thought and tried not to laugh at the ludicrous appearance of my sponsor. He was an eccentric rich man though I'd never heard my parents mention how he'd achieved his wealth.

"Mr. Bryan, thank you for having me." I didn't bother offering my hand as I fell into stride with the man. He didn't shake hands.

"Call me Eugene, Ally. There is no need to stand on formality. We are family."

We weren't family. This man, who didn't shake hands, had always seemed weird to me. Knowing that things could quickly fall into uncomfortable silence around him, I continued, "What have you discovered that prompted you to invite me all the way here?"

"Take a look." He gestured towards the screen of moving images that sat atop the contraption he continued to push, covering every bit of ground. "There is something there, a large something, and I'm hoping this machine," he patted the handlebar, "and your expertise will tell me what lies beneath the dirt."

I frowned at the screen and could make out what appeared to be a long continuous straight line and then something solid. He had made enough passes back and forth across the area that I could see that something square or rectangular-shaped sat waiting several feet below the dirt and grass. However, with every pass he made, the structure grew bigger. "I think you have some sort of building, Eugene."

"Precisely, but of what sort?"

I scanned the open pasture. There had been no digging here. The ground remained undisturbed. "How did you find this?"

"I had a hunch." He explained no further as he finished scanning the area. "Well, would you look at that? It's a large rectangle."

"Who owns this property? We will need permission and permits before we go any farther." I've been told many times that I am all work and no party. That may be true, but my current grumpiness derived from a feeling of being misled. Over the phone, Eugene had implied that I was coming to an active site, but no earth had been upturned here.

"I've taken care of all that." He waved my questions away as he walked me towards a sturdy canvas tent.

I sighed, inwardly knowing that I would have to go into town the next day to make sure he'd done just that. My reputation depended upon my forthrightness and my respect for the land.

"This will be headquarters for us, and you and your crew can set up your tents in that area right there." He pointed to the empty clearing beside a large open-sided tent.

I nodded and checked my watch. My crew consisted of Joe, who explained every mystery away as proof of alien existence, and Kaylee, a young woman who always complained about dirt but had made digging in dirt her profession. They would arrive soon with our tents and the most rudimentary of exploratory tools.

While I waited, I veered away from Eugene to do a proper walk of the site and surrounding area. This place felt off, or maybe it was the job itself, and I could not put my finger on the problem. The land was beautiful. The wide open field was surrounded by walnut and cedar trees. Wild blackberry bushes mingled with wild roses and honeysuckle vines, creating what I imagined would soon be a fragrant natural border. I found no clues as to what could be lurking beneath the ground here, and so, when my crew pulled into the muddy makeshift entrance, I abandoned my fruitless search and headed towards them.

"Eugene, these are my assistants, Joe and Kaylee." I introduced everyone as they were swiftly unloading the gear in an attempt to beat sunset.

They were well trained. Neither of them needed direction from me on how to set up camp.

"Good, good. Everyone is here. In the morning, we will break ground." Eugene rubbed his hands together with excitement.

"We need more information before we begin. What is the history of this property?"

We were far enough away from town that I doubted we'd run into gas or water lines, and I hadn't seen any electric lines, but it didn't hurt to have facts. Not to mention that the large rectangular shape could simply be the foundation of a house or where someone built a basement but never built a house. Eugene was loaded with money, but I saw no reason to spend it until we knew what we were dealing with.

With a jolly smile, he insisted. "We have all the information we need. This property has been owned by the same family for two hundred years. Before that, no one is known to have lived on it except maybe the Cherokee."

"So, we could be dealing with a house foundation."

"Absolutely not. I've done all the research. There has never been a house here." His insistence caught my attention. I suspected that Eugene was withholding information.

Joe, having overheard the conversation, looked at me in earnest when he approached and said, "This could be it. The proof I've been looking for."

"Proof, my boy?" Eugene's eyebrows rose.

"Aliens," I sighed. He thinks that every unexplained occurrence relates back to aliens.

"It's going to rain," Kaylee snarled as she, too, approached where we all stood in the main tent, looking out over the field. "I suppose tomorrow will be a muddy work day."

Normally, I would laugh at both Joe and Kaylee, but I didn't have the heart. I felt a little paranoid.

We had supper around a fold-out card table and listened to Eugene tell stories of his adventures around the world. Several times we attempted to bring the conversation back around to the excavation at hand, but he had a way of diverting our questions off to some other topic. After several fruitless attempts, we all readied for bed.

Later that evening, while sleeping fitfully in our tents, a terrible cry wrenched into the night, jerking me from my sleeping bag. Grabbing a flashlight, I quickly unzipped my tent as a bone-chilling wail permeated the silence. Disheveled, my crew joined me.

"What the bloody hell is that? Is that a woman screaming?" Kaylee asked. Her teeth chattered as she shivered at the chill in the air.

Joe opened his mouth to reply, but I held my hand up to him and spoke instead. "I am not sure. It isn't aliens, Joe."

"It sounds like a woman. We should..." the screeching ended abruptly, and Kaylee's words fell short.

We stood there, trying to decide what we had just heard when a cracking of limbs sounded off to our left. Kaylee inhaled so sharply it made an audible sound.

"Hello." I peered out into the darkness, shining my flashlight in the direction we'd heard the rustling.

"Don't shoot!" Eugene joked as he walked into the beam of my light with his hands held up high.

"Did you hear that?"

"It sounded like a woman screaming, like a woman being murdered," Kaylee muttered.

Eugene shook his head and laughed. "I didn't hear a thing."

I did not believe him. The sound had been so loud that I could still hear the haunting screams ringing in my ears. The echo of it could have been heard quite far away.

"You really didn't hear it?" Joe looked Eugene straight in the eyes.

"No, my boy. I heard nothing but night crickets."

Joe's eyes grew wide. "Then it must have been..."

"Joe!" Kaylee and I both exclaimed.

I wasn't in the mood for theories. Instead, I debated on going to investigate the sound.

Eugene must have seen it in my face. "I wouldn't worry about it, dear. The sound you heard was probably coyotes. We have them here, you know."

Coyotes were a perfectly plausible explanation, but I didn't believe it. "Maybe, but I'd rather have a look around to be sure. I'd hate to think that anyone was in distress, and I did nothing."

"No, no," Eugene emphatically insisted. "It's much too dangerous at night. If you must search, do so in the morning."

I shook my head. His warnings made sense, especially if it was coyotes out there in the dark, but I hadn't heard a pack of animals. I'd heard a woman screaming, and I didn't believe that he hadn't heard the sound. I couldn't rest until I was sure.

Joe and Kaylee must have been in the same mindset as me, as they were already tugging on boots and grabbing head lamps and lanterns. If it was animals, maybe all the lights would deter them from thinking we looked tasty.

Within moments, we were ready to set out on our trek through the dank darkness. A slow drizzle began to fall. Eugene remained unusually quiet as he followed behind us. This, too, felt strange to me. He knew this property better than we did, yet he did not lead the way.

Our way through was hindered by wet slosh, grass and mud. The rain made visibility poor. I'd stopped along the way to pull my honey-colored hair back into a messy bun. I didn't think sleep was in the near future for any of us, so I fastened it out of my face and out of my mind in order to get down to business.

"We should really go back," Eugene urged as we ignored him and trudged on in the muck.

We were nearing the edge of where I knew the rectangular shape rested beneath our feet and would soon be to the hedge of blackberries. I began weighing the dangers of proceeding into the woods and was startled by a manlier scream.

"Ladies, don't look," Eugene commanded. "Don't take one step closer."

I realized he'd been the one to scream, and rather than listen to him, I focused the beam of my flashlight down onto the ground in front of where he stood. There, just at Eugene's feet, was a woman, bruised and battered, and most definitely not breathing.

I dropped my flashlight as I lowered to the woman to listen for her breath, preparing to administer CPR. At the periphery of my conscious, I heard Joe placing a call to 911. Kaylee had come around to the body, ready to help me keep up the rhythmic compressions should I tire out. In the background, Eugene mumbled to himself. His words were unintelligible.

It seemed like it took hours for the first responders to arrive. We were in the middle of nowhere Tennessee, so maybe it did take longer than usual, but it didn't matter. Even with Kaylee's help, we'd been unsuccessful in reviving the woman, and she was declared dead before her poor body was placed into the ambulance.

I was still sitting back on my knees on the wet ground when an officer approached me.

"I'm Chief Hawkins."

"Dr. Ally Whitcomb." I answered as I stood up and made a useless attempt to brush off my sopping pants. I cast a glance over to see that my crew and Eugene were being interviewed by detectives.

"You've had quite a night," the police chief observed. He was a quiet sort of man, the kind whose presence instantly calmed a situation.

"You could say that. It's not exactly what I expected to find on a pastoral dig."

"Yes, I heard that old Eugene asked y'all to come down and plow his old place up. I'm not sure what he is hoping to find. Would you mind telling me what happened tonight?"

"Not at all," I complied. I began the story with the loud screaming, and I paused after I got to the bit about the coyotes. Chief Hawkins just nodded as if coyotes could have indeed made those kinds of screams. So, I continued telling every minute detail I could recall until a thought occurred to me. "Wait! Did you say this property belongs to Eugene?"

"Yes, it's been in his family for a very long time."

"Why would he ask me to come excavate his own property? Wouldn't he know what is here?" I asked no one in particular. Chief Hawkins nodded as if he'd wondered the same thing all along, but he made no comment on the matter.

"When are you supposed to break ground?" Chief Hawkins asked.

"Tomorrow morning."

He nodded again and then took his leave from me without giving me any reassurance on how or why the woman had been murdered.

As dawn approached, we'd all been told to stay close to town, so as much as I wanted to grab my crew and head back to Spain, it wasn't possible. Until we were given clearance by the police, we could not go anywhere.

"I suppose we should all get some rest." Now that the body had been removed and the sun rose in the sky, Eugene had stepped back in as the authoritative figure at the site.

"I don't think I will be sleeping for a long time," I admitted. "Might as well get to work." I wanted to ask him about his property, but hesitated. Previous attempts to gain that information had been thwarted.

"Come now," Eugene said with an unusually bright smile. "Don't you come across dead bodies all of the time in your line of work?"

Suspicion rose within me at his blasé response. After his initial scream upon finding the body, Eugene hadn't seemed bothered in the slightest that someone had been killed on his property.

"Sure, but they aren't usually murdered within earshot," Kaylee snapped. She was covered in mud. The rain had dissipated, but everything was a begrimed mess. Her mood would not improve until she got somewhere warm and dry.

Eugene scoffed at Kaylee and chuckled. Grabbing the keys, he winked at me and tossed them to Joe. "Start her up. We marked the edges yesterday, so you won't hit the structure. Let's see what we are working with."

His excitement worried me more than anything we'd encountered so far, including the dead woman. Eugene already knew what was under the ground. I could see it all over his face. We were a part of a game, his game. I just didn't know what that was yet.

Soon, smooth concrete came into view, and not long after that, Joe was able to hop down off of the bulldozer and use a smaller version of the ground penetrating radar to confirm that it was a hollow structure, like that of a building.

This should have thrilled me. Even my crew had that telltale gleam in their eyes that only occurred right at the brink of discovery, and Eugene had grown quiet, rocking back and forth on the balls of his feet rather than speaking.

"There must be an entrance," Kaylee spoke as she looked to me.

"Unless. Aliens…"

"No, Joe... no." I half-hoped that someday we did stumble upon proof of alien life forms, if only just to fulfill Joe's dreams.

I turned to Eugene to implore, "Thoughts?"

"I'm not sure what you mean. I agree that there must be an entrance, but I've no idea where that could be."

I bit the inside of my cheek to keep from telling him to cut the crap. And then I realized what he'd just said. *Where that could*

234

be...but not what side the entrance was located? Full on panic struck me. Eugene knew where the entrance was located. He knew what waited beneath the ground. I needed answers, now.

By all accounts we were digging up a large rectangular building. It stood to reason that the entrance would be on one of the four sides. I recalled how undisturbed everything had been and looked to Eugene once more. "The entrance isn't on the building. It is somewhere else. Where is it Eugene? You went through all of the trouble of having us fly to America. Why did you have us come all the way here?"

I expected him to brush my questions off as had been his way since we'd arrived, but he only met my gaze with that infernal smile he always had plastered on his face.

"My, aren't we impatient! I thought you, Ally, would be the one to understand, the one to take the time to uncover the beauty the way it should be, to discover it as it was meant to be discovered."

The hairs on my arms and the back of my neck rose high.

"Very well, follow me, children, and all shall be revealed."

I should have refused.

Eugene bid us to follow him into the woods past the inviting tree line and thorny wild rose bushes. Longing for clarification, I motioned for my team to follow me, and, feeling cautionary, I simultaneously reached into my pocket and pressed the emergency button that would dial the Chief of Police on my cell phone. I'd saved the number as an icon on my screen. Being careful, I did not pull my phone out of my pocket as we followed dutifully behind him, and I prayed to all of the gods I'd unearthed in previous shrines that there was enough signal that Chief Hawkins could hear us walking, that he would somehow sense that I wouldn't call him by accident. I had a bad feeling. Since my arrival, Eugene's behavior had been strange, and now, I had this inkling that we could possibly be in some danger.

"Where are you taking us, Eugene?"

"You'll see, soon."

I cursed inwardly. I'd hoped he'd reveal something for the Chief to go on, but he'd not. "You are taking us pretty far into the woods."

I said this loudly, hoping it would help the Chief. I didn't dare say more.

"Mr. Bryan, erm Eugene," Joe began. "It's an awful mess today. Perhaps we should go back to camp and get some rest and start again tomorrow."

Joe's voice shook a little, which further validated my worries. Until now, it had been only me who had been suspicious, but now I could tell by their demeanor that both of my crew were also concerned.

"Why would we do that? We're here." Eugene announced with a chuckle.

The entrance consisted of two leaning old rusted storm cellar doors surrounded by leaves, twigs and bracken curling and spiraling across them, like a crypt long forgotten. Eugene easily opened the dilapidated entry, creating even more anxiety to course through me. This entrance to the supposed "unknown" structure had been used recently and often.

Without a word we followed Eugene down into the darkness as the cellar doors closed behind us. We were forced to creep in the silent oppression, listening only to the sounds of our racing hearts and ragged breaths while smelling what surely was the awful, unmistakable scent of death. Along the way, I had begun to beat myself up for not having the foresight to put a stop to this charade earlier. We should never have followed him down to this pit. I'd had a bad feeling from the beginning, and now, we were underground in the middle of nowhere, walking into what I imagined would be a horrific death. I opened my mouth to shut this mission down. For the first time ever, I did not care what waiting in the unknown. I did not even care if my suspicions were unfounded. "It's time we…"

"We're here." Eugene's excitement filled the cold space. "This isn't the way I'd hope you'd discover my treasure trove, but, Ally, I'm so glad it is you. I'd always hoped your parents could come here. But alas, they were the ones who got away. Not you, Ally. I knew I could depend on you."

Darkness thickened around us, and I fought an urge to tell my crew that I was sorry, though I didn't know for what, when Eugene struck a match and lit a couple of old oil lanterns, casting an eerie, dull light around a large chamber illuminating an unimaginable sight.

"What the hell?" Joe wrinkled his face in disgust. "Ugh, the scent of death."

"Eugene? What is this?" I looked around at what must be thirty, maybe forty concrete cavities, exactly like a crypt, filled with bodies crammed into each one. There were no coffins, nothing to preserve or decompose the bodies, just dead people shoved carelessly into cold caverns. I'd entered many such places in my line of work, but nothing compared to this horror. These weren't bodies from the past. In various examples of modern clothing such as blue jeans and t-shirts, these dead were relatively fresh in my way of thinking. All had died within the last thirty or so years.

"Bodies are everywhere," Kaylee whispered. I could hear frightened sobs building in her chest.

"My masterpiece," Eugene's laughter caused my heart to skip a beat. "I wanted to leave this so that, someday, when an archaeologist such as you broke ground here, I would be remembered, immortalized."

His voice was steady.

As he revealed his thoughts to me, I froze in disbelief. Standing before me was not the man that I'd considered a family friend. "You want to be remembered in the annals of time as a serial killer? Where is the glory in that?"

Suddenly, my disgust with him banished my fear of imminent death, at least temporarily. This ghastly crime scene made a mockery of my life's work.

"Killer?" He seemed honestly stunned. "No, look around. These are all different, but perfect, specimens of the 21st century. Once they decompose, scientists and other archaeologists will have examples of every age and culture currently in our world to study."

Bile rose in my throat. I didn't want me or my team to become part of this macabre exhibit. "I see." I said, but I didn't. "They aren't ready yet. Why did you have me come now?"

"You are a top-notch archeologist, famous in your field. You, my dear Ally, complete the collection."

The fear returned instantly. My heart thumped so loud my ears pulsed. I looked around for an escape and noticed Joe and Kaylee. "Let them go. They have nothing to do with your masterpiece," I begged.

"So that they can go and tell the authorities? Now, Ally, dear, why would I do that? Wouldn't that ruin this experiment?" Eugene's smile disgusted me.

He began walking towards me, his hands outstretched as if he planned on just grabbing my throat to choke the life out of me. Without moving, I glanced around. There were no weapons that I could see. For that matter, none of the dead bodies looked as if they'd been assaulted beforehand.

Keep him talking, I thought.

"What happened with that woman last night?"

For the first time since we'd arrived the night before, his grin faltered. "She was suspicious. They never suspect a gentle old man."

Eugene froze, staring behind me. His hands still held in the position to reach out and choke me, when a shuffle from behind caught my attention.

"Drop your hands, Mr. Bryan, and step away from Dr. Whitcomb." Chief Hawkins spoke calmly as other officers filed into the room, moving Joe and Kaylee back through the tunnel to escape.

A prayer of thanks ran through my mind. Chief Hawkins was a dull, quiet man, but Eugene's strange behavior must have made him apprehensive as well. I hadn't been sure he'd pay attention to my call.

"Dr. Whitcomb, step back, please. Go with one of my detectives."

I didn't hesitate to obey Chief Hawkins' orders and quickly made my way out of that macabre cavern

"Ally!" Kaylee and Joe rushed over and embraced me.

We stood silent for a minute, absorbing the atrocious twenty-four hours we'd just had. Soon, Chief Hawkins came up from the opened cellar doors with Eugene handcuffed before him. Two of the detectives then took the disturbing man, who was no longer smiling, off in the direction of where I supposed their police squad vehicles were waiting on the outside edge of the woods.

Chief Hawkins walked over and handed us a business card, "Here, this local bed and breakfast will have rooms available. Hot showers, food, and rest wait for you. Come to the station tomorrow to give your statements."

"Chief Hawkins."

He turned to face us once more.

"Thank you."

With a brief nod, Chief Hawkins motioned for us to follow him out of the woods back to where our belongings could be found.

We walked in silence for a few minutes, too stunned to make any real comment on what we'd just witnessed. The ground was still muddy, but this time, Kaylee made no complaint.

"Geesh!" Joe shuffled disappointedly.

We all stopped. Even Chief Hawkins paused.

"What, Joe?" I asked, knowing what his reply would be.

"Why couldn't it have been aliens?"

EPILOGUE: Now Comes Death
part two

And now my time has come to pass
The sand has left the hourglass.
The stories, frightening and true,
Their messages I've shared with you.

Fifty summers gone since Blane was here
And helped me cope with my own fear
Of what beyond awaited there
Past Heaven's gates to anywhere.

And many times in life I'd see
A cemetery filled with families.
Of lovers, friends, and loners, too;
A melancholy witches' brew.

I remember, long ago, a tale
Given to me amidst a gale.
The crystal warned me in its glow,
"Beyond is but for Death to know."

*If you enjoyed stories from this anthology, please post a review
on Amazon.*

31347940R00137

Made in the USA
Middletown, DE
30 December 2018